Praise for *POISON TOWN*

"With *Poison Town*, Creston Mapes has crafted quite the thrill ride. He explores the evils of corporate greed and exposes an even more menacing enemy lurking inside all of us. Warning: once you pick this book up, you will not want to put it down." **Mark Lee, guitarist and founding member of the Grammy Award-winning band Third Day**

"A wild roller-coaster ride! I thoroughly enjoyed *Poison Town*." **Francine Rivers, bestselling author**

"Every time you think the tension can't be more intense, Creston Mapes ramps it up a notch. Be prepared to stay up late (and make sure the doors are locked) when you start reading *Poison Town*." **Robert Whitlow, bestselling author of *The Choice***

"Mapes has crafted a David versus Goliath tale that reaches toward Grisham greatness and will keep you turning pages long into the night." **Harry Kraus, bestselling author of *An Open Heart***

"*Poison Town* is another winner from Creston Mapes. I was on the edge of my seat and read it in one gulp. Highly recommended!" **Colleen Coble, author of *Rosemary Cottage* and the Lonestar series**

"Grab an oxygen tank and a tall glass of water—you're going to need them when you read *Poison Town*. A powerful tale of suspense! Intriguing and compelling—an absolute must-read!" **Ronie Kendig, bestselling author of *Trinity: Military War Dog* and the Discarded Heroes series**

"In *Poison Town*, Creston Mapes weaves conspiracy, corruption, and murder into a gripping tale about the damage done by justice delayed and forgiveness denied." **Athol Dickson, author of *River Rising***

"*Erin Brockovich* on steroids! A suspense-filled journey into the world of a corrupt corporation, the blue-collar workers who are being 'poisoned,' and a reporter's determination to tell the truth. Mapes keeps the tension high as he realistically portrays Christians wrestling with fear, forgiveness, and the need to stand up for what's right." **Elizabeth Musser, author of The Secrets of the Cross trilogy: *Two Crosses, Two Testaments, Two Destinies***

"I was quickly pulled into this story through the believable, quirky, and endearing cast of characters and their deadly situation. Creston's novels thrill as well as challenge readers. You'll be glued to the page as these flawed p   ıth, fighting for justice, and having the faith to fac   right thing. Can one person make a difference? Yo   ıt question in the climatic conclusion. I highly r   ıt this on your Book Club reading list!" **Nora St. Lá   Network**

ALSO BY CRESTON MAPES

SIGNS OF LIFE SERIES
Signs of Life
Let My Daughter Go
I Pick You

STAND ALONE THRILLERS
Nobody

THE CRITTENDON FILES
Fear Has a Name
Poison Town
Sky Zone

ROCK STAR CHRONICLES
Dark Star: Confessions of a Rock Idol
Full Tilt

CrestonMapes.com

POISON TOWN

THE CRITTENDON FILES

CRESTON MAPES

POISON TOWN

This story is a work of fiction. All characters and events are the product of the author's imagination. Any resemblance to any person, living or dead, is coincidental.

Published by Rooftop Press

To Steve Vibert

As iron sharpens iron, so one man sharpens another.

"Anyone can hold the helm when the sea is calm."

— Publilius Syrus —

"Courage is being scared to death…and saddling up anyway."

— John Wayne —

"Courage is contagious. When a brave man takes a stand, the spines of others are often stiffened."

— Billy Graham —

1

Jack could see his breath even inside the car as he dodged potholes on the Ohio interstate and maneuvered his way into Trenton City at daybreak. He blasted the heat, but was getting nothing but cool air. The gun he'd bought three days earlier still felt bulky and foreign strapped to his ankle.

Wiping the moisture from the side window, he glimpsed one of the city's sprawling industrial plants, its web of mechanical apparatuses and smokestacks silhouetted by the dawn's red-orange glow. He didn't like keeping the gun a secret from Pam, but with Granger Meade out on parole, it was for her own good—hers and the girls'.

Jack put the windows down to clear the windshield. It was below freezing outside. "Shoot!" He laughed at how cold he was and how ridiculous he must look with the windows down in the dead of winter. Cars hummed alongside his, covered with clumps of snow and ice and white stains from the rock salt on the roads.

He'd been taking the cars to Randalls' garage for repairs on the east side of Trenton City for years. Galen, the elderly father, and his two fortysomething sons, LJ and Travis, knew cars like a cardiologist knows chest cavities.

He glanced at the digital clock in the dash: 7:17.

The fact that Granger had returned to Trenton City made Jack sick to his stomach—especially when it was time to leave Pam and the girls each morning. The man had come to Trenton City to track Pam down a year and a half ago, because she was the only person who had ever cared two cents about his life. She had paid for that compassion—they all had.

Jack rested a hand on his chest. His sternum had been severely cracked that night when he slammed into the guardrail. The bone had eventually healed, but his heart had not. But Jack didn't care. It was his right to despise Granger. He had zero sympathy for the man, even though Pam—the real victim—had mustered the mercy to forgive.

He recalled driving hopelessly in the dark, through sheets of torrential rain, in search of any sign of his wife—then spinning out of control. Jack realized he was clamping the steering wheel like a vise. *Ease up.* He tried to relax his hands, neck, whole body.

He shook away the disturbing vignettes of that night.

At the last second he spotted the Tenth Street exit sign, shot a glance back, and veered off the interstate. When Granger got into his head, the memories possessed him. Just like that—almost missing the exit.

He looped around the exit ramp, past the new soup kitchen, which was lined with dark figures—standing, sitting, sleeping—trying to stay warm on sewage grates billowing clouds of steam. He hit green lights for several city blocks. Once past the library, thrift shop, and triple set of railroad tracks leading to the east side, he slowed along the narrow streets.

The houses were shoeboxes whose colors had faded long ago. Many were trailers, yet almost every one supported a monstrous, leaning antenna or satellite dish. Smoke chugged from tiny chimneys, and he imagined the warmth inside. Beater cars and trucks were parked at all angles in the short driveways and right up against the shanties and shotgun shacks.

Jack's phone chirped. He knew without looking that it was a reminder to attend an editorial board meeting at nine thirty. He had tons of work on his plate. He took a left on Pell Lane and a quick right at the Randalls' place, easing the Jetta up to the large doors of the auto shop. It was a leaning, rusted silver metal building the size of a barn, sealed up tight with no windows or sign.

A hint of snow fell as Jack turned the car off. The Randalls' one-story house was situated about fifty feet from the shop. It was faded green with a big metal awning over the back. Next to it was a rusting white propane tank that looked like a giant Tylenol capsule. Out back were a red tool shed, an ancient doghouse, and a broken-down sky blue Ford Pinto.

The Randalls' orange dog with the corkscrew tail was lying on the back stoop, which led to the rear entrance of the house. A cozy yellow light shone from inside. The instant the mutt saw him, it bolted upright and howled.

"Hello, Rusty." Jack continued toward the back door. "It's okay. I'm here to see the boys. Are they up?" Rusty quieted and sniffed at his coat.

Jack went up the steps slowly, still not used to the feel of a gun on his ankle. Through the screen door he could see Travis sitting hunched over an enormous plate of food at the small kitchen table. Jack knocked at the leaning screen door, and without any change in facial expression, Travis lifted a hand and motioned him inside.

Jack nudged the tightly sealed back door, scaring a gray cat away as he slipped in. "Morning, Travis."

The kitchen was small and toasty warm, permeated with the smell of cigarettes and dotted with NASCAR posters, hats, and paraphernalia.

"Jack." Travis nodded casually, as if Jack lived there and had just meandered in for breakfast. He sat with his right leg crossed and his right foot gently bouncing. He was distinctly bony, like a caveman, from his large hands and sinewy arms to his long, sculpted face. His fork tapped and cut and diced its way into a pile of yoke-smothered eggs, bacon, grits, grilled potatoes, biscuits, and white gravy.

"Could it be any colder?" Jack took his gloves off.

Travis continued to work on his breakfast, his elbows resting on the Formica table. "I guess it could, but I wouldn't want it to be." He chuckled at his own joke. "What's the word at the *Dispatch*? Any new scandals? You can wipe your feet right there on that rug."

"Nothing earth-shattering." Jack wiped his feet.

"You still doin' the city hall beat?" Travis spoke slowly, in a deep voice. He wore faded jeans with a small rip above one knee, a soft brown T-shirt, and thick gray socks.

"Yeah," Jack said. "And I'm the features editor now, so I've been doing some personality profile stuff. We ran a story about a neighbor of yours recently—Jenness Brinkman."

"They live right 'round back, I think. Jenness is the handicapped girl, right?"

"Yep. Top of her class at East High. Got a full ride to Yale to study criminal law. Wants to work with the FBI in Washington."

"I'll be," Travis said. "I missed that one."

"The features usually run on Sundays."

"Well, that answers that. Bo's always runnin' off with the Sunday paper. Uses it to clean car windows. You hear he's detailin' cars now?"

Bo was Travis's seventeen-year-old nephew, who was always into something new.

"No, I hadn't." Jack heard a sound from the other room.

"Yup. Ask him 'bout it. He's startin' off really cheap."

"I might do that."

"You want somethin' to eat? Biscuit? I got some a daddy's homemade sawmill gravy over there. A little go-joe?"

It all sounded good, but he'd had fruit and eggs with Pam. "No, thanks. I appreciate it, though."

The smell of a freshly lit cigarette wafted in from the next room, but Travis didn't seem to notice.

"What brings you out this mornin'?" Travis scratched his dark, sparse beard, which was peppered with gray.

"I've got my '98 Jetta out there. The fan is barely working and there's no heat. Plus the muffler's sagging."

Just then LJ rounded the corner from the dark room, a lit cigarette dangling from the corner of his mouth, the usual black eye patch covering his left eye. He wore dark blue jeans, a white T-shirt, an unbuttoned blue and red flannel shirt, and white socks. "You want the good ole boy fix on the muffler, Jack, or you want me to get the parts from Volkswagen?"

"Hey, LJ," Jack said. "The good ole boy fix, if you can."

"What you doin', boy?" Travis suddenly came to life. "Sneakin' round here in the dark." He looked at Jack. "He's been doin' that since we was boys. Ears like radar. Stickin' that crooked nose into other peoples' beeswax. Ain't no such thing as a private conversation 'round here."

LJ smirked as he stirred the grilled potatoes in the frying pan above a blue flame. With the cigarette pinched at the end of two fingers, he took a heaping mouthful. "Momma used to call me Ghosty. Remember, Trav?"

The most prominent feature on LJ, besides the eye patch, was his Adam's apple, which protruded an inch from his long, skinny neck. He was about six foot four and balding. The blond hair he did have on top was long and thin; on the sides it was full and flowing.

"Momma had your number," Travis said. "Remember how she got onto you for spying on Daddy's customers? Hey, don't smoke around the food!"

"How long ago did your mother pass away?" Jack asked.

LJ ran his cigarette under water, threw it away, and got into the eggs, eating right out of the pan. "Two thousand and seven," he said with a mouthful. "These need salt. Want some grub, Jack?"

"I already asked him. . . but now that you've gone and stuck your greazee grubs into everythin' . . . Sorry, Jack. LJ, mind your manners."

"Same thing's gonna kill Daddy that killed Momma." LJ shook the big spoon toward the window as he spewed the words: "Demler-Vargus."

"Is something wrong with Galen?" Jack asked.

"He's in the hospital." LJ tossed the spoon in the sink. "They's callin' it emphysema, and maybe it is, but we know what caused it." He jabbed a finger toward the window. "That plant. It killed Momma and it's killed others. But nobody wants to listen to us poor east-siders. We got no voice in this town."

Travis calmly tapped and scraped at the remains on his plate.

Jack knew that Demler-Vargus, the massive fiberglass manufacturing plant that employed half of Trenton City, had been the recipient of complaints in the past for emitting hazardous pollutants. But as far as he knew, the corporate giant had only received several slaps on the wrist from the EPA.

"How bad is he?" Jack said.

"He's gonna be okay." Travis didn't look up. "Passed out the other night. Wasn't gettin' enough oxygen to the brain. Scared the starch out of us."

"I thought he was dead." LJ came over and stood by Travis. "He was purple. Sprawled out yonder in the TV room."

"Lucky there was no brain damage, they said." Travis picked at his teeth with his upside-down fork. "It's my day at the hospital, so LJ will be takin' care of your car." He looked up at his brother. "You hear all his Jetta needs when you was listenin' in?"

"I heard. I gotta take care of the fuel filter on that Volvo first, then I got that little day care bus out back, door's busted—"

"But you gonna get to it today, right?" Travis said.

"I might could. But it might be tomorrow."

Travis craned his neck toward Jack. "That okay?"

"That's fine."

"You need a ride to the paper?" Travis stood and took his dish to the sink.

"That would be great." Jack put his gloves on. "You know, we just ran a feature story about the CEO of Demler-Vargus. He was voted Trenton City's Person of the—"

"That is *the* biggest load of horse manure." LJ scowled and pulled at his thick brown mustache that reached to the bottom of his chin. "Don't get me started, Jack. That man is nothing but a murderer, plain and simple."

"No, please don't git him started." Travis finished rinsing his things and put them in the dishwasher. "I can take you to the paper on my way to the hospital."

"Great." Jack guessed LJ was frustrated and looking for someone to blame for his parents' struggles, but his own curiosity was piqued. He'd come away from his interview with Leonard Bendickson III thinking the fiberglass CEO was intelligent, cocky, and filthy rich. "Why are you so sure Demler-Vargus is hurting people?" he asked. "What do you know?"

"Whatever that plant is spewing, it's killing people," LJ said. "It's in the air and the water. I've heard *plenty.*"

"Like what, specifically?"

"Uh oh," Travis said. "Here we go."

"You know what fiberglass is, Jack?" LJ whirled around like a raging pirate, with his arching brown eyebrows and long, crooked nose. "It's tiny slivers of actual *glass.* We breathe it in day in and day out in this crummy neighborhood. Momma and Daddy been breathin' it in they whole lives. Some days we can *see it* on the cars and houses. You know what that does to your innards? That plant shouldn't be anywhere close to any neighborhood."

"What did your mom die from?" Jack said.

"Lymphoma, eventually," Travis said as he hoisted on a heavy blue-and-yellow parka. "But she had respiratory problems the last three years."

LJ slammed things in the sink. "Her mouth was covered with sores." He stopped, gripped the sink, and stared out the window. "She had a sore throat for years. Used an oxygen tank."

"Did she smoke?"

"All her life," Travis said.

"That ain't the point!" LJ kicked away the gray cat that was poking around the dishwasher. "Smokin' don't make you twitch and break into hives till you itch yerself raw!"

Travis snatched his keys from a wooden key board. "We know people who work in there whose health is broken down somethin' miserable. They's some horror stories, how it affects the central nervous system."

"Big joke at the plant is, none of 'em collect on their retirement 'cause they all dead shortly after they retire," LJ said. "If they last *that* long."

"I've heard things from time to time at the paper," Jack said. "But it always sounded to me like when there was any wrongdoing, Demler-Vargus complied and cleaned things up."

LJ closed the dishwasher with a bang. "Jack, this is dirty, filthy politics and greed and cover-up. Nobody wants to do nothin' about it 'cause Demler-Vargus employs the whole town. It would cripple the entire city if they got shut down. That's yer bottom line."

"Daddy got us a big-shot lawyer." Travis knelt to pet the cat. "Says we're gonna pursue it hot an' heavy. Lawyer says we got a good shot at winning some big moolah."

"Other people have gotten payoffs from Demler-Vargus, but you wouldn't know about that down at the *Dispatch*," LJ said. "Probly wouldn't write about it even if you did."

"Sure we would."

LJ shook his head like a spoiled child. "No sir. I'm tellin' you, Jack, this here is a can a worms. The *Dispatch* don't cover it, and neither does AM 550; Demler-Vargus is too powerful. They're Goliath. No one's got the guts to call 'em out and say what's really goin' on."

"That's enough, LJ." Travis headed for the door. "Jack's gotta get to work and I gotta get over to see Daddy. Oh, that's right . . ." Travis rattled around in a drawer until he found a brown bag. "I told him I'd bring him some biscuits." He dropped three in the bag and wrung it closed. "That'll do it. You ready?"

"Yep." Jack followed him to the door. "Look, I'm not promising anything, but if I can get my editor to agree, would you guys be willing to give me names and details?"

"Shoot, yeah. Daddy's got all the facts. You need to talk to him." LJ stretched his long arms, touched the low ceiling, ran his fingers through his thin hair, and snapped the elastic band that held the eye patch in place. "But I bet you a six-pack you won't do nothin'—beverage of your choice."

Jack reached his hand out and it was engulfed by LJ's massive, calloused paw, clean except for the dirt beneath his fingernails.

"You're on."

2

It was getting light and snowing when Travis dropped Jack out front of the big *Dispatch* building downtown. From there, Travis rocked and rolled his dark green Jeep Wrangler through Trenton City slush puddles and backstreets, on over to visitor parking at Cook County Hospital.

Up on the modern fourth floor, he quietly entered the dark, sterile-smelling room. Daddy was upright in bed, sleeping. Travis set the bag of biscuits down, then went to the window and pulled up the blind, knowing his father would want to see out when he awoke. His color looked better, more like the ruddy brownish-reddish color he usually was.

Travis ducked back out into the hallway, keeping the door open with his foot. "Excuse me—Candace, is it?" He addressed a plump young nurse in aqua scrubs, whose shiny brown hair was pulled back in a ponytail.

"Yes?" Her eyes shifted and cheeks reddened, as if she was surprised he knew her name.

Shoot, they'd been there how many days now?

"Has Galen Randall eaten breakfast yet? Right here in 411?"

She looked at her watch. "It should be coming soon. You're one of the sons, right?"

"Travis." He nodded. "I know I asked this before, but can he have waffles 'stead of eggs?"

"They should know that by now in the kitchen."

Travis smiled and went back into the room, doubting they would get the order right. People didn't care about their jobs anymore. Not like Daddy had taught LJ and him—to do your job well, respect others, please the customer, go the extra mile.

Travis sat himself down in the green vinyl chair. His father was fit as a fiddle for seventy-eight. He only stood about five foot nine, but he was lean and stubbornly strong. His forearms were thick and his hands were small and tough as metal. He could reach unreachable places on an engine, unscrew things, bend, clamp, tighten, and manipulate a motor like most people couldn't do with a full set of tools. And nothing ever seemed to hurt those hands, or him—until now.

His father's face was full of gray beard stubble. He looked older. Of course he had to be fatigued from all this hospital business. They still had the oxygen tube stuck up his nose, but it looked like they had reduced his IVs from two bags of fluid to one. *Good.*

Travis just hoped he could get Daddy home soon, because that house and that garage and that piece of property were his life, especially since Momma died. He'd been going to church quite a bit since then, too, and that seemed to give him a lot of comfort, which was fine with Travis. Daddy even managed to get LJ and him to church once in awhile, when he promised to take them to Ryan's afterward for the all-you-can-eat buffet.

It wasn't like Daddy to sleep late, but he was probably still drugged up. Travis stood, took his parka off, and laid it over the chair so Daddy would see it when he awoke. Then he set out to get a paper and some of the vending machine coffee he "loved" so much.

He had the route down pat—out the door, turn right, down the hall, around the nurses' station. He admired nurses and doctors—people who helped people. Maybe they didn't make them like they used to, but most were still compassionate and good at comforting those who were hurting in all kinds of ways.

The cramped sitting room was bordered by red chairs. Only one was occupied, by a middle-aged man with blond hair and a cleft lip that had been surgically repaired, and poorly at that. He wore a black overcoat and sat hunched over, elbows on knees, cell phone glued to ear. Several coffee tables were strewn with newspapers and magazines. A TV in the corner blared *Good Morning, America.* The vending machines were in a nook off to one side.

The seated man didn't acknowledge Travis, which he thought was rude. But the man looked like he was in a pretty deep discussion and, who knew, his wife or momma or daddy might be on their deathbed.

Travis put his money in and hit dark roast. It was as weak as the coffee they served at Daddy's church, but he needed some go-joe. He picked up the steaming cup from the machine and turned around, and the blond man was gone. *Good.* He plopped down on the edge of a chair and went through the reading materials.

Wouldn't you know it . . . smack-dab on top was a recent Sunday edition of the *Trenton City Dispatch,* featuring a huge color picture of Leonard

Bendickson III, CEO of Demler-Vargus. And sure enough, it was written by none other than their buddy Jack Crittendon, who had just ridden in Travis's Jeep!

How do you like them apples?

Bendickson's picture had been taken as he stood inside the plant in an expensive-looking suit with a roll of blueprints under one arm, a hard hat and goggles on his head, one shiny shoe perched on the edge of a fancy fiberglass boat. Behind him was a massive puzzle of heavy-duty machinery, tanks, air ducts, conveyor belts, tubes, scaffolding, drums, gauges, and a giant furnace throwing flames and sparks. Travis dropped back in the chair and began to read.

Trenton City's Person of the Year — Leonard Bendickson III
Mastermind of the Fiberglass Universe
By Jack Crittendon

As one might guess from his formal name and expensive taste in clothes, Leonard Lee Spalding Bendickson III, known as Lenny B to his yacht club pals, was reared in a wealthy Virginia home, attended Ivy League universities, and never wanted for anything.

And he doesn't plan to.

Since taking the helm as CEO of Demler-Vargus thirteen years ago, Bendickson has steered the Fortune 500 company to unfathomable heights. On its climb, the $7.9 billion corporation has consistently surpassed Wall Street expectations on its way to becoming one of the world's most prolific manufacturers of fiberglass—all kinds of fiberglass.

"When I was asked to takeover as CEO, the Demler Corporation mainly produced fiberglass insulation. I knew that was the tip of the iceberg," Bendickson said.

It didn't take him long to make waves. Within eight months of his arrival, the Demler Corporation had acquired Vargus International, a huge player in the fiberglass arena, based in Brussels and with plants around the globe. Over the next five years the companies consolidated nine plants into five. Since then, each has

become a perennial powerhouse in the world of fiberglass
manufacturing.

Travis let the paper crumple in his lap. He had never met Bendickson, though he'd seen him once at the bank on the square downtown. He wondered what the truth was. Could LJ be right? Were pollutants from Demler-Vargus hurting employees and neighbors? Were they what killed his mother and made his father sick?

The Demler-Vargus plant on Winchester Boulevard on
Trenton City's east side is the largest of all, churning out dozens of
kinds of fiberglass, which is then shipped to manufacturers worldwide
and used to produce boats, car parts, buildings, sporting goods,
windmills, insulation, fabric, bulletproof vests, and more.

"We hit our stride when we purchased the old Trenton City
refinery and its 225 acres," Bendickson said. "We built the new plant
and that was the turning point for Demler-Vargus. We've never
looked back. We are always exploring new ideas, techniques, and
venues for our products."

Although Demler-Vargus has been the subject of complaints
about air pollution from Trenton City neighbors over the years,
Bendickson insists the company has worked diligently to comply with
the Occupational Safety and Health Administration and the
Environmental Protection Agency.

"I love the natural beauty of our land, lakes, rivers, and seas;
that's one of the reasons I studied environmental engineering at
Rutgers," Bendickson said.

"Being a good environmental steward and a leader in green
initiatives is one of my passions. When it comes to educating and
properly fitting our employees with the safest, most state-of-the-art
equipment and resources, we lead the way. And when it comes to
reducing overall hazardous air pollutants in our community, Demler-
Vargus is at the cutting edge. You won't find a more conscientious
corporation."

Travis couldn't take anymore in one sitting. He glanced at the elevators outside the waiting area and noticed a boy in an Ohio State ski cap pushing his gray grandpa in a wheelchair. If LJ saw the story, he would go directly to the moon, do not pass go, do not collect two hundred dollars. But if Demler-Vargus was dirty, wouldn't OSHA and the EPA have caught on and stopped them? Was Bendickson lying or was he running a clean shop?

Jack was a good writer. Travis wondered if he would really pursue a story about Demler-Vargus. He took the paper and coffee and went back around the nurses' station.

"Good morning." A different nurse was behind the counter now, an attractive brunette.

Travis looked behind him and, seeing no one there, concluded she was speaking to him. "Hello. How is the morning treating you?"

"Very well." Her name tag read Meredith. "Can I help you with anything?"

"Ahh . . ." Travis wanted to keep the conversation going. "I'm Galen Randall's son, he's in room 411. I was wonderin', is he gonna get to go home today?"

She flipped through pages on a clipboard and paused. "His doctor is supposed to come by this morning and give him a look. He has definitely shown improvement. It shouldn't be too much longer."

"Very good, then." Travis tapped the counter, wishing there was more to talk about. "By the way, my name's Travis—Travis Randall."

Meredith lost her pretty smile for a split second. She shot a glance at another nurse seated behind the counter, who made eye contact and then looked back down at his paperwork. Meredith gave Travis a sealed-mouth smile. "Nice to meet you, Mr. Randall. I hope your father gets to go home soon."

Mr. Randall. See how she immediately shut him down? Slammed the door right in his uneducated, country-bumpkin face.

"Thank you." Travis headed back toward his father's room.

He was forty two. His folks had married in their twenties; they were together over fifty years. They'd had their two sons, built a business, taken care of each other and their neighbors—*that* was living.

Travis was sick and tired of being alone. It frustrated him that his life was half over and he had no one. The problem was, he never had any opportunities to meet nice women. He didn't hang out in the bars. Most of the clients at the garage were men or housewives. Daddy told him he needed to go to the singles' class at church, and he was half tempted to try it. What did he have to lose? But he'd probably only embarrass himself there too.

'Course LJ was in the same boat as Travis, but his brother hung out at the Twisted Tavern and the East End Grill now and again, so he had a bigger pool of ladies to draw from—if you wanted to call them that.

LJ had been married once, to Roxanne. They were the proud parents of Bo. When LJ got a tip Roxanne might be seeing somebody on the sly, he went after the fella in the Big Lots parking lot; tore him limb from limb. But then the man sent a posse after LJ one night, and they carved him up so badly he lost his left eye. After the divorce, LJ got shared custody of Bo.

Rounding the corner and walking back down the long hallway, Travis said hey to the nurse Candace, who was typing something at a workstation in the hallway. *'Course she didn't mention nothing about Daddy's waffles.*

Down the long hallway near his father's room, Travis suddenly saw the man in the black overcoat pop into the hallway. He glanced both ways, held his eyes on Travis for a second, and whipped off in the opposite direction.

That's odd.

The man practically ran out of there.

Travis picked up the pace. He'd take a look into the room the man had come from. He walked faster. Then his heart kicked up a notch.

Wait a minute . . .

It hit him like a bomb.

The man had not been *near* his father's room—he'd been *in* it!

Travis busted through the heavy door, past the bathroom, hoping to turn the corner to see a nurse doting over Daddy, hoping to see his father awake with his glasses on, eating his waffle, looking out the window, complaining about how much longer he would have to stay.

Travis jammed on the brakes at the foot of the bed.

The room was still. Everything was fine.

Daddy slept.

The breakfast tray had been delivered; it sat on the swinging table next to the bed, but the food hadn't been touched. Nothing was beeping on the monitors. Travis stared at Daddy's chest until he saw movement.

"Phew-wee."

Travis hurried back into the hallway, looking for the man in black, but he was long gone. Could he be sure the man had left this room? Perhaps he was mistaken.

He went back in and plunked into the chair, still holding the crumpled newspaper.

He reached over and lifted the silver lid off the main breakfast plate.

Egg

"Dang." He dropped back into the chair.

Incompetents.

Travis was worn out already and the day had hardly begun.

He leaned back, folded the newspaper, and found his place.

> *Bendickson felt so strongly about Demler-Vargus's green initiative that he appointed his son, Devon Bendickson, 28, as the company's environmental liaison. Devon has degrees from Furman and Rutgers and is Bendickson's only child, by his first wife, Patricia.*
>
> *Enjoying his third marriage, this one to concert pianist Celeste Excelsior, Bendickson resides in a 15,000-square-foot solar-powered mansion in Cool Springs. The glass, metal, and stone architectural award-winning structure has indoor and outdoor pools and spas, tennis and basketball courts, and a professional par-three golf hole designed by golf great and Columbus native Jack Nicklaus.*
>
> *Although Trenton City residents may see Bendickson cruising around town in a silver Range Rover, his daily vehicle, the fiberglass king also has a collection of automobiles in his seven-car garage, including his prized-possession, a 1982 DeLorean. He loves boating, mainly in the Atlantic, on his 32-foot yacht, aptly named* Fiberglass Slipper, *which he docks at the Sea Pines Resort on Hilton Head Island in South Carolina.*

Travis wasn't interested in finishing the story. He tossed the paper aside and looked at his father. Why was he sleeping so long? The food had to be cold by now, and Daddy detested cold food.

Travis would have them heat it up when his father awoke. Until then, he decided to turn on the TV, real low.

He scanned the room for the remote.

Wait . . .

The silver IV stand had been moved.

It had been back toward the wall earlier.

He looked from the wheels up the silver pole to the IV bag.

A pinkish solution floated with the clear liquid in the bag.

With three giant steps, Travis grabbed the pouch and followed the tube leading to Daddy's right arm.

A sudden, violent cough from his father jolted Travis, drawing his attention away from his task. Daddy's face was purple as a bruise. His coughing turned to choking, then to a loud, alarming screeching for air.

"Oh dear Lord." Travis's hands shook violently.

His father gasped and his arms flailed. His hands moved to his throat. His brown eyes searched Travis in despair.

Travis snatched Daddy's wrist and pulled it toward him, fumbling for the IV tube and ripping it away.

His father's body was limp, his head grotesquely twisted to one side, and the color was draining from his face like antifreeze flushing from a radiator.

The monitor next to him pinged and flashed, pinged and flashed.

"No!"

"Mr. Randall?" came a voice from the intercom.

Travis grabbed it with trembling hands and pressed talk. "Hurry! We need a doctor! *Emergency!*"

Going one way, then another, uncertain what to do, Travis straightened his father's torso and shifted his head back to a normal position, trying to make him look right. But the older man's lips were almost as white as his ashen face.

Travis sprinted into the hallway and yelled as loud as he could toward the nurses' station. "Emergency. Room 411! Get a doctor!"

Seeing they were scrambling, Travis ran back in and took his father's face in his hands. "Come on, Daddy. Hang on. Please . . . "

Travis put his arms around him and hugged. "Hold on, Daddy. Hold on." As he rocked him, Travis's eyes fell to the dangling IV tube, dripping a steady flow of the liquid that, he was certain, had been tainted by the stranger in black.

3

Jack scratched images of smokestacks with a black felt-tip pen on his yellow notepad as he rocked and squeaked in the fake brown leather executive chair. He was seated at an ancient conference room table on the third floor of the *Trenton City Dispatch*, just off the newsroom. The enormous table, with chairs for twelve, now accommodated six. The brown-paneled room, with stained Styrofoam ceiling, overlooked the Trenton City courthouse, whose clock read ten twenty-five.

"That's a wrap," said Editor Cecil Barton, whom Jack had worked with for seven years. "Let's remember to help each other. Your reporters should be sharing leads, sharing information. It's your job to make sure they *communicate*. That's how we stay on top."

Although everything was an emergency to Cecil, whose nerves carved lines around his frazzled eyes and narrow forehead, Jack had to admit he was one of the finest journalists he knew. Not a great manager, but a great journalist.

"Questions?" Cecil stood and stroked his mound of thinning brown hair. Obviously, from his stature and coloring, he was a man who cared little about food or sunshine.

"I've got something." Jack stood as the others gathered their things to adjourn. "I know some residents on the east side who think Demler-Vargus is making people sick over there. We've covered bits and pieces of their pollution issues, but have we ever done anything in-depth? An investigative series?"

Cecil took a giant breath and slouched. He was about to respond when his right-hand man Nigel Waheed chimed in. "That was Amy's beat. Whenever complaints were filed, she got wind of them through her contacts at the courthouse. Demler-Vargus has been fined before, but they've always complied. We've covered all that."

Dark-skinned, dark-eyed Waheed—who was always trying to schmooze Cecil—was referring to reporter Amy Sheets, who had covered the east side for years, until she moved to Columbus to be closer to her aging parents.

Pete Forbes spoke up. "Whittaker's got that beat now."

Jack was privately of the opinion that Forbes, the city editor, was going through a midlife crisis. The guy was on a no-carb diet, had a personal trainer, wore orthodontic braces, and had recently shown up at work in a yellow Miata.

"Of course, Whittaker doesn't have the contacts at the courthouse that Amy did," Pete added.

"Never will." Cecil crossed his arms in a huff.

Derrick Whittaker, a thirtysomething African American reporter, was one of Jack's best friends. Although he was a fantastic writer, Derrick sometimes lacked speed at deadline time. Jack coached him whenever he could, and truly believed he was becoming a star reporter.

"My contacts say they know people who've gotten payoffs from Demler-Vargus," Jack said, "but it's all been hushed up." He knew that would ruffle Cecil's feathers. The editor hated missing a story or getting scooped, especially by the news team at the popular local radio station, WDUC-AM 550, which *Dispatch* reporters fondly called "the Duck."

"For the love of peace, Crittendon," said Cecil, "if anything earth-shattering was going on over there, I'd have thought you would have dug it up during that feature you did on the CEO. What did *he* have to say about it?"

"He's insists they're green; all kinds of clean initiatives. But before I interviewed him I looked at Amy's stories. They dealt more with government compliance issues than with personal complaints. What I'm getting from my sources is that there's a whole lot of animosity on that side of town toward the company."

"What sources?" Nigel snapped.

"Just a family of long-time residents. They have a small business there. The mom died of respiratory failure, but she had mouth sores, hives, chronic sore throat."

"Who?" Cecil said.

"The Randalls. Galen's the dad. LJ and Travis are the sons."

"Amy told me once she was working on a story with an employee of Demler-Vargus," said copy editor Jocelyn Jenkins. "Actually, it was a couple— they both worked in the plant. Amy was going to meet with them."

"What came of it?" Cecil threw his bony hands in the air and glared at Pete, then Nigel.

"I don't know anything about it." Nigel shrank up like a prune, his black eyes enormous, apparently shocked something might have gotten passed him.

"She must've been flying under the radar on that one," Pete said. "I never heard about it."

"Well . . ." Cecil nodded rapidly, as if he was the only one who understood, "obviously it was a dead end or she would have told us about it."

"When was that?" Jack asked.

Jocelyn pursed her lips and shook her head. "A year ago? Nine months? Something like that."

"Would you consider letting me spend a few hours on it?" Jack asked "See if there's anything to it?"

Nigel groaned and closed his notebook.

"It might make a good community interest series," Jack said. "If it pans out."

"Depends." Cecil shrugged. "It might be hard news, it might be a softer feature series. I have a hunch it's *nothing.*" Cecil was animated, his small brown eyes forced wide open by his taut nerves. "Jack, you've got a full plate, and that's Whittaker's beat, anyway. It's time he got his big boy pants on. Pete, have Derrick interview Jack's sources over there and see what he finds. But no more than a couple hours. That's it. If there's nothing there, forget about it."

"I'll go on record saying he's not gonna find a thing," Nigel said. "Amy was the best. If there was anything there, she would have dug it up. But knock yourself out."

The meeting broke up, and Jack stopped in the break room for a cup of coffee to take back to his desk. The sprawling newsroom, with its maze of cubicles and computers, was dotted with a person here and there staring at a glowing computer screen. Since the *Dispatch* had an evening deadline, many reporters and photographers were out on their beats until after lunch.

Jack had worked with Cecil long enough to realize what his editor was doing, and it bugged him. He was throwing Pete and Derrick together on Demler-Vargus, knowing they had bumped heads about Derrick's supposed lack of productivity. Cecil wanted them to work together in hopes things would magically resolve themselves. That was one of the editor's managerial weaknesses—not addressing personnel issues head on. Not only that, but Jack was certain the Randall family wouldn't talk to Derrick as readily as they would to him.

He got to his desk and found his notes from the recent Trenton City municipal meeting. He slipped on his headset, plunked into his chair, and opened a Word document where he would keystroke notes during his phone interviews. He had to track down five city council members, make a two o'clock water board meeting, and write two stories before deadline.

Jack knew what was going to happen. He would get swept up in all his assignments, more work would be thrown at him, and he would forget all about the Randalls and Demler-Vargus. And he'd buy LJ his six-pack.

But something about the situation was nagging at him. He felt for the Randalls, having lost their mother to such a cruel sickness. And what about the other victims in that neighborhood? If Demler-Vargus was hurting people, Jack wanted to know—and believed Demler-Vargus should be held accountable.

His phone vibrated. At the sight of Pam's number, his heart jumped—even after so much time had passed since her kidnapping.

"Hey darlin'," he answered quietly.

"Is this Jack Crittendon, famous reporter and feature editor at the award-winning *Trenton City Dispatch?*" Pam said.

"You got him."

"I have a story to report . . ."

Jack smiled, glad to hear her voice, but uptight about all he had to do.

"What's happening?" he said.

"Girls off to school, laundry in. Did you get the car to the boys?"

"Yep. Galen's in the hospital with respiratory problems, but he'll be okay."

"Oh no . . . maybe you can go see him."

Sometimes Jack wondered if she realized how busy he was.

"Maybe," he said. "Got a lot cooking here."

"How'd your editorial meeting go?"

"Not bad. Remind me to tell you about the Demler-Vargus thing."

"You sound busy. I'll let you go in a sec. I just wanted to tell you two things."

"Shoot."

"My mom called this morning. She said Daddy hasn't been himself."

Ugh. Pam's mom, Margaret, was extremely paranoid. Her husband's "illness" was likely all in her imagination.

"He hasn't had any appetite—or energy. You know my mom, she's a wreck. I was thinking it's about time I got up to see them anyway. Maybe we could all go some weekend."

"Okay." Jack really didn't want to make the two-and-a-half hour trip to Cleveland any time soon. "It depends on the weather. Let's look at the calendar . . ."

"Okay." Pam hesitated. "I was hoping we could do it soon—like this weekend or next?"

Jack took a deep breath, leaned back in his chair, and grimaced, glad she couldn't see his reaction. "Let's talk about it tonight."

"Okay."

He could tell by her voice that he had burst her bubble. Now she was debating whether to even tell him the second thing.

"What else?" he prompted.

"I'll tell you later." Her voice fell into a monotone.

She had come to him recently with several things that meant a lot to her, and he had squelched her every time—it seemed to be the norm lately.

"Go ahead, really," he said. "I want to hear."

"I was just going to tell you I talked to Wendy McDaniel."

Jack sighed. Wendy was the wife of Evan McDaniel, a local pastor who, clinically depressed and facing serious pressure at his church, had left town at the same time as the Granger Meade fiasco. In a stranger-than-fiction scenario, a suicidal Evan ended up in a crucible with Granger, and the two down-and-outers made a pact to live. Evan then counseled Granger during the latter's incarceration at Mansfield Correctional Institution and now insisted Granger was "reformed"—that he was "a different person."

Jack refused to believe it.

"Yeah?" He tried to sound upbeat. "What's going on with the McDaniels?" He knew Evan had stepped down as pastor of his church and had been working at an art supply store in Trenton City.

"Evan helped Granger find a job."

Really? Jack dropped his head. "Where?" That was all he could muster. Was he supposed to jump for joy that her abductor had found employment?

"Crafts Galore." Pam spoke quietly, all emotion gone. "In Mount Camden. I just thought it was a good thing."

"They're going to let him be around all those attractive housewives?"

Dead silence.

Jack knew his burning comment had hurt Pam. He stood, realizing it was too late to take it back.

There was a long pause. "I'll talk to you later," she said finally.

"Pam, what do you want me to say? I'm so thrilled your kidnapper got a job? Be serious."

"You know something, Jack? You have to let this go."

"I just find it hard to believe—"

"This bitterness is poisoning you. You get so angry at the littlest things—ever since it happened."

"And you can't understand that? My wife was stalked by some pervert high school classmate. He invaded our home—took things. Tore you away from us for a night of pure hell!"

"Have *you* not been forgiven?"

"Pam—"

"You forgive to a point, but if it's too big of a sin or too personal, forget it?"

"He's dangerous! Okay? My job is to protect you—and the girls."

"We've been through this. God's big enough, Jack. He's big enough to protect us. He showed us that. He's big enough to make something of Granger, if that's what he wants to do. But who are we to make that call?"

Jack knew she was right, but he had not been able to forgive, period. As far as he was concerned, it wasn't even a topic for discussion. He had only agreed to drop charges to appease Pam.

"Look, I just don't want any part of the guy and, no, I don't like knowing he's free and living near us. That's ludicrous. I don't want to know anything about him. Can't *you* understand *that?*"

"It's not like we're going to have him for dinner. I was just sharing something uplifting.. Wendy said they're making progress. Evan is really helping him."

"Evan's wife wasn't kidnapped by that freak!"

"Jack, he is not a freak. He's a person who was mentally abused by his parents his entire life. Can't you put yourself in his shoes?"

"No. I can't! I can't understand anyone who could steal a mother from her children. I don't think I ever will."

"Does it matter to you at all that Evan has talked to Granger about God?"

But all Jack could think about was what might have happened if Pam hadn't escaped. Rape? Murder? Another unthinkable headline in the news?

"Answer me, Jack. Does it matter to you that Granger is considering God?"

"No," he said flatly. "It doesn't. It just doesn't."

Pam sniffed and there was a long pause.

"I know I'm not perfect," she said. "But you need to examine yourself on this. You need to forgive—just as much as you've been forgiven. I've gotta go."

He sighed, not wanting it to end like this, trying to think of something to say.

"Bye." Pam hung up.

He looked at the phone. His face flushed. He debated whether to call her back. But all he would be doing was confirming what she had said about his temper.

"What up, dude?" Derrick Whittaker slung his leather satchel into the chair in Jack's cubicle and peeled off his enormous green coat. Running a flat hand along the right side of his buzz-cut Afro, as if giving the side of a car one last polish, he said, "Dig the new do?"

"Nice."

"What's with you?" Derrick was big into weight lifting and was built like a brick house; not huge but lean, with zero body fat.

"What do you mean?"

"Dude, you're usually in, like, this incredible mood. Something must be up."

"Had it out with the wife." Jack put his phone back in its holster.

Derrick jumped back two feet, looking as if he'd smelled a skunk. "For real? You guys fight?"

Jack raised his eyebrows and tried to get back to what he was doing.

"What about?" Derrick made himself at home, resting an arm along the top of Jack's cubicle.

"Granger Meade." Jack leaned way back in his chair and clasped his hands behind his head.

"What about him?"

"She insists on keeping tabs on him. Evan McDaniel helped him find a job. Big deal."

"Hmm. Where?"

"Crafts Galore. Mount Camden."

Derrick blew out through lips that formed an O, as if he was about to whistle. "I can see the rub. At least when you guys argue, it's about something. Zenia and I argue about nothing, all the time."

"Well, I got news. It doesn't get any better when you walk down the aisle. Over time, all the little stuff gets magnified."

Jack had met Zenia at the Public Safety Director's office at City Hall, where she worked, and had introduced her to Derrick at a Christmas party several years ago. The two formed an immediate bond. When they were on, they sizzled. But when they were off, they were like bickering siblings.

"Dude, you're killin' me. What are you trying to do, scare me out of it?"

"No, man, I'm just being real. Marriage is *tough*. You gotta give, give, give—and not expect a whole lot back. And then when you have kids . . . look out."

Jack knew he had it good. Pam was special and beautiful. She still struggled with fear and paranoia handed down from her mother, but she was generous and compassionate. She did for others, all the time. She was a true gift from God.

"Man, I'll be honest," said Derrick, in a rare serious moment. He glanced around with those big brown eyes and shiny black retro glasses, making sure no one else was listening. "Sometimes I wonder if I'm ready, if I have the maturity—not only to be a good husband, but a good dad. I'm one selfish dog."

"Dude, that's half the battle, right there, realizing you're selfish. We all are. At least you know it and can work on it."

"That doesn't come easy for me—or Z."

Jack was about to "say something Christian," but he stopped before he made a hypocrite of himself. After all, where was the Spirit five minutes ago when he belittled Pam for caring about the well-being of a mixed-up individual whose rotten misdeeds she was willing to overlook in hopes that he might find God?

"Me either," Jack said. "We're all a work in progress . . . And speaking of work, I gotta get busy."

As Derrick hung his coat and began unloading his bag, Jack bent over, elbows on knees, staring at the gray carpet beneath his desk. At one time in his life, he would have taken a minute to pray, but as fast as that thought came, it went, run over by a freight train of revulsion toward Granger and apprehension about his family's safety.

He had a problem.

But that was just how it was—he was powerless against it.

Or had he made a calculated decision to deny God's way? Was it really his pride that had convinced him that this was his right—to harbor bitterness toward the demon who had invaded their lives?

But he *was* right to be cautious—and vigilant. It was his job as husband and father to protect his family.

That's why he'd bought the gun the day Granger got out.

For protection.

Who could blame him?

But Pam still doesn't know.

And that was another problem: it was getting easier and easier to lie.

4

A gob of money must have gone into furnishing the plush waiting area near ICU, where Travis sat on a hard, shiny leather chair, squinting at his worn-out notepad, making calls to clients. He gave the same explanation to each: his father was out of commission, there'd be a delay getting their vehicles fixed.

Nephew Bo was slumped on a big comfy couch, black earplugs stuffed in his ears, blasting away at some shoot-'em-up game on his handheld. At seventeen he was tall and lanky, black hair shaved to the scalp, low-riding baggy jeans, silver chain, the works. LJ, who should have been curbing his son's time on that idiot box, stood staring out the window at the end of the hall.

Travis figured the hospital made the ICU area extra cozy because the people who were waiting there were nervous and worried, suffering, probably doing some grieving. A large old woman across the room looked sick with sorrow.

He licked his fingers and leafed through the little notepad till he found Jack Crittendon's cell number.

"Jack, I'm real sorry, but your Jetta ain't gonna be ready till tomorrow or the next day. Daddy took a turn for the worse today. Me and LJ and Bo's all at the hospital."

"No worries about the car. What's going on with Galen?" Jack said.

It still didn't seem real to Travis. "It's a long story. He's stable now, but all we know is he was poisoned."

"Poisoned? You mean food poisoning?"

"I wish. He was drugged on purpose, through his IV."

"*What?* By who? What kind of poison?"

"I saw a man leave his room. The police got here right away. They're working with hospital security, checking all the video cameras. Only a trace made it into Daddy's system, but the doctor said whatever they gave him would have made his whole respiratory system shut down in another couple minutes."

"Who would do this, Travis? Did you recognize the guy from anywhere?"

"No sir. And I got a clear look at him at one point, in the waiting room. And I can assure you of this—I ain't gonna forget that face."

The only long-shot idea Travis had was that LJ had got vengeance on the posse that carved his eye out, and this was some sort of payback. He'd be asking his brother about that in about one minute flat.

"But he's going to make it?" Jack said.

"Yeah, yeah." Travis sighed, feeling like a slow-leaking tire. "They gave him an IV with some medicine that counters the effects of the bad drug. He vomited twice from it, but he's resting good now. We're hoping he gets back to a private room by tonight."

"I'm going to try to get over there to see you guys."

"You don't have to, Jack. Besides, you ain't got no car, remember? Sorry to leave you stranded."

"Don't worry about it. Pam can get me."

Bo had managed to unfold his lazy bones from the couch and made his way over to Travis. "Can I have some coin for the snack machine?" he whispered. "I'm starving."

"Hold on a minute, Jack." Travis looked up at Bo with a snarled face and covered the phone. "Did you ask yer daddy?"

"He ain't gonna give me nothin'."

Travis was a darn softy. "In a minute," he whispered.

Bo nodded and meandered away.

"Jack, sorry. I guess that'll do it. I'll let you know when your car's ready."

"Okay. We're flexible."

"All righty then. I gotta make some more calls—one to that big-shot lawyer I told you about."

"The one helping you with Demler-Vargus? What's his name?"

"Ralston Coon." Travis chuckled. "How could you forgit that one, right?"

"Do you know how often your dad has met with him?"

"Only once I know of. I drove him downtown to Coon's office—it's only a couple blocks from the *Dispatch*, in the Flat Iron Building. You shoulda seen that place. Whew-golly, it was polished."

"Did you meet Coon yourself?" Jack said.

"Yeah. I went in with Daddy to make sure he got up to the office okay. Coon came out and we said hey. I left Daddy there to tell Coon all the stuff he knew, and I ran errands."

"What kind of stuff?"

"Daddy keeps notes—dates when we can actually see pink fiberglass all over the neighborhood. Names of neighbors who's ailing from it. Names of employees who had the inside dope on what really goes on in the plant."

"And your dad shared all that with the lawyer?"

"Yeah. Coon made copies of his notes. Daddy felt real good about the whole thing."

There was a long pause.

"What's wrong, Jack? Daddy felt like we was finally gonna get some justice. You think we did wrong?"

"Not if Coon's honest. How did Galen hear about him?"

"His best buddy, Charlie Snellinger, recommended him."

"And is that the only time they met?"

"They've talked on the phone a couple times, but I'm pretty sure that's it. We keep pretty close tabs on Daddy. He's been strugglin' with rememberin' things lately, like where he put his keys and his chewing tobacca."

"Has he mentioned that to a doctor? They have patches you put on your skin now to slow down memory loss."

The gimmicks people don't fall for these days.

"We might look into that," Travis fibbed.

"Do you recall when it was your dad met with Coon at his office?"

"Second Tuesday of the month," Travis said. "You know how I remember that so quick? 'Cause down at Gebralter's Grocery, Mr. Gebralter makes his homemade sausage the first Tuesday every month. That's where I went after I dropped Daddy."

"Travis, I talked to my editor today, about doing an investigative piece on Demler-Vargus."

"You get the green light?"

"He gave it to another reporter, a good friend of mine, Derrick Whittaker."

"Hmm."

"But I'm going to see if I might be able to work with him on it. Do you have those notes your dad kept?"

"They're in Momma's old desk in the kitchen. You was standin' right by it this mornin'."

"If it's all right with you, I'd like to see those notes."

"Sure, sure. How 'bout when you come by to get the Jetta?"

"Yeah. I might want to see them before that. I'd like to talk with Coon, but I want to know what's in those notes first."

"Good idea," Travis said.

"Is anybody around the house—if I were to get a ride over there?"

"Shoot, it's open, Jack. Just go on in, same way you came in this mornin'. Daddy's notes is in the drawer on the far left, in one a them manila folders. It's got D-V written on it. Can't miss it."

"Okay then. I might have Derrick run me over there."

"Jack, you think Demler-Vargus did this to Daddy?"

Jack exhaled loudly. "I can't imagine that. It would be very sloppy."

"Well, *someone* poisoned him." Travis stood. "And whoever did it is gonna face the wrath of the Randall clan—and that ain't gonna be purty."

5

Jack was jealous of the heat blasting in Derrick's maroon Toyota FJ Cruiser, which had him sweating within minutes of their drive to the Randalls' place. He felt quite hip riding shotgun in the Cruiser, which Derrick had decked out with the all-terrain package: rock rails, fog lights, side steps, roof rack, tow kit, and black wheels.

As they rolled through slushy backstreets beneath a dreary winter sky, Jack explained all he knew about the Randalls' accusations against Demler-Vargus and Galen's apparent poisoning.

"That is crazy," Derrick said. "They're sure he was poisoned?"

"Yep. I got a feeling about this one," Jack said.

"Barton's gonna lose his marbles when he finds out we're both working on this thing."

"Look, he told Pete to give you the story, and for me to give you my leads. That's what we're doing. Finding Galen's folder will get you started. You can take it from there." Jack wanted to be more involved and had a hunch he would be.

"You believe how these people live over here?" Derrick scanned the drab, impoverished landscape. "Never fails to remind me of Detroit."

"That's right, you're a Motor City kid."

"Lower east side. Mostly single-parent homes. Food stamps. Drugs. Gangs."

"You had both parents, didn't you?"

Derrick nodded and tugged at his black leather gloves as he drove. "We were the exception. Had a lot of love between my folks and my three sisters. All my buddies wanted to hang at my house. It always amazed them—how calm things were, when right outside the door there was gunfire and all kinds of chaos."

"Where'd your dad work?"

"GM. Mom too. We got out of that neighborhood eventually."

"Turn left here, and that's it on the right." Jack pointed.

Jack's Jetta and several other vehicles sat covered in a dusting of snow in front of the large metal garage. Derrick pulled into the driveway over some tire tracks and footprints that were fading with the new snow.

"I can't believe they just leave it open." He parked, yanked the brake, and turned off the car.

"If you knew them, you'd understand. Very simple people." Jack opened his door. "Brrr."

Rusty, stationed on the back porch, howled with such zeal that he came off his front paws.

"Hey. I don't do attack dogs." Derrick got out of the Cruiser slowly and stood behind his open door. He tugged his green ski cap low over his forehead and remained there.

"He's harmless." Jack trudged toward the steps. "I was just here this morning and walked right past him. Come on."

"Man, they don't pay me for this." Derrick slammed his door. "Wait up, Critt." Derrick slipped, but grabbed the big side mirror on the Cruiser to stabilize himself.

"Watch yourself," Jack kidded. "Calm down, Rusty," he said in his nicest tone. "Be nice to Derrick." He looked back at Derrick, who was ten steps behind him. "I hope this dog's not prejudiced." They both laughed.

Jack trudged up the steps, which were covered with a half inch of snow and a bunch of old footprints.

"Just wait for me, would you?" Derrick was right behind him. "Easy, Fido, ea-sy."

The dog pranced in a circle and sniffed them with his dirty nose, then gave a low growl.

"Hurry up, man. He's seriously deranged."

Jack snickered as he opened the squeaky screen door and nudged the heavy wood door open, Derrick pushing from behind.

The place did not resemble the kitchen Jack had stepped into that morning.

"Hold up." Jack threw an arm up to stop Derrick.

Derrick froze and looked around. "No way."

"Shhh." Jack held a finger to his lips.

The kitchen cupboards and drawers were open at cockeyed angles, their contents spilled over the counters and floor. Broken dishes, pots, silverware, pans, and shattered glass were everywhere.

Standing completely still, they listened. Something moved in the adjacent room. Jack bent down, hiked the leg of his pants up over the black holster, and yanked the gun out. He rose, caught a glimpse of Derrick's gaping mouth and huge eyes, and cocked the gun with his thumb instead of racking the slide, to keep it quiet.

A skinny gray cat slinked around the corner.

Both men exhaled, and Jack lowered the weapon.

With its back arched, the cat tiptoed through the broken plates and strewn silverware.

"What're you doing with that?" Derrick eyed the gun.

Jack ignored him and took in the scene. The kitchen table where Travis had eaten that morning was overturned, and the desk where the Demler-Vargus folder was supposed to be had been smashed onto its side, its drawers and contents scattered everywhere.

"I think they're gone." Derrick's voice broke. "Don't you?"

"Yeah." Jack holstered the gun.

Someone had been searching for something.

Whoever it was knew the Randalls were away.

Jack's head got fuzzy as he contemplated the danger the Randalls were in—and the potential story he and Derrick were sitting on. He made his way across the kitchen and peeked into the TV room—a complete demolition site.

"There too?" Derrick asked.

Jack nodded.

The couch was overturned, its cushions knifed open and gutted. Everything was smashed, from the big-screen TV to an antique glass cabinet that looked like it had held a coin collection.

Jack assumed the rest of the little house was in similar condition, and his heart broke for Galen and the boys.

He came back into the center of the kitchen. Whoever had ruined the place had done so with a vengeance. The kitchen chairs were broken like kindling. The dishwasher door was dented from a boot.

"I'll call Travis." Jack got his phone out. "Let's look for the folder."

"You think that's what they were after?"

"Who knows? It might just be random, but somehow I don't think so."

"Should we call the cops?" Derrick bent down over one of the desk drawers on the floor and began sorting through what was left in it.

"Yeah . . . I'll ask Travis if he wants me to."

Jack dialed Travis's cell phone and got no answer, so he tried LJ.

"LJ, is Travis available?" Jack knew Travis had the cooler head.

"He's indisposed right now, if you know what I mean. He told you the Jetta's gonna be late, right?

"Yeah, how's Galen?"

"Steady. Should be back to a private room right quick here."

"Good." Jack hesitated, knowing he needed to tell LJ about the break-in. "LJ, did Travis tell you he gave me permission to go to your house and get your dad's notes on Demler-Vargus?"

"No, but it's fine. The house is open."

"Yeah, me and another reporter from the *Dispatch* came over to get the folder."

"Knock yerself out."

"There's a problem, LJ. Your house has been . . . searched."

"Searched? Whatcha mean, Jack?"

"When we got here, we found it—pretty badly torn up. Someone was looking for something."

"Tore up? You mean *robbed?*"

"We don't know if anything's missing. Do you want me to call the police? I kind of wanted one of you to be here . . ."

"Just wait, Jack. We'll be right there, fast as we can."

"Okay, we're going to keep searching for the notes."

"How bad is it, Jack?" LJ's voice was low and cold.

"It's pretty bad, LJ . . . I'm sorry."

"Bo!" LJ had covered the phone, but Jack could still hear his booming voice. "Git yer coat. Find your uncle. We gotta go . . . Jack?"

"Yeah."

"We're coming."

Jack put his phone away and examined the mess as Derrick made his way to another of the strewn drawers on the floor.

"Which ones haven't you looked in?" Jack asked.

"Those two." Derrick pointed toward two small desk drawers lying on the floor near the sink. Jack tiptoed through the maze of broken dishes and picked up one of the drawers.

"Hold up. Got something." Derrick turned a manila folder toward Jack. "Says D-V right here in pencil." He opened it, stared down, then lifted the manila folder so that it dangled open—empty.

Derrick's face was stone. "This is all that was in it." He waved a small piece of white paper in two fingers, then held it up and read it aloud to Jack: "LEAVE IT ALONE."

6

Although you wouldn't guess it from the clothes he wore, Travis was a neat freak. He tried to keep the house clean, because that's what his mother had always done. So when he walked into the foul mess at the house, a sick feeling gnawed at the pit of his stomach and he got right to work picking things up.

Who could do this to another person's property? It was downright heartless. There just wasn't any respect any more.

Jack and the black reporter, Derrick, had stayed at the house till Travis and LJ arrived. When Travis saw the note he was scared and blazing mad at the same time. LJ was just blazing mad. They scanned the house and quickly determined nothing else was missing. To Travis's way of thinking, that meant the break-in and his father's poisoning had something, if not everything, to do with Demler-Vargus.

LJ wanted to wring somebody's neck, but didn't know whose. Instead, he ended up kicking things around, muttering to himself the whole time, making things even more tension-filled than they already were. Bo had stayed behind at the hospital to keep an eye on his grandfather. So it was pretty much up to Travis to do the work, picking up that cruel mess until the winter sky turned dark at suppertime.

The cop who came to the house was a skinny, nervous wreck of a kid named Delgado who Travis was sure was a rookie right out of officer training. He basically took a few notes, stuttered that he would file a report, and advised the boys to keep the door locked. Trenton City's finest.

"What you want to do for dinner?" LJ lazed into the TV room where Travis had finally plunked down in Daddy's blue corduroy recliner to take a blow.

"This mess and Daddy's poisoning . . . they got nothing to do with you, right?" Travis said.

"Me?" LJ craned his neck. "What would they have to do with me?"

"I want to make sure there's nothing you're not telling me, like, if you're in more trouble with Roxanne's crowd."

"No sir. Whoever did this is the same person who poisoned Daddy, most likely."

The phone rang, and Travis answered.

"Travis, it's Jack. Just calling to see how Galen is."

"Bo is with him. He says they done moved Daddy back to a private room. Nurse said he's in 'good condition.'"

"Is Bo going to spend the night there?"

Travis raised an eyebrow. "Why? You think they're gonna try something else?"

"This thing isn't sitting right with me," Jack said. "I think one of you should be at the hospital overnight. Did the police ever get back to you on the video from the hospital?"

"Tomorrow," Travis said.

"Think about it, Travis. They poisoned Galen. They ransacked your house. These guys are playing hardball."

"What do you think we should do?"

"Let's meet at the hospital, see if we can talk to your dad. I've got some questions for him. And meanwhile, you need to tell your lawyer what's happened."

"How soon can you be there?" Travis was already heading for his coat and keys.

"I'm about to grab a bite with my family," Jack said. "But I can be there in an hour. I'm going to have Derrick meet us there too."

"We're going now. They moved him to room 356."

"See you there."

• • •

Rebecca and Faye loved eating at Campolo's, the cozy Italian restaurant nestled along the sidewalks near their Merriman Woods neighborhood. Pamela sat on one side of the booth watching for Jack, while across from her Rebecca and Faye colored away at their kids' menus, sipping their lemonades through straws, gabbing like old ladies, and looking out the window every once in a while at the gently falling snow.

After the awkward call from Jack, when he told her he needed to work that evening, they had agreed to meet for a quick bite. Pamela placed their order when she and the girls arrived so the food would be ready when he got there.

"Look, girls, here comes Daddy." Pamela tried to sound excited as she shooed them off to greet Jack. With a solemn face, he peeled off his heavy coat on the way to the booth. As the girls reached him with squeals and hugs, he couldn't help but smile as he knelt and engulfed them in his strong arms.

He hung his coat and gave Pamela a quick kiss as he slid into the booth next to her. "So tell me . . ." He leaned over the table toward the girls. "How was your day today, young ladies?"

The girls' eyes flashed as they jabbered about spelling bees, a butterfly collection, and a pet hamster named Golem that visited Faye's second-grade class. They were oblivious to the tension that sizzled like an invisible electric fence between their parents.

"So, what are we having? One large kitchen sink pizza pie?" Jack kidded.

"Noooo!" Nine-year-old Rebecca shook her head vehemently. "We girls are getting a medium cheese pizza pie with extra cheese. You and Mommy are getting a *medium* kitchen sink pizza pie, but no sausage, because Mommy says—"

"It's greasy," Jack finished, pretending he was going to faint.

The girls laughed, and he and Pamela exchanged obligatory smiles.

"Let me guess, did Mommy get extra black olives?"

"She most certainly did," said Faye. "And if you don't like it, you may pick them off—one by one."

So there, Pamela thought.

Jack took Faye's little hands in his big ones and shook them. "Did Mommy say that? Did she?"

Faye nodded and smiled broadly. "She most certainly did."

"And if you have a problem with it," Rebecca chimed in, "you don't have to eat."

Pamela felt her cheeks warm.

Jack changed to Rebecca's hands. "She did not say that!"

"Uh huh." Rebecca nodded. "Yes, sir, she most certainly did."

The girls giggled and went back to their coloring. Jack turned toward Pamela. "So, I'm going to need to pick off the black olives one by one, am I?"

He teased her, trying to gloss over what had happened earlier. "Any more word on your dad?"

Jack was ignoring the obvious elephant in the room.

"No." She fidgeted with her napkin and stared out at the crisp winter night, at the patches of snow beneath the streetlamps, at the cars and people heading to and fro.

"Maybe we can get up to see them soon. My car won't be ready for a few days." He told her about Galen's poisoning and the break-in at the Randall house.

Pamela had always believed in choosing her battles wisely; if it wasn't worth an all-out war, let it die. But this was worth going to battle over. It was time. For the past year and a half, even before Granger got out of prison, Jack's unforgiving spirit had worsened. Now that the topic was out on the table, she wasn't going to drop it until she had spoken everything that was on her heart.

"What do you think about what we talked about on the phone today?" She examined his eyes.

Jack searched beyond the window, then glanced at the girls, who were busy with their creations.

"You have your opinion and I have mine." He lowered his voice. "Pam, it's my job to protect us, okay? Think about what we went through, what he did to us—to *you*. Cut me some slack. You don't have to agree with the way I feel. I'm doing the best I can."

"You know what you remind me of? You remind me of *me*, right after he first broke in and I wanted to get a gun. I was so furious I couldn't think straight. I wanted to take matters into my own hands. That's how you're acting. And your temper is always right there, ready to blow at the drop of a hat. You were never this way before."

Jack lowered his head and slumped his shoulders. "I'm the husband, Pam. Okay? The protector."

"I was in denial about who was in control," she said. "*You* were the one who asked *me* if I thought God wanted us to have a gun, if he was big enough to protect us. Thanks to you, I took a hard look at myself. Remember? I realized I needed to give all my rage to him?"

Pamela caught a chill from a cool breeze that swept through the restaurant. The voices and laughter of other dinner guests and the sound of clattering dishes filled the stillness between them.

"Maybe I'm the voice you need to hear right now," she said, "just like you were the voice I needed to hear."

"I don't see why you can't understand my feelings toward the guy. I'm not ready to be his friend. After what happened, doesn't it make sense that I want to be a little . . . vigilant?"

"Vigilant is one thing." She paused, praying she would come across as humble. "But there's hate in your heart, honey. I can see it. It consumes you sometimes."

Jack's head swayed.

She hesitated, but decided there would never be a better time to lay it on the line. "I haven't seen you do your quiet time lately. What's going on?"

"Since when do you monitor my quiet time?" He squinted at her. "You don't know what I do and don't do."

A myriad of emotions rushed up and warmed Pamela's face. "See? You get angry about everything! You can't take any criticism. Listen to yourself."

"The guy kidnaps you, and you want me to celebrate that he got a minimum-wage job someplace? Nope. Can't do it. Sorry."

Rebecca had stopped coloring and was staring at them.

"We're having an adult conversation," Jack said to Rebecca. "Just keep doing what you're doing and try not to listen."

"This isn't the place," Pamela said softly.

"I'm not the one who brought it up."

Pamela shook her head and tried to rise above the tears that threatened to gush over.

"I'm going to say something, and I'll be done." She held her napkin beneath her left eye for a few seconds, then her right, then stuffed it in her lap.

"Mommy, are you crying?" Rebecca said.

Faye stopped coloring and stared, her mouth open.

"Girls," Jack said. "We'll be done talking in a minute."

Bella, their favorite waitress, showed up just then. "Hey, Jack. Your pizzas are almost up."

When she was out of earshot, Pamela whispered. "All I'm asking you to do is consider what I'm saying. Pray about it. See if there's anything God wants you to deal with. This affects all of us."

Jack stared at her, mouth sealed.

"I'm done," she said.

He locked his fingers under his chin in front of him, elbows on the table, and turned his head ninety degrees, staring out the window as if he wished he could disappear.

It was time for Pamela to flip on her happy switch. She dug into her purse, opened her compact, fixed herself up, and put it away, along with the conversation. "Let me see what you've colored." She reached for the girls' drawings.

Bella whirled around the corner with arms held high, a pizza tin in each mitted hand. "These are hot, hot." She slid them onto the table. "The Crittendon special. One extra cheese. One kitchen sink with extra BOs. Remember girls, hot trays, don't touch."

Jack asked Rebecca to say grace. He always asked someone else when he was in a bad mood.

Pamela slid Faye's plate in front of her. "Let me cut that for you so it cools off."

"I'll cut my own," Rebecca said. "Mm-mmm, yumalicious."

"Yumalicious," Faye echoed.

"That's *him.*" Jack shoved the table toward the girls with a loud scrape. Faye let out a scream. Everything flicked to slow motion, as each head turned toward their booth—and Jack dashing from the restaurant.

The girls cried aloud and Pamela quickly slid around to their side of the booth and took them in her arms.

Bella was there in an instant. "What's wrong, Pamela? What's happening?"

As Pamela held the girls, she leaned around Faye to look out the window where Jack had been gazing. Could he have seen Granger Meade? Her heart thundered, and her pulse pounded at her temples. She could not muster an answer for Bella or even look up at her, but simply squeezed the girls, closed her eyes, and prayed for Jack to come back.

7

Once Jack came back inside, he and Pam ended up taking the girls and pizzas home. He'd seen Granger Meade driving slowly past Campolo's in a small, dark pickup truck.

Jack had sprinted three blocks to catch up, but his ankle holster came loose.

What he would have done if he had caught up with Granger, he didn't know.

"We haven't seen him for a year and a half," Pam said, back at the house. "Surely he looks different now—somehow. Are you positive it was him?"

Jack knew it was. He would never forget that face, no matter how fat or skinny, young or old, no matter what length the dirty orange hair. It was Granger.

"We're bound to see him around town," Pam said. "We might as well prepare for it, mentally. The thing to do is ignore him."

Jack was dumbfounded at the way she had handled the whole thing, from the night she was kidnapped right up to that moment. Pam's mother would have had to be medicated. But Pam had steadily managed to sever those generational traits of fear and paranoia. She had long fought those wars, but had overcome, connecting with God in a way Jack only used to know.

He knew she was right about his own waning faith.

It was the weirdest thing, because he *saw* what was happening to him. He was spending less and less time reading his Bible, praying—the things he used to do with such zeal. He was like an apathetic bystander, watching his own demise, unable or unwilling to do anything about it. His venomous attitude toward Granger seemed to be creeping into other parts of his heart and mind, causing him to be outspokenly negative at some times, and just plain dead at others.

He'd left Pam and the girls at home, and now was riding toward the hospital with Derrick in hopes of speaking with Galen.

"You're sure quiet," Derrick said.

"It hasn't been the best day."

"Why would Granger pick Trenton City, of all the places he could live? That's crazy."

Derrick wheeled the FJ Cruiser into visitor parking at the hospital, which was lit up like a baseball stadium, making the patches of snow on the ground look neon.

"I know," Jack said. "Part of it has to do with the fact that he's been meeting with Evan McDaniel ever since the whole thing happened. Evan thought it would be a good idea if they were close when Granger got out."

"Dang, that would tick me off." Derrick found an open space and parked. "Are you worried about Pam and the girls?"

"You saw my gun. I didn't want to leave them tonight; I never do. A guy like that? He's messed up in the head. He could've been meeting with Evan all this time just to make it look good, so he could get out early. I don't care what Evan says—the guy is sick."

They got out. It was biting cold. The rock salt crunched beneath their feet as they hurried across the breezeway and through the automatic sliding glass doors into the warmth of the hospital lobby.

"His folks were some real wing nuts, weren't they?"

Jack paused at the welcome desk and asked the white-haired volunteer lady to confirm Galen's room number: 356.

"Oh, yeah." Jack led them to the elevators and hit the up button. "Heavy mind games, mental abuse."

The elevator doors opened. They got on and Jack hit 3.

"Who knows," Derrick said. "Maybe Evan really did help him."

Jack rejected the possibility. Gone. Wouldn't even consider it.

They got off on the third floor and followed the signs to Galen's room.

Jack felt he owed Derrick a response. "The dude is a bad seed. Guys like that are evil to the core. Birth to death. It's not gonna change."

"Hold up. You think God *makes* people like that?"

They stopped outside Galen's room, and Jack lowered his voice.

"Look at Pharoah. Look at Judas. The Bible says God made everything for its own purpose—even the wicked for the day of evil."

"But people can change, dude. I'm not saying he has, but it's possible."

"Okay." Jack held up a hand. "We need to shift gears. We can talk theology later. You got a pad and pen? We both take notes."

Once ready, they nodded at each other, and Jack knocked on the door. After a moment he knocked louder.

Finally LJ opened the door, adjusting his eye patch. The TV blared from within. "Hey Jack, come in." He nodded at Derrick and went back into the room with a bounce in his long stride, as if he was welcoming them to a New Year's Eve bash. "We got the race on, and Daddy's feeling spunky as ever."

"Hey, Jack." Travis got out of his chair and shook hands with both men. "And it was—"

"Derrick," Jack reminded them. "Hey, Galen." Jack crossed to the bed where Galen sat was fully upright, glasses on, glued to the roaring TV. When Galen didn't look at Jack, he rested a hand on the older man's shoulder.

Galen looked up. "Oh, hey young man."

"Jack Crittendon."

"I know that."

"And this is my buddy from the *Dispatch*, Derrick Whittaker."

Galen gave him the up-and-down and shook hands. "Good to meet you. Who you pullin' fer?" His eyes went back to the colorful race cars blowing around the brightly lit track. Galen had an oxygen tube hooked to his nose and an IV in his arm, but he looked like he could get out of bed and walk five miles. A small, worn-out brown leather Bible sat on the nightstand next to the bed.

Derrick gave Jack a quick shake of the head.

Jack looked up at the screen and figured out it was NASCAR.

"I'm not really too up on it myself," Jack said. "Jimmie Johnson?"

"Crashed in the second lap," LJ said.

"Dale Earnhardt Junior?"

"Mountain Dew car. Number eighty-eight. Back of the pack," LJ said. "You like the old-timers, Jack."

"Hasn't won anything in three years." Galen's watery eyes were fixed on the screen. "Shadow of the driver his daddy was."

"That old Impala don't help things none," LJ said. "He needs a faster car."

"Who's driving the Target car?" Derrick asked. "My fiancée loves Target."

All three Randalls turned to Derrick, then back to the screen.

"That's Montoya," Travis said. "He's got the same problem as Earnhardt. What he needs is that new Dodge Charger just got announced for the Sprint Cup Series. That thing is a rocket."

"What race is this?" Derrick asked.

Even though the noise was mind-blowing and all three of the Randalls had their eyes fixed on the TV, when Derrick said that, it was if a skunk had just let off its spray. All heads and eyes locked on Derrick.

Then they all burst out laughing.

"Daytona, for crying out loud." LJ turned to Jack as if wondering who Jack had brought with him.

"Oh, the 500?" Derrick said.

That brought even more knee slaps and howls.

After several minutes more of education about Fords, Chevys, and various drivers, Jack finally got up the nerve to ask if they could turn the TV off for ten minutes to talk about Demler-Vargus.

LJ and Galen scowled, but Travis went for the remote. "They're just drivin' to work this early in the race, anyway," Travis said. "Real action comes later."

The TV flicked off, and Travis pushed the only two chairs in the room close to Galen's bed. LJ went to sit down, but Travis shooed him away, making room for the reporters.

"Jack and Derrick want to ask you some questions, Daddy, 'bout Demler-Vargus and all that," Travis said.

Galen started the interview. "Who busted up the house?" he demanded, his sharp chin jutting out.

"That's what we want to find out." Jack spoke loudly so Galen could hear him. "Who do you think did it? You know that all they took were your notes on Demler-Vargus?"

Galen fidgeted with the sheets and didn't make eye contact. "My lawyer, Ralston Coon, has copies of those notes, so we're good."

"What was in the notes, exactly?"

"Names, mainly," Galen said. "Neighbors. Employees. People I learned were more than likely suffering and sick because of that dirty operation."

Galen's voice quavered. He had a lean, ruddy face with brown splotches on his forehead. His mouth formed a sad horizontal line. Perhaps he was thinking of his deceased wife?

"Travis said you had dates in there when you could actually see the fiberglass spewed all over the neighborhood?" Travis said.

"You know it's a fact they killed Betty Jo, my wife." Galen eyed Jack, then Derrick. "It ain't right. It ain't fair. And it ain't American. There wasn't no other way for me to go against them than with a lawyer."

Jack scanned his notes. "But two attorneys you pursued didn't want to work with you on this?"

"I should've known better." Galen rubbed his beard stubble. "They was just ambulance chasers. Think I saw 'em on the TV. Charlie finally put me in touch with Coon; he swears by him."

"And Charlie is your best friend, is that right?" Jack said.

"Since we was boys." Galen shook his head, and his eyes wandered. "Walkin' the railroad tracks in our bare feet; fishin' down at Kline's Pond . . ." Galen had returned there in his mind. "Takin' our nickels to Drucker's General Store for fresh-squeezed lemonade . . ."

"What else you wanna know, Jack?" LJ snatched the remote and tossed it back and forth in his large hands.

"We need for Galen to try to recall for us as many of the names as he can think of from his notes." Jack waited for an objection from the boys, who'd had a long day, were tired, and wanted to watch their race.

"I'll tell you who you need to talk to," Galen said. "Spivey Brinkman. Lives right round back of us in the double-wide."

Travis snapped his fingers, loud and quick. "That's the handicapped girl's daddy, Jack. The one you said you wrote the story about. Remember?"

"Jenness Brinkman, the East High honors grad? That's Spivey Brinkman's daughter?"

"That's it." Travis was so proud he looked as if he'd just won a contest.

"I met Spivey when I was there." Jack recalled the short, plump gray-haired man with round glasses, who seemed quiet and polite. An older sister was at the house too, but Jack did not spend much time with her.

"He's your ticket," Galen said. "Knows people. Got the inside dope on Demler-Vargus. More than me. I just jotted down things here and there. Spivey is like the underground know-it-all. He's got connections."

Jack checked Derrick to make sure he was taking notes.

Galen yanked the bedcovers, puffed them up, and wiggled back and forth.

"Look at you, Daddy." Travis leaned him forward and flipped his pillow. "You're like a fart in a skillet."

"I'm ready to git *home*. Had far 'nough a this hospital."

Jack eyed Derrick. "We need to talk to Spivey Brinkman, pronto."

"I talked to the *Dispatch* about this whole thing once, long time ago," Galen said. "Ain't nothin' gonna come of this. No offense toward you boys."

It took a second for Galen's comment to hit Jack.

"What do you mean, you talked with the *Dispatch*?" he said.

"Gal named Sheets." Galen said matter-of-factly. "Don't recall her first name."

"Amy Sheets?" Derrick said.

Galen nodded. "That's it. She done interviewed me about Demler-Vargus long time ago. Never heard another word about it."

"You never told me that," Travis said.

"Me either," LJ said.

Jack underlined Amy's name on his pad. "This is the second time her name's come up." He looked at Derrick. "Jocelyn told me Amy was nosing around Demler-Vargus nine months or a year ago."

"You need to get with her," Travis said.

"She's gone," Derrick said.

"She moved to Columbus," Jack said. "Jocelyn said Amy was interviewing a couple who worked at Demler-Vargus. But then it just dropped. No one in editorial even knew about it."

"I never heard about it," Derrick said.

"What did you tell Amy Sheets, Galen?" Jack said.

"I had some friends worked in the plant—Emmett and Barb Doyle. That's who she interviewed." Galen closed his eyes, took a deep breath, and let it out. "They was trying to get some money out of Demler-Vargus for their ailments. Barb struggled something awful with eye problems, breathing trouble—" Galen coughed. His voice was weakening. "Git me some of that cranberry juice, would you, Travis? With the crushed ice?"

Travis crossed to the sink.

"Did they have an attorney?" Derrick asked.

"Naw," Galen said. "They went direct to Demler-Vargus. Told 'em if they didn't help pay for their medical bills, they'd go to the media, tell the whole world. They had some gumption."

"Did it work?" Derrick said.

"No sir," Galen said. "That's why they contacted the Sheets girl."

"They told Amy about all this?" Jack said.

Galen took the cranberry drink from Travis and practically drained the plastic cup, dribbling some down his chin and onto the white blanket. "Ahh, thanks, son."

LJ hurried over with some paper towels to clean him up, but Galen shooed him away.

Jack was on the edge of his seat. So was Derrick, who breathed audibly through O-shaped lips.

"The Sheets girl came to me because Emmett and Barb told her about Betty Jo, my wife." Galen rested his head back on the pillow and closed his eyes. Thinking about his wife again, probably . . .

"Jack, we're gonna need to stop soon." Travis moved toward his dad. "Daddy's gettin' wore out."

Jack knew he was right.

Galen lifted his head and looked at Jack. "Barb and Emmett knew that I thought Demler-Vargus was responsible for Betty Jo's death. Barb's symptoms was just like Betty Jo's. Eyes burnin' like blazes. Headaches. Dizzy. At times her whole body felt like a pin cushion. She needed oxygen all the time."

Galen's head dropped back onto the pillow.

Travis moved over and squeezed his shoulder. His father patted his hand.

"Where are Emmett and Barb now?" Derrick said.

There was a knock at the door.

"Good grief, what now?" Still holding the remote, LJ lumbered to the door.

Galen was distracted, but continued. "They moved south. Doctors said it might help Barb."

"Do you know where in the south?" Derrick asked.

"Nope. They was up and gone faster than a bee-stung stallion."

Jack eyed Derrick as they closed their notepads and stood. "We need to find Barb and Emmett Doyle."

LJ reappeared, rolled his eyes and motioning backward with the remote. "Look what the cat drug in." He was followed by a bulk of a man wearing a heavy overcoat over an expensive suit and polished black shoes. He had a wide face, neck, and nose, and wore sleek silver glasses. His eyes narrowed when he saw Jack and Derrick.

"Mr. Coon!" Travis jumped two feet. "We been tryin' to reach you all day."

Ralston Coon set down his brown briefcase, removed his fedora, and held it in front of him with both hands. Smoothly, he ignored Travis's outburst, as well as Jack and Derrick, and crossed directly to Galen Randall's bedside. "Mr. Randall." He patted Galen's shoulder. "I'm sorry to hear about your complications. How are you feeling?"

"Galen. I've told you before, call me Galen. I could've gone home today if it weren't for the paranoid doctors round here. So afraid of lawsuits they keep you till you git sick all over again."

Coon smiled. "Well, you look very good, I must say."

"Do you know what's happened today?" Travis pushed up his sleeves. "Did you get my messages?"

Coon's eyes flicked to Jack and Derrick.

"It's okay," Travis said. "These are friends. Jack Crittendon and Derrick . . . what's the last name?"

"Whittaker," Derrick said.

"I tried to reach you today too," Jack spoke up. "We're with the *Dispatch*."

"You know Daddy got poisoned this morning?" Travis said.

Coon nodded. "Yes, I got your messages."

Travis unfolded the piece of paper he'd finally found in his pocket and stuffed it in Coon's hand. "Our house got busted into this morning."

Coon stuffed his hat under his armpit, unfolded the paper, and read the note the intruders left at the Randalls' house. His eyes locked on Travis. "Was anyone hurt?"

"No one was hurt because no one was there," LJ spouted. "But whoever it was took them Demler-Vargus notes of Daddy's."

"The ones you copied," Travis said.

"What else did they take?" Coon said.

"That's it—after they destroyed everything," LJ said.

"Mr. Coon, I'd like to see the copy you have of Galen's notes," Jack said. "We're doing an investigative piece on Demler-Vargus."

Before Jack had finished speaking, Coon gave a shake of the head. "I'm afraid that won't be possible. The Randalls are my private client. Those notes are confidential." He looked at Travis, then Galen. "You've got to understand that giving those notes to the press would impede our case."

"What exactly is your case?" Jack said. "How far have you gotten with Demler-Vargus?"

"Excuse me, Mr. Crittendon, with all courtesy, this is all confidential."

"You can answer," Travis said. "Where are we? We must be getting close if they're goin' to all the trouble to poison Daddy and ransack our house."

Coon shook his head at Travis and spoke in a firm, parental tone. "I would not be serving in your best interest to talk about the case here, now, with these men present. I hope you haven't divulged too much already. I'll be glad to give you the latest once they've gone."

For an awkward moment everyone looked at everyone. LJ slapped the remote against his thigh repeatedly.

"Look." Coon sliced the air with a karate chop. "I understand you are all friends. But we are at a crucial place in our negotiations. I urge you, Randalls, to refrain from speaking with these gentlemen—with *any* representative of the media—about Demler-Vargus until we reach a settlement."

Jack understood where Coon was coming from and wanted the Randalls to win whatever case they had. Even if he and Derrick couldn't get their hands on Galen's notes, they had a handful of fresh leads to pursue: Spivey Brinkman, Emmett and Barb Doyle, Amy Sheets, for starters.

With both hands on his waist, Travis arched way backward and let out a groan. "We need to wrap this up for today. Daddy needs rest—"

"Not till I see the checkered flag," his father said. "LJ, hand me that clicker."

LJ hit the power button, the volume blared, and he handed the remote to Galen.

Travis's eyebrows arched. "Well, I think that's it for today, gentlemen."

Jack was glad he would get to spend time with Rebecca and Faye before bed. As he and Derrick headed for the parking lot, he mentally juggled the leads he planned to follow the next day. He would get into the paper early and explain everything to Cecil, in hopes that the editor would allow both him and Derrick to dig into the Demler-Vargus story full force.

"Right now, Demler-Vargus doesn't know we're looking into this," Jack said.

"Was that a question?" Derrick hit the unlock button and the lights blinked on the Cruiser as they hurried toward it in the cold night.

"I'm just trying to keep everything sorted out."

"I know, this thing is feeling big."

"You're feeling it too?" Jack said. "It's not just me?"

Derrick hopped into the driver's seat, started the car, and flipped the heat on. "Are you kidding me? I feel like we're standing on top of a hornets' nest, but the hornets don't know we're there yet."

"I gotta get Cecil to turn us loose on this."

"He'll be all over it. Nothin' he likes better than a scoop."

Jack's phone vibrated as Derrick maneuvered the Toyota out of the parking lot. Seeing Pam's number on his phone made Jack's heart skip; she usually just texted him while he was working, unless it was something important.

"Hey, hon," he said.

"Just be calm, okay?" Pam whispered. "Granger Meade is at our front door."

8

As she crouched in the dark by the window in the dining room with her back to the wall, Pamela made herself take deep breaths, in . . . very deep . . . as far as she could, and out . . . phhheewwwwww.

She had sequestered the girls to Faye's closet, upstairs in her bedroom, with the door locked. Jack and Derrick were on their way. So were the police.

Stay calm.

She thought of how her mother would be freaking.

She thought of the gun they'd never bought.

It's okay.

Keep the girls calm, Lord, please . . .

Rebecca had spotted him first, and casually called from her bedroom upstairs, "Mommy, someone's parked out front."

She knew her mom would want to know. Ever since the home invasion, Pamela checked the street frequently out of habit.

Granger had unfolded out of the tiny truck and walked slowly and purposefully toward the house. His hands were chest high, as if someone was behind him with a gun telling him to keep them in the air. He was thinner, but still huge and broad, with a thatch of oily red hair.

When she heard his footsteps on the front porch, within inches of the door, within several feet of her trembling frame, Pamela's breath departed. Her head buzzed as she waited for his shoulder to hit the door as it had before, like a medicine ball, busting through the glass and splintering the wood.

She felt worthless cowering there, paralyzed by the memory of him driving her through the night in the horrendous rain . . . as he smoked . . . talked nonsense . . . sweated . . . tore beef jerky with his crooked front teeth.

The first ring of the doorbell had jolted her back to reality. That's when she fumbled for the phone and called Jack, and he'd said he would call the police.

Now the doorbell rang again, echoing in the foyer of the still house. Her heart ticked rapidly, like that of a frightened animal.

Breathe.

The girls would be worried.

Blanket them in peace, Lord.

His knocks reverberated in her chest like gunfire.

Tilting her head ever so slightly so she could see more out the front window, she saw he had backed away from the door seven or eight feet after knocking, and was standing with one foot on the driveway and the other on the porch step. He wore a waist-high black leather jacket that appeared two sizes too big.

What was he doing out there?

He stood with his hands clasped behind his back. He examined the house, the windows—downstairs and up—then gazed up at the clear night sky, as if waiting for the girl he was courting to come out and meet him.

Is he here to apologize?

Although Pamela wanted that, wanted to forgive, wanted the air to be cleared between them—especially if he was going to be living in Trenton City—why would he come to their home? Why would he scare the girls? Why would he come when Jack wasn't home? Why at night?

If that's what Granger was there for, Pamela pitied his complete lack of protocol or understanding of acceptable behavior.

Jack will be livid.

She tilted her head again. *Thank God!* He was retreating, as slowly as he had come, toward the pickup truck parked along the front curb. Her shoulders went limp. She breathed again.

Half of her wanted Granger to hurry out of there before Jack or the police arrived, just to avoid a nasty confrontation.

The vehicle bounced when Granger got in. He shut the door, but Pamela did not hear the engine start. He just sat there with the dim streetlight casting a soft, yellow hue onto the old truck.

• • •

"You better be dang careful." Derrick flicked his eyes toward the gun in Jack's hand, then back to the road as he rushed them through Trenton City toward Jack and Pam's house. "You know how to use that?"

Jack was in no mood for small talk. "Just hurry."

Somehow Granger had known Jack was working late.

How dare he even think about returning!

Jack would hurt him.

"Dude." Derrick kept his eyes on the road. "I know you're ticked. I would be too. I just don't want you to do anything you'll regret."

"The only thing I'll regret is letting him leave unharmed. Hit this green light. Hurry."

Derrick gunned it beneath the yellow light, bouncing them through the intersection of Perkins and Baker. Almost there.

"Take this next left," Jack ordered.

Derrick hesitated, but obeyed. Not many people knew about the shortcut.

"Now, right down this one-way," Jack said. "You know the way from here?"

"Up here on the right?"

"Yeah. Hurry, dude."

Derrick turned onto Jack's street and floored it. The Cruiser seemed to lift off the ground as it roared toward Jack's house.

"Hit your brights," Jack said.

Derrick did so, casting floodlights on a small pickup truck parked along the curb directly in front of Jack's house.

"That's him!" Jack yelled. "Hurry."

Jack examined the windows in every room of the house, but saw no movement.

As Derrick's vehicle drew closer, Jack noticed steam coming from the exhaust pipe of the pickup.

"He's in the truck!"

The pickup's headlights flicked on, and it began to roll.

"He's moving. Cut him off!"

"Hold on!" Derrick ripped the wheel left and screeched to a halt directly in front of Granger's truck.

Jack flew out of the car into the night, racked the slide, and braced both arms in front of him with the gun pointed at Granger's chest.

"Get out!" he screamed.

Derrick pulled his parking brake and was out too.

Granger's enormous frame filled the pickup like an overstuffed suitcase. His elbows and arms were scrunched up in front of him, his pudgy hands in the air. Jack immediately remembered those tiny eyes and the chronic sadness etched on his round face. His blocky head moved side to side. He was saying something from behind the dirty driver's window, as if explaining he had a good reason to be there.

No reason would be good enough.

Jack's mouth was clamped shut. Without moving the gun from Granger, he said, "Derrick, check on Pam and the girls."

"Okay." His friend trotted for the house. "Stay cool, man."

Jack's face was on fire.

He could actually pull the trigger and end all the insanity.

Granger's left hand lowered and his door began to open.

"Don't you even *think* about it!"

"Jack!" Pam was out the front door, arms crossed, no coat, moving down the driveway toward him.

Derrick stopped her.

"Are the girls okay?" Jack yelled.

"Yes," Pam cried. "He didn't come in. He rang the doorbell and went back to his truck."

"What about you?" Jack yelled, stepping closer to Granger's door.

"I'm fine," Pam called. "Jack, don't do anything. Just wait for the police."

"Jack." Granger craned his neck up through the ten-inch opening in the door. "Let me get out. I came to say I'm sorry. Please hear me out . . ."

"Stop right there, or so help me I'll blow a hole in your chest." Jack stepped cautiously within three feet of the truck and spoke through clenched teeth. "How *dare* you come here."

"I'm sorry," Granger said. "That's what I came to say. For all the trouble, for everything I put you through. Please . . ." He pushed the door open more and started to get out.

"Stop!" Jack pointed the gun straight up and blasted a shot into the night.

Pam screamed. "Jack, the girls!"

He racked the gun again.

"Jack, dude," Derrick called. "Stay calm."

"I understand your anger." Granger put one foot on the ground and started to get out. As he did, the pickup rolled forward. He plunked back inside, his one booted foot dragging outside, and jammed on the brake. The pickup banged to a stop three feet from Derrick's car.

Granger dropped his head. Frustrated and embarrassed, he ran a hand through his hair. "Let me say what I came to say—"

"You don't make the rules!"

"Jack, please," Pam cried. She tried to come closer, but Derrick held her back by the shoulders.

"Just wait till the police come. Don't interact with him."

"Stay out of this, Pam. Go inside with the girls."

Jack heard her ask Derrick where he had gotten a gun.

"Your number was unlisted." Granger had his hands up in front of him. "Or I would have called."

"So you come here at night, when I'm not home." Jack inched closer to him. "I *saw* you at Campolo's."

"When?"

"Tonight! Stalking us."

"I was not. I was at the library. I passed Campolo's, driving home . . ."

"Phh." Jack shook his head in disgust. "Get out."

Granger opened the door and bent out of the pickup with his hands up. He was taller than Jack remembered, and thinner. "Pam, I'm sorry," he called. "I've changed—"

"We don't care about your personal life!" Jack said. "Say what you have to say. Clear your sick conscience before the cops get here."

"I wanted you to know, you helped me, Pam—and I'm sorry for everything I put you through. You too, Jack. I apologize."

Pam cried and nestled closer to Derrick.

"Something was terribly wrong with me back then. Evan has helped me. God has helped me."

Pam sobbed.

"I thought maybe we could do this differently—"

"Oh, yeah, like what?" Jack hoisted the weapon closer to Granger's chest. "Come in for coffee and dessert? Maybe read the kids a bedtime story?"

A siren sounded in the distance, and Granger dropped his head.

"Let him go, Jack." Pam shook away from Derrick. "Let him go, now."

With the gun still locked on Granger, Jack examined Pam. Her watery eyes were fixed on his. He knew she already felt betrayed because he'd bought the gun without telling her. Now Granger had done the most humble thing a person could do, and Jack was cutting him no slack.

The sirens drew closer.

Jack slipped the gun into his coat pocket, stepped toward Granger, and grabbed him by the jacket with both fists, shoving him with his forearms.

There was no resistance.

"If I *ever* see you near this house again, you are dead. You read me? *Dead.*" Jack spoke within inches of Granger's indifferent face, so Pam couldn't hear. "This is your last warning. Don't go near my family, ever again, or it'll be the last thing you do."

He bashed Granger into the pickup. "Now get out of here."

"Will you forgive me?" Granger spoke softly, as if not to make him answer in front of Pam and Derrick.

Jack stared at the sad-looking stranger who had tormented their lives.

"Please," Granger pleaded. "I need to make this right."

The police cars were almost there, but Granger didn't care. He stood unmoved, waiting for the words he was desperate to hear.

"Just go. *Now.*"

Without a word, his eyes closed, his countenance fallen, Granger slipped into the pickup, backed up, and scooted into the night.

9

Pamela closed the door to Rebecca's room ever so gently; both girls were finally down. Rubbing her stomach, she walked the hall to the dark master bedroom and peered through the slats at the dimly lit street below. Jack stood next to the black Trenton City police car talking animatedly to their friend, Officer Dennis DeVry, who had handled the original Granger home invasion.

Dennis was one of the first officers to arrive, just seconds after Granger left the neighborhood. He took a report and concluded that, although no crime had been committed, Jack and Pamela could request a restraining order, which wouldn't go over well with Granger's parole officer.

But in Pamela's mind, Granger wasn't the problem.

Jack was.

Oh dear . . . how should she handle this? Her temples pounded.

She grabbed three tissues and crossed to the bay window, turned on a small lamp, and sat in one of two upholstered chairs. This was the sitting area where they sometimes curled up before bed to read or watch TV. Pamela sat there to pray when she needed a quiet place away from everyone.

She needed God now.

Oh . . . this hurt.

So this was what it felt like to be married, joined together as "one flesh," but to have that flesh torn apart. Separated.

Jack had always been such a godly example.

What was happening?

How had things gotten so out of whack?

Jack's change had been evolving ever since Granger showed up in their lives. She'd tried to sympathize. Tried to be a good partner by listening when he vented. But he'd crossed a line somewhere.

Too bitter. Too violent.

And now this . . . *betrayal.*

He had lied to her—to her, his wife—about the gun.

The front door opened and closed downstairs.

Pamela dried her eyes and wiped her nose.

He was probably turning the lights off, locking up for the night.

She heard him on the steps. Her heart rate increased.

"Hey." He stepped into the room, took his watch off, and began emptying his pockets at his tall dresser just inside the door.

She waited for him to say something else, but he headed for the bathroom.

"Will you sit down—so we can talk?" she said.

"Yeah. Let me get my pajamas on real quick. I'm bushed."

She wasn't ready for bed yet. Surely he'd noticed that.

"Jack . . . now. My gosh! I think you owe me that much."

"Okay." He went to her, sat down in the free chair, and began taking his shoes and socks off.

"Are you just going to act like nothing happened?"

"No." He looked up. "I've been in these clothes all day. I'm ready to change."

"Well, go ahead and change then!" She shot up, crossed to the door, and looked back at him. "I can't believe you." She burst into tears.

He stood. "Okay, let's talk."

"You bought a gun—without telling me?"

He sighed. "When I heard he was getting out, I went to Amiel's." Their friend's gun range in Trenton City. "I didn't intend to buy one—"

"Oh, no," she said sarcastically.

"No. I shot some different guns. I didn't buy one."

"So there's one big thing you did that you didn't tell me about. Keep going."

"I was going to tell you about it that night. I was leaning toward getting one. I'd been up at night thinking about it—that we needed protection. But I knew you wouldn't go for it."

"So you got one anyway."

"Yes." He approached her. "Because I knew he'd come back!"

"To say he was sorry!"

"Oh, right. You believe that?"

"Stick to the topic." She was unraveling. "You lied to me. More than once! And you would have kept lying—"

His head dropped back so he was looking at the ceiling.

"What else have you lied to me about?"

"Nothing!" He evened his gaze with her. "And I didn't consider the gun a lie."

"Well, I do." All the emotion in her gut came rushing to her eyes. "It's like you cheated on me, Jack. Don't you see?"

He reached for her elbows, but she shoved his hands away.

"I'm sorry, Pam. I am. I'm sorry for keeping it from you. It was wrong."

"Where did you keep it?"

"In my sock drawer. But I kept the magazine separate. It was no threat to the girls."

"Where is it now?"

He bent down and pulled up the cuff of his pants, revealing a black ankle holster, the gun in it.

She shook her head. "I can't believe you," she said again.

"But he did come back, didn't he."

"This is about *trust*. You should have talked to me! It makes me feel betrayed."

"I understand. It won't happen again. It was for your good, and the girls."

She shook her head vehemently. "No, Jack! We discuss things. It was not your decision to make alone. And you're not sorry. You still think you were right. You're apologizing to get through this so you can go to bed."

His mouth closed and he frowned.

"I think we should see a counselor," she said.

"For what?"

"This whole thing."

"This whole thing—with Granger?"

"Yes."

"Look." He put his hands on his waist. "You're tired, I'm tired—"

"No." She shook off the tears and spoke evenly, firmly. "I've been thinking about this for a long time. We need guidance. Someone who can hear us both out and give some good, biblical advice."

"About what?" He was turning sour. "The gun thing? I told you—"

"It's more than that."

"Oh, great. Now we're going to get into all the things I do wrong that you haven't told me."

"You're such a smart aleck. No one can tell you anything anymore."

"So it's all about me and my problems."

"It's about *us!* Your problems are my problems. Mine are yours—"

The phone on the nightstand rang. She didn't want it to wake the girls. Jack got to it quickly. "Hello."

Was it more about Granger?

"This is he."

What now?

"Oh . . . How are you? Is something wrong?"

Jack was standing with his back to Pamela. Staring down at the floor. Phone to his ear.

"Oh my," he said quietly. "When did this happen?"

He put his shoulders back, turned slowly, and stared at Pamela with a solemn face.

Her heart sank for what seemed like the hundredth time that day.

Jack reached his hand out. "Come here," he whispered.

She went and took his hand. He sat them down close on the edge of the bed and covered the phone. "It's your dad."

She hadn't even thought of her folks.

"What is it? What's wrong?"

Jack's eyes and mouth turned down.

Oh no. She knew that look. This was bad.

Jack shook his head. "He's gone."

10

Jack opened his eyes the next morning in the bright bedroom where Pam had grown up in Cleveland Heights. He was alone in the bed beneath a snow-white down comforter. The old house was stifling hot, even with his shirt off. He folded the comforter down to his waist and wondered how Pam's mom was holding up. A terribly heavy feeling came over him as he recalled the previous night's events.

They had thrown some suitcases together, packed Pam's car, and awakened Rebecca and Faye just long enough to get them into the vehicle. The girls slept the entire three-hour drive and were delighted to see three inches of snow covering everything when they arrived.

Jack and Pam had driven in silence most of the trip. The friction from their argument was fresh. But her dad's death had brought a sorrow they both shared, which seemed to make other things not quite so important—at least for a time.

Pam had said her mother would be completely distraught, and she was right. When they arrived well after midnight, Margaret was not ready to let the funeral home take Benjamin's body. The men in black suits waited in their van outside, trying to stay warm. They got out every now and then, lit smokes, and tossed snowballs; they'd even built a leaning four-foot snowman.

When Pam finally convinced her it was time to let Benjamin go, and the men rolled and bumped the stretcher to the waiting vehicle, Margaret tripped over them every step of the way, wailing and talking to Benjamin as if he were still alive.

Jack closed his eyes for one last quiet moment before starting the day. He heard Rebecca and Faye running about downstairs. Pam was probably helping Margaret write the obituary, make plans for the service, determine who they needed to call.

His eyes fell to a gold crucifix above the closet. He hadn't prayed in days. He knew he'd wandered, knew he was ignoring sins. To fire a gun in the middle of the neighborhood? To even *have* a gun without Pam's consent? Pam insisted he was angry and impatient. His unwillingness to forgive Granger was clearly wrong. He was failing on so many fronts.

He shook away the memory of Granger pleading for forgiveness, sat up on the edge of the bed, and scrolled through his e-mail. He had called Cecil on the way to Cleveland to let him know about Pam's dad. Now he found an e-mail from his boss letting him know he had successfully divvied out Jack's pressing assignments to other reporters. *Good.*

Jack had held off telling him more about the Demler-Vargus story, but planned to do so that day. First, he dialed LJ. After explaining where he was, Jack inquired about Galen's health and was glad to hear that he was fine and getting stronger, and would be going home that afternoon.

"We talked to Ralston Coon a good while after you left last night," LJ said.

"Anything I should know about?"

"No. That's just it, Jack. Me and Daddy and Travis is convinced old Coon has a good plan cooking."

"What is it, exactly? Did he tell you how he's approaching it?"

"See, Jack, he wants us to keep things on the hush-hush. You get me? So I really can't say no more. Now, them's Coons' instructions. Nothin' personal, you understand. It's just how lawyers do things."

"Oh . . . okay." In his boxers, Jack crossed to a small desk and took a seat where he'd put his notepad the night before. "Look, LJ, I understand what you guys are trying to do. I would probably be doing the same thing. But I'm concerned."

"About what?"

"Well . . . your dad."

"Oh, he's gonna be fine, Jack. The doctor said—"

"No, I'm talking about his safety. After the poisoning and the break-in? I mean, do you guys really want to be negotiating with the very people who might be responsible?"

"Look, thank you and all that, Jack, but Coon guaranteed us he's close to striking a deal with some top dogs at Demler-Vargus. Dang it, there I go, openin' my big trap. Anyhoo . . . we decided last night to keep our mouths shut and let him move forward real quick-like to see if we can't make this thing happen. By the way, I'm gonna have your Jetta ready real soon; should be done by the time you get back."

Jack hung up with LJ and was glad to reach Cecil at his desk. He explained all that was happening with the Randalls and Demler-Vargus, and encouraged Cecil to at least put Derrick on the story full-time. Cecil said he would consider it.

"By the way, I need Amy Sheets's contact info," Jack said.

"Amy? I'm not sure I have it," Cecil said.

"Can you check? She interviewed a couple that was going after Demler-Vargus."

"Who?"

"Emmett and Barb Doyle."

"I thought we agreed if she had found anything newsworthy, she would have told us."

"I know. But she also interviewed Galen Randall and who knows who else? She was onto something. I just want to ask her about it—you know, find out why it fizzled."

There was a long pause.

"Cecil?"

"Jack, you can't contact Sheets."

"Why not?"

"Just drop it, will you, Jack? Trust me."

"What's going on, Cecil?"

Another long pause. "I know you won't let this rest. You're that kind of a *dog* reporter. Okay . . . here it is. She was pregnant and she was embarrassed. She decided to have the baby and raise it, with her parents' help."

"Whoa." Jack never even knew there was a man in Amy's life.

"Yeah."

"In Columbus?" Jack said.

"Last I heard, yeah. But this is for your ears only."

"But listen, Cecil . . . she wouldn't even have to know that I know about the baby. I could just tell her the only reason you gave me her number was because of this story.."

"Look, Jack, I'm going to make an executive decision here. Amy was a star reporter and a good friend. I promised her I would keep her secret, and I don't want to take any chances on messing that up. If she'd found anything, we would have known about it. That's gonna have to be the end of it, as far as she's concerned."

There were more ways than one to find a person. "Okay. I understand."

"Good. I'll see what I can do about getting Whittaker more hours on the D-V thing."

One more quick call and Jack would get downstairs. He reviewed the items he wanted to discuss with Derrick and called his cell.

There was a soft knock at the bedroom door. It opened and Pam shuffled in, cradling a cup in both hands. "I come bearing coffee."

Jack set the phone down. "Ahh, what incredible timing. Thank you."

He set the cup down and put his arms out. They embraced lightly, but she quickly backed away a foot or two.

"How are you holding up?" he said.

She nodded. "I'm okay. Numb, but okay. Glad we came last night. Mom needed me. Thanks."

"Good. I'm glad we did too."

"Mom wants to have the funeral tomorrow."

"Wow, that fast?"

Pam nodded. "Calling hours this afternoon and tonight."

"Man. Why so soon?"

She shrugged. "You know her, she wants to get it over with. She'd already called a Realtor before I got up this morning. She wants to sell the house and move into St. Edwards, the assisted-living place I told you about, like ASAP."

"It's too soon."

"I told her that. She's convinced herself she can't be alone. It's her worst fear."

He paused. "And when she's afraid, she drinks . . . more."

Pam was silent. Jack thought she purposefully ignored her mom's drinking at times.

He knew what they needed to do. He didn't want to do it, didn't think it would be good for their marriage—especially now—or for the girls. But he knew it was the right thing.

"She needs to come stay with us," he said. "At least for a week or two. Just get out of here, away from the house and memories. It'll give her time to think, be with the girls, you . . ."

Pam's eyes filled with tears. She hugged him. "Thank you." She held him for a moment.

"I'll talk to her about it, if you want," Jack said softly. "Everything will be okay. We'll take good care of her."

She nodded and broke away. "I'll see you downstairs." She ducked out of the room.

Jack flipped the pages of his notepad, reviewed what he wanted to go over with Derrick, and called him.

"I just ran into Cecil in the break room," Derrick said. "Sorry to hear about Pam's dad."

After small talk, Derrick said Cecil had instructed him to spend one hour a day on Demler-Vargus.

"An hour? That's it?" Jack said. "That's ludicrous."

"He also wants me to give him a rundown of what I find each day, so he can—"

"He's not gonna hold you to that. He's told me that before and he never follows up."

"By the way, the police finally got back with Travis about the video footage from the hospital. It confirmed the guy in black leaving Galen's room. He got into a silver Toyota Celica. They got partial plates. They're working on it."

"Good." Jack eyed his notes. "Here's what I think you should do, top of list. Contact this Spivey Brinkman. He lives right by Randalls'."

"Dude, I already talked to him. Heading over there later this morning."

"Sweet. You are on it, dog."

"He wants to talk off the record first. He wanted to know all about me and who else is working on the story, so I told him about you. He wants to hear what we know, then go from there."

"That's okay."

"He asked if Cecil was still editor."

"Why, does he know him?"

"Not sure. He just seemed surprised we were reaching out to him."

"Hopefully, he'll talk."

"I'm also going to try to track down Barb and Emmett Doyle," Derrick said.

"Man, you've had your caffeine today; you're two steps ahead of me." Jack went down his list. "I'm going to try to set up a face-to-face with the CEO, Bendickson, for when I get back—and maybe his son, the kid that leads their green initiative."

"What about Amy Sheets?"

Jack thought for a moment. "Cecil wouldn't give me her contact info. This is between you and me; she got pregnant and left to raise the baby near her parents, probably in Columbus."

"Whoa, man, are you serious?"

"We don't mention that to anyone. You just need to track her down. We don't have to bring that up with her at all."

Jack finished the call, got up, and knelt over his suitcase to find his shaving kit. The gun was in its black nylon ankle holster below some clothes. He felt its bulk. Should he get rid of it, apologize to Pam, make things right?

But who knew if and when Granger would show up again?

Jack found the gun's loaded magazine in the side pocket. He put the gun and mag back in their places. He was not ready to go anywhere without them.

Heading to shave and shower, he was determined to hang out with the girls so Pam could spend as much time as she needed with Margaret. Rebecca and Faye would love to play in the snow, make a snowman, maybe even find a cozy coffee shop for hot chocolate before the afternoon calling hours. For the next few hours, he would forget everything else and focus only on the family.

At the sink, he dug for his razor and shave cream.

Leaning over, about to wet his face, he stopped and stared into his own tired eyes.

Yes, for a few hours, he would be the model dad, the Christian role model—the one with the gun strapped to his ankle and the malice hidden in his heart.

11

It didn't take Travis twenty seconds to spot the silver Toyota Celica once he and Bo pushed Daddy in the wheelchair through the sliding glass doors of the hospital into the frigid Ohio air.

So, the guy thought the Randalls were stupid. Had no brains.

Uh-uh, buddy. *Wrong.*

The man in black was slouched in the driver's seat of the Celica, backed into a space three rows beyond Travis's Jeep.

Who was the dumb one now, boy?

Travis said nothing to Bo or Daddy about the man's presence. He thought about going back into the hospital to find security, but that would take too long. And what did they have the authority to do, anyway?

"Dang, it's cold," Bo said. "Granddaddy, you warm enough?" Bo removed his own black stocking cap and worked it onto Galen's head, his white hair dull gray against the snow.

Galen bumped along in the wheelchair with his big green coat on, his hard old hands resting relaxed atop his thighs. His normally straight mouth curled up on the right side; he was glad to be heading home.

Travis didn't want to ruin it for him by getting sidetracked in a hostile episode with the stranger, but he wasn't about to lose the guy, either. As they got closer to the Jeep, he thought about trying to drive around behind the car to get his full plate number, but he didn't want to take any chance that the guy could pull out and lose him.

Nope.

That wouldn't do.

Even though it was freezing as he opened the passenger door of the Jeep, Travis's face was on fire. He felt three times as strong as normal, like he could go over and flip the guy's car. But was confronting him the smart thing? He could let the guy follow him, call LJ, and they could ambush him.

"Can you make it, Daddy?" Travis locked the wheelchair.

"I'm no invalid." His father stood with the help of Travis and Bo. Both of his legs were bent, and he was hunched over and unsteady. "Bo, you better git yer skinny behind in back."

"Yessir." Bo leaned the seat forward and disappeared into the backseat like a lizard slithering into a hole.

"Okay, Daddy, here we go." Travis took his elbow.

Galen shook his hand away. "I can do it, son."

Once in, he said the same thing when Travis tried to buckle his seat belt.

Travis finally shut the passenger door, walked around the front of the Jeep, careful not to look at the stranger, and hopped in. He started the engine, cranked the heat, and glanced in the rearview as he looked over at the others.

"Don't turn your heads and don't move." Travis spoke loudly and clearly. "The man with the black overcoat is in a silver Toyota behind us right now. Don't look."

Bo's neck craned toward Travis and his brown eyes doubled in size as he made himself stay focused forward. Galen eyed Travis with the cool gaze of a codger who had been to war and back, which he had.

Travis backed out of his parking space, his heart pumping like a piston. "I'm going to pay him a visit." He put the car in first, a quick second, zipped around the lot, and jerked to a stop three feet in front of the Toyota, which was blocked in from behind by another car. "You boys get nice and warm till I git back."

Travis yanked the emergency brake, ripped his door open, jumped out, marched around back of the Jeep, and made a beeline for the man's door. He could see movement behind the reflections—the man was suddenly fully upright, but couldn't find the door lock fast enough.

Travis ripped the door open. "What were you doin' in my daddy's hospital room?" He jerked the lapels of the black coat.

"What are you talking about?" The man had food in his mouth. It was him, all right. Middle age. Curly blond hair. Cleft lip.

Travis shook him. "What were you doing in my daddy's room yesterday morning? I ain't gonna ask nicely agin."

"Wh . . . who is your daddy?" The man shriveled up, a convincing question on his face.

Travis looked quickly at the Jeep. "That man"—he yanked the guy—"right there."

Daddy was staring right at them, not smiling any more.

"Room 411!" Travis jerked. "Yesterday!"

"It . . . it was an accident," he said. "Wrong room. I had the wrong—"

"What are you doing back here now?" Travis had him pinned to the seat.

"My mother . . . She's here. Audrey Jacobs. Check and see. I swear to you . . ."

Travis's heart sank and he immediately released his grip.

"I'm sorry . . . someone . . . my daddy . . ."

"Get away from me, before I call the police." The man shook the intrusion of Travis away, brushing at his coat and shirt, scrunching a half-eaten biscuit in its wrapper and tossing it aside where there was more trash on the floor.

"Look, I apologize," Travis said. "I saw you leave his room. He was poisoned . . ."

With mouth sealed shut, the man burned holes in Travis with his blue eyes and reached for his door handle. "Move. Your. Car." He slammed his door.

Debating whether to try to explain further, Travis thought better of it, held his hands up, walked back, and got in the Jeep. As soon as he got moving, the man in black gunned that little Celica for all it was worth, skidding sideways on some ice before gripping the pavement and zipping out of the lot.

• • •

Pamela stared out her mom's back window. Pink-faced, runny-nosed Rebecca, Faye, and Jack were on their knees, bundled in bulky winter clothes, rolling the third large snowball for the snowman they were building. They had been laughing, eating snow, patting the big ball, and wiping their noses with mittens and scarves. Jack stood and pointed to where he wanted them to roll the ball so it would go right up to their snowman—which stood next to the small one the men from the funeral home had built the night before.

It warmed her to see them playing together. Jack had been such a good daddy. Although the whole Granger fiasco had done something to him, his passion for Rebecca and Faye had never wavered. He went out of his way to ask about their schedules and plan when he could spend time with them.

Does he have that gun with him now?

Her stomach ached because they were at odds; it always did when they argued. They were meant to be of one heart and mind, and it felt as if half of her had been torn away. She truly believed a counselor could help, but she didn't have time to think about that now.

The funeral home was due to call any second on last-minute details for the calling hours and graveside service. Although Jack had convinced her mom to stay with them in Trenton City, Margaret still insisted on putting the house up for sale immediately. The Realtor was due any minute to take photos, put the lockbox on, and stick the sign in the frozen yard.

"You know, I'm going to need two suitcases if I'm going to stay more than a week." Margaret's sudden presence startled Pamela. "Will we have room in that little car of yours?"

Her mom—who looked smaller, grayer, and more fragile—tidied the pillows on the couch. The pouches beneath her eyes were purple from all the crying; decades of fear were etched on her face.

"We'll find room, but if you can fit everything in one, that would be best," Pamela said.

"Well, winter clothes are just so bulky."

"Mom, I need to tell you something."

Her mom put her hands on her slender waist and tilted her head in anticipation.

"Granger Meade got out of prison a few weeks ago."

Margaret dropped to the couch.

"Pastor Evan is convinced he's changed. He's been counseling him the whole time."

"Why are you telling me this?" Margaret seemed to have fallen into a trance. "Where is he now?"

No matter how Pamela couched it, it wasn't going to be pretty. "Well, when he left the prison in Mansfield, Evan thought it would be best if they were close, so—"

"Evan lives in Cool Springs, which is basically *in your town.*"

Pamela nodded. "Granger's in Trenton City."

Margaret gasped.

"He's got a job. He's starting over."

Pamela wondered why she was the only one who seemed to have any sympathy for the man—and she was the one who had been kidnapped.

Margaret turned away. "This isn't going to work. I'm going into St. Edward's."

"Mom, not yet." Pamela went over and sat beside her. Her mom stared out the large back window. "Trust me. It's all fine. Granger apologized. He's not the same person—"

"Apologized?" Margaret turned to face Pamela. "How? When?"

"That's not important."

"It's important to me!"

"Mom, please." If she told her Granger had shown up at their house, Margaret would never come home with them. "This is already difficult enough . . . losing Dad. Please, just trust me. This is not even a topic—"

"You know, your father never said so, but he wanted you to press charges; so did a lot of people who didn't have the courage to come out and say so. You could've put that monster away for the rest of his life—*and you should have!*"

Margaret got up and went into the kitchen.

Pamela followed. It hurt her to think her dad hadn't voiced his opinion about pressing charges, but it wouldn't have changed her mind.

Her mom rifled through her address book. Pamela knew what she was looking for, and reached for the book, but Margaret jerked it away.

"I am not about to go to your house with that *fiend* on the loose. I wouldn't even stay here. Pamela, you need to think of Rebecca and Faye. Sometimes I wonder if you have any sense."

Let her go. Just let her go into the nursing home! Maybe it would be best. They wouldn't have to worry about her drinking around the girls, locking all the doors, freaking everybody out...

"Mom," Pamela said as calmly as she could, "we want you to be with us." She gently squeezed her mother's shoulder. "I need you. You need us. Believe me, Granger Meade is not going to bother us. I know it. I promise you."

Margaret pursed her lips and shook her head. "You know what happened to me . . . in college."

Pamela nodded.

"I still think I see him." Margaret spoke as if in a trance. "I imagine what he would look like now, all these years later. I can see him so clearly."

Her mother's fear and hatred were palpable.

"The smell of him. That gaunt face. Those crazy eyes." Her head dropped. Her shoulders bounced.

Pamela took her mom in her arms and let her cry. Margaret dropped the address book and embraced her. "Oh, Ben," she moaned. "Why did you leave me? What am I supposed to do?"

"Daddy would want you to be with us, Mom."

Margaret cried harder.

"You know that. He wouldn't want you to go right into St. Edward's— not yet. He'd want you with Rebecca and Faye, with me and Jack."

Margaret leaned back and examined Pamela. "I won't sleep." Her mascara and tears mixed. "You don't know what I'm like. You haven't lived here in years. You don't want the girls to see that."

"Mom, the girls adore you. They accept you, no matter what."

Pamela snatched a tissue from a nook in the kitchen and handed it to her. Margaret wiped the tears and blew her nose.

"I can't go." She shook her head and her mouth curled into a frown; she fought back more tears. "I would have a nervous breakdown. Trust me. It would be much more trouble than you bargained for."

Pamela tried to reason with her, to assure her they could deal with anything. But Margaret bent down, retrieved the address book, and reached for the phone.

Pamela's heart broke.

12

It had stopped snowing. Derrick relished the rays of sun poking through the dark gray sky as he drove to Trenton City's east side once again. This time he was heading to the home of Spivey Brinkman, the man who was supposed to know a great deal about the alleged misdoings at Demler-Vargus.

Derrick went through a mental list of the odds and ends he had to tie up before the evening deadline at *The Dispatch* and his date with Zenia. He had finally talked her into trying La Gloria's, his favorite Cuban restaurant. But he was running behind because he'd spent most of the morning trying to track down the whereabouts of Barb and Emmett Doyle and Amy Sheets.

He hadn't had any luck on the Doyles, but oddly enough, had almost surely tracked down Amy's mother on Facebook. With the help of the city search, he found a Rebekah Sheets in Columbus, Ohio. Although she had posted no photos and only had sixteen friends, she listed herself as the mother of Amy, Bruce, and Brendon.

Derrick sent Rebekah Sheets a message on Facebook, introducing himself as a *Dispatch* reporter and stating that he was trying to track down Amy for some input about a story he was working on. He sent a similar message to Amy's brother Bruce, who also had a Facebook page; the other brother seemed to be invisible. If Derrick didn't hear anything quickly, he would search further for phone numbers, but he had run out of time.

The NAV indicated he was almost to Spivey Brinkman's house. He recognized the street he and Jack had turned on the day before to get to the Randalls' place. Sure enough, Spivey's double-wide was just in back of the Randall property.

Derrick parked in front near the beige plastic mailbox. He headed for the door and heard dogs barking all around in the distance. Smoke from nearby furnaces and fireplaces permeated the air. It was a wooded neighborhood, dotted with trees a hundred feet tall. Derrick figured the smooth, unblemished blanket of snow covered a multitude of unkempt lawns, dirt, toys, and junk. An old red clunker was parked near the trailer with a torn ARMY bumper sticker and one that read *Horn Broke—Watch for Finger.*

He went up the wooden steps and rapped at the aluminum door. The muffled beat of rock music reverberated from the rear of the small dwelling. He knocked harder.

Finally the door opened and Derrick got the full force of the music.

"You must be Mr. Whittaker." A young woman reached up to shake hands from a wheelchair with neon pink wheels. "Sorry about the music."

Derrick smiled and shook hands. "Call me Derrick."

"Come in." The girl backed her wheelchair away from the door. "My dad said you were coming."

Derrick entered and took his hat off. The pulse of the music pounded from the back of the house. "And you are . . ."

"Jenness. Sorry about that." She wheeled over to a small living area with a couch, two chairs, and a fake fireplace that was turned on. "Have a seat." She was a slender girl with light skin, a beaming smile, and a beauty mark at the top corner of her mouth. "My dad should be here soon. He's running errands."

"Okay." Derrick wished she had told him at the door that her father wasn't home. He wouldn't have gone in, alone with a young girl; it didn't look or feel right.

"Do you know Jack Crittendon?" she said.

"Sure, yes. He and I are good friends. We work together."

Derrick smelled something. Not cigarettes or cigars . . . marijuana?

"He wrote a story about me in your paper." She smiled brightly and curled her shiny brown hair behind an ear.

"Oh yeah, that's right." Her gray Yale sweatshirt made sense now. "You're the Yale girl. Criminal law, right?"

"That's me!"

The bass from the music rumbled beneath Derrick's feet. It was The Pretenders, some seriously old stuff.

"So you graduate this fall?" He practically had to yell.

"From East High." She nodded. "I can't wait. Pardon me for a moment, will you?"

"Sure."

She shot Derrick a forced smile and wheeled down a narrow hallway toward the back of the house.

In about thirty seconds the volume went down and Derrick heard two female voices.

Jenness rolled back into the room and stopped near the kitchen. "Can I get you something to drink? We still have coffee on. I'm actually surprised my dad's not back; he's usually quite punctual."

"No thanks. Maybe I should call him?"

"You can if you want. So you're here to talk about Demler-Vargus."

"That's right . . ." Derrick reached for his phone.

"Give him another minute. I'm sure he'll be right back." Jenness rolled over and parked closer to him this time. "They really are hurting people, you know. It's not right. My dad knows a lot of people whose lives have been ruined by Demler-Vargus."

"That's what I want to talk to him about."

"My dream is to come back here someday and make things right for all our neighbors who've been adversely affected."

Derrick liked her spunkiness. "So, you'd file a lawsuit against them . . ."

"You're darn right. I've told Daddy that if someone would take the time to research back far enough, it could be a class action lawsuit where all these poor people around here finally get redress for their suffering."

A girl in her early twenties slinked into the room like Cat Woman. Derrick had the impression she had been standing silently in the hall, listening.

"Hey." Colored tattoos swirled up her arms, around her neck, and on her calves. She had short jet-black hair with a white streak on one side, a diamond nose stud, and various silver hoops dangling from her ears. She swirled a red Tootsie Pop in her mouth. "You're a reporter."

Derrick stood. "Derrick Whittaker." He reached his hand out. She eyed it, then his face, then simply gave his hand a soft pet, rolling her fingers over it. She gyrated to the window and peered out. "Another beautiful day in paradise." She wore a bright aqua T-shirt and tight black knee-high yoga pants that showed off her figure.

"This is my sister, Tatum," Jenness said with a pink face.

"So . . . *Derrick.*" Tatum turned back into the small room. "What do you want to talk to my daddy about?"

"I told you, Demler-Vargus," Jenness said.

"Since when is the *Dispatch* interested in Demler-Vargus?"

"Tatum, don't start."

"Hey, I'm just trying to help the poor guy. Save him some time." Jenness pursed her lips.

"They must not have a heck of a lot of faith in you." Tatum's mouth curled sarcastically and she lowered her gaze at Derrick.

Derrick squinted. "Pardon me?"

Tatum laughed. "Anybody they'd send out here on this wild goose chase must be a real prize—"

"Don't listen to her," Jenness said. "She does this to everybody."

Derrick was almost certain he smelled pot.

"What?" Tatum threw up her hands. "He should know what he's getting into."

"You've said enough. What he needs to know, Daddy will tell him. I'm sorry, Mr. Whittaker. It seems like that's all I ever do, is apologize for Tatum."

"She does have my curiosity up," Derrick said. "What do you know about Demler-Vargus, Tatum?"

"It's just some in-family talk"—Jenness shot a glare at Tatum—"that I'm sure our father will tell you all about."

Tatum worked her way over to Derrick. "I see you're not married, Derrick."

"Engaged," he said, feeling especially uncomfortable now that Cat Woman had come closer. "Jenness, can I get your dad's cell number? I'm going to give him a quick call, make sure he's on his way."

He punched the number Jenness dictated and got an automated response telling him to leave a message. He walked away from the girls, toward the window. "Hey, Mr. Brinkman, this is Derrick Whittaker with the *Dispatch*. I'm at your house for our appointment. I waited as long as I could, but I've got to run. Give me a call and we'll set up another time, okay? Thanks."

He clicked off and looked at his watch.

"I'm going to take off. I'll reschedule with your dad and probably see you girls again, okay?" He handed each of them his *Dispatch* business card. "Anything at all about Demler-Vargus, give me a call."

He got to the car, started it, got the heat cranking, and went through the messages on his phone. Nothing important. Then he checked Facebook and found a message from Amy's mom:

Mr. Whittaker,

We have not had contact with Amy and are unsure of her whereabouts. Sorry we could not be of help.

Rebekah Sheets

Derrick punched in a quick response:

Mrs. Sheets,

Thank you for your prompt response. May I ask Amy's address the last time you knew of her whereabouts? And, when that would have been?

Thank you again for your help.

Derrick Whittaker

Derrick scanned the snowy neighborhood one last time in hopes of seeing Spivey Brinkman driving up, but no such luck. Jenness's face was pressed low against one of the windows, which was half covered in condensation. She saw him looking back and waved. Derrick shot a wave as he rolled away.

That Tatum was a piece of work. What had she meant about a wild goose chase? Those girls knew something. Derrick needed to see Spivey Brinkman.

His phone rang. *Cecil.*

"Whittaker."

"Where the heck are you?"

"Heading back from the east side."

"A train derailed in Royston. I need you over there pronto. You got your camera?"

"Yeah. Where in Royston?"

"Take Highway 21 all the way. After it intersects with Bowman, go to mile marker 138. You'll see it."

"On my way."

"Whittaker."

"Yeah?"

"An hour a day on Demler-Vargus, you got me?"

"Got it."

"No more."

13

Travis had never cared for Roxanne, LJ's ex-wife. Even before LJ married her, Travis had a feeling deep in his skinny bones that she was trouble. Now she bustled about their kitchen, fixing things up and chattering away as if she were part of the family again. She claimed she'd heard about Daddy's poor health and rumors of the break-in, and had to get over and see what she could do to help. Of course, nothing stayed a secret too long in Trenton City, and Travis was convinced she was just there to confirm the latest gossip.

They were all there—Daddy, pleased as peaches to be sprawled out on his corduroy recliner with a stomach full of Roxanne's peanut butter pie; LJ, still stomping and steaming over everything that had happened the past two days; Bo, following his momma around like a long lost pup; and Roxanne, with her tight Wranglers and frizzy brown hair, teasing old LJ, who still really loved her, deep down.

Travis pulled his father's shoes off and handed him the brown blanket his mother had knitted for him just before she passed. Galen was supposed to be on the portable oxygen machine, but he would have nothing to do with it. Instead, he had his old transistor radio up to his ear, tuning into WDUC, the local AM station.

"This always happens when Momma comes around." Bo wandered into the TV room, looking over his shoulder. "Chores, chores, chores. You forget what it's like till she shows up again."

"Tell me about it," LJ said. "Woman's a slave driver."

"You love it, both of you," Travis said.

LJ and Bo exchanged a sheepish glance. Those boys wished they could be a family again, Travis knew, but Roxanne had proven she couldn't be trusted. Travis never wanted to see LJ get hurt like that again.

"Bo, flick them back floodlights on, would ya?" LJ said.

Once his son was out of the room, LJ whispered to Travis, "Daddy's shotgun's loaded—hall closet; just in case they decide to come back."

Travis nodded, hoping there would be no more trouble.

"I wish Coon would hurry up and seal this deal. I don't like this whole mess," said LJ.

Bo returned, snatched his handheld from the end table, and dropped onto the couch.

"I just don't get it," LJ said. "If the guy in black didn't have nothin' to do with the poisoning, who did?"

"We know that for a fact?" Daddy said.

"Yessir. He was just visiting his momma," LJ said.

"So he said," Travis mumbled.

LJ turned on a dime. "So he said!"

"Yeah . . . that's what he told me."

"But you checked it out . . ."

"What do you mean?"

"You made sure that lady's in the hospital?" LJ's one big, blazing eye bore into Travis and read the answer in his brother's blank face.

"Travis, you idiot!" LJ scrambled for the phone. "What the heck were you thinking?"

"I don't know. I . . . I . . . I believed the man."

"Watch your lip." Daddy eyeballed LJ, who was punching at his phone like a mad man.

Roxanne rushed into the room. "What's wrong, what's wrong, what's wrong?"

"Would you be quiet!" LJ said. "What did the man say his momma's name was?"

"Audrey. Audrey Jacobs," said Travis, who felt sick as a dog.

LJ stuck the phone to his ear and darted out of the room, mumbling as he went.

"Shoot, he had to have been tellin' the truth." Travis was bewildered.

Bo patted Travis on the back. "Don't worry, Uncle Travis, I know just how you feel." Roxeanne insisted on knowing what was going on and Bo gave her a thirty-second recap.

"Sheesh, Travis, what were you thinking?" she said.

"Shhh," Daddy said, as they listened while LJ asked to be connected to Audrey Jacobs's room at the hospital.

Travis heard him say, "Are you sure?" and he knew what was coming.

LJ filled the doorway looking like the creature from the black lagoon.

"Ain't never been no Audrey Jacobs at the hospital. That was our man."

Before the funeral, Jack grabbed his notepad and headed downstairs to find a quiet place where he could call Derrick.

Margaret approached in the hallway wearing a formal black dress, pearl necklace, and black high heels; those shoes would be a challenge in the snow. She was carrying a pair of black leather gloves, and would need them today.

"You look very pretty, Margaret. Here, let me straighten your collar. It's wanting to stand up in back." Jack touched her shoulders gently.

"Thank you. You look handsome, Jack."

Margaret reeked of alcohol. And it didn't smell like her usual peppermint schnapps. This was stronger. Her red lipstick was uneven on the top lip. Jack would get Pam to help her fix it, and to find some mouthwash.

Rebecca and Faye came out of the kitchen, mouths full.

"Girls, we just ate. What could you possibly be into?" Jack said.

"MawMaw has a gigantic tin of candy mint sticks dipped in chocolate," Rebecca said.

"They are de-licious," Faye added. "Would you like one, Daddy? MawMaw?"

Margaret laughed heartily, not feeling any pain. "They're fine, Jack. Let them be."

If this was any indication of what she was going to be like when she came to their house, it was going to be a challenging few weeks. St. Edward's was full and had put Margaret on a waiting list, so whether she liked it or not, she would be returning to Trenton City with them.

"When do you think we should leave?" she asked.

That was new. Usually she *told* him that sort of thing. Jack looked at his watch.

"I say we go in about fifteen minutes. I need to make one quick call first."

Margaret waved clumsily toward the back of the house. "Go in the den where you'll have some privacy. You'll be fine in there."

Sheesh. She was half in the bag.

After a quiet word to Pam suggesting she give her mom a little assistance, Jack entered the den, his father-in-law's space. It was still and silent. His dress shoes tapped loudly on the dark wood floor. How very odd that Benjamin would never again touch the books on the room's many shelves, or scribble a note at the antique desk, or take a lazy afternoon nap on the leather couch.

Jack parted the curtains and peered out at the snowy backyard where Pam had played as a child. He bent over, lifted the cuff of his pants, and tightened the Velcro on the holster. The last thing he needed was for that thing to drop off while he was carrying the casket.

He phoned Derrick and found he had been sidetracked the day before by a train wreck Barton had sent him to cover. It turned out to be minor, just some cargo cars that tipped during a track change; no injuries.

"The big news is Spivey Brinkman's missing," Derrick said. "He never showed for our appointment. I met his daughters. Hung around for a while and left. I talked to Jenness today, and he never came home; been gone over a day now. He's been known to drink, but hasn't for almost two years."

"Of all times to fall off the wagon."

"Jenness doesn't think so. She called the cops. But because he used to disappear when he drank, they're not going to consider him missing until three days go by. Jenness thinks Demler-Vargus has something to do with it."

"You're kidding me."

"No. Those girls know more than they're telling."

"Maybe Spivey just got nervous about meeting with you. Maybe he *has* started drinking."

"The girls say no way. He's kicked the bottle. And he wouldn't leave overnight without telling them."

"Man. What is going on?"

"I know, right? Barton asked me last night how many hours I put in on Demler-Vargus. I told him I wanted more; he said not yet."

"Hmm." Jack sat on the couch and looked over his notes. He told Derrick he had phoned the Randalls and learned about the man in black who lied to Travis in the parking lot.

"So he really is the one who poisoned Galen," Derrick said.

"Yeah, only now he knows the police are on to him—and the Randalls. LJ's fit to be tied."

"Dude, this thing is getting weirder by the second."

"I know, but there's no story yet. I've got an interview set up when I get back with Bendickson and his son."

"Maybe I can go with you. Hey, I almost forgot. Amy Sheets's mom wrote back again on Facebook, after I asked her for Amy's last address. Let me find it . . . here:

> Mr. Whittaker,
> Please respect our privacy and leave us alone. We have no idea where Amy is and are certain she would not want to be contacted.

"They don't even know that we know about Amy's baby, right?" Jack said.

"No! I just told her I wanted to talk to Amy about a story. But listen, here's the kicker. I went to her mom's Facebook page to dig around some more—and it's gone. She must've closed her account."

Jack dropped back on the couch. "Something's wrong."

"I know, right?"

"All we wanted to do was talk to Amy on the phone. Now we really need to find her."

"I messaged the one brother again on Facebook. I'll keep looking," Derrick said.

"Anything new on Barb and Emmett Doyle?"

"Nada. Still searching."

"All right. I've got a funeral to go to. Hope to be back tomorrow, mother-in-law in tow."

• • •

Lake Erie was living up to the "eerie" part of its name—vast, dark, raging—water splashing over the sea wall, mocking the huddled funeralgoers whose breath hit the cold air as steam. Thirty-three degrees for a high and a lashing wind that stung Pamela's cheeks and numbed her ears, fingers, and toes, even though she had dressed for it. The darkness made it feel more like evening than midafternoon; a typical February day in northeast Ohio.

The landscape seemed like a dream. Daddy . . . gone. Mother . . . alone. Who knew what a day would bring?

With her stylish brown wool cap pulled down over her ears, Pamela stood erect and sober, one gloved hand on her father's casket and the other around both girls. Rebecca and Faye were holding up like troupers, more concerned about doting on their grieving mom and grandmother than about the frozen tundra beneath their shiny black shoes. The crowd was dotted with aging relatives, family, friends, and some people Pamela didn't recognize.

Jack stood at her side wearing a full-length black overcoat. She hadn't seen him in a suit in such a long time—he looked dashing. When she'd slipped back into their room that morning she'd been carrying something much bigger than a cup of coffee: a suspicion that she might be pregnant. She'd wanted to tell him, but the timing hadn't been right. As she'd thought so many times recently, perhaps a new baby was what they needed to come together as a couple again.

She glanced down at Jack's shoes, but couldn't tell if he was wearing the gun. It still absolutely miffed her that he had made such a monumental decision without telling her. They had always talked about everything, and that had always given her security. It was one way Jack showed he cared, by being patient with her and talking things through—even if he had already made up his mind.

They sat down on the row of folding chairs, and Pamela tried to focus on what the stoic, brown-haired priest was saying, as he stood next to her father's dark coffin. Clad in a black robe, purple silk stole, and brown earmuffs, he spoke in a monotone and rarely looked up from his notes. When he did, it was either to rub his dripping nose with a handkerchief or to extend that same hand toward Margaret with a stony look.

Margaret sat between Pamela and the girls, wrapped chin-to-toe in a brown blanket, petting the funeral program in her lap as if it was a purring kitten. Pamela had made her brush her teeth and put on fresh lipstick. With her husband gone, Margaret's paranoia and fears would only be magnified. The next few weeks would be challenging, to say the least.

Pamela surveyed the frozen ground. She and her friends used to hang out in that cemetery on summer nights, discussing who had the latest crush on whom. She could walk home from there, it was so close. Granger's house was close too. Of course, he was never included in anything back in school.

Pamela exchanged a solemn glance with Jack, and he gave her a sympathetic smile. She didn't hear the priest's closing words, but snapped out of her daze when people started moving, shaking hands, hugging, heading for their cars.

"I'm going to get the girls to the car and get the heat on," Jack whispered. "Stay as long as you need. When I see you're ready, I'll come help your mom."

"Thank you." She bent down and hugged the girls. "Go get warm. We'll have cocoa when we get back."

"Who's that?" Margaret muttered.

Pamela took a deep breath of cold air in an attempt to clear her mind and shore herself up for this last round of embraces and condolences. The two sets of calling hours the day before had sapped her; she didn't have much "social" left.

Her Uncle Phillip shuffled toward her, cane in hand, coming to say good-bye before his drive back to Michigan. Pamela headed to greet him.

Margaret stood abruptly, her blanket dropping to the ground.

"Who is that?" Her right arm was straight out, pointing. Her mouth was agape, her eyes enormous.

Pamela followed her finger, but saw only the parking lot where Jack was walking hand in hand with the girls. People were getting in their cars, or standing there talking.

"Get him! Stop that man!" Margaret screamed.

Everyone turned to look.

"What is it, Mom?" Pamela tried to touch Margaret, but her mother shoved her hand away.

"He was here! The whole time! Sitting in that gazebo!"

Pamela saw the white gazebo. No one was in it. "Who? Who did you see?"

"He's gone . . . He's gone . . ." Each word got softer, till Margaret's voice finally trailed off. "He's gone . . ."

"Who, Mom? Who did you think you saw?"

Margaret's head snapped toward her daughter. "Granger Meade." She raised her right hand and pointed. "Right over there, watching your father's funeral." Her head swiveled toward Pamela. "They're all watching . . . all of the bad ones."

14

Galen insisted LJ, Bo, and Travis get their lazy bones out of bed early Sunday morning and go with him to church. Between his father's poisoning, the break-in, and the confrontation with the man in black, Travis was wide open for some spiritual intervention. And, based on the vision standing next to him in the narthex, God was indeed still on his throne.

Her name was Claire Fontaine, and she and Travis had been in the same class in the second and fifth grades at Trenton City Elementary. They remained friends through high school, after which Claire went off to college and eventually became a social worker in downtown Columbus. Since then, she'd worked in many different roles with various grassroots organizations, always helping people who were less fortunate. Travis spotted her thick, shoulder-length auburn hair and pale freckled face several rows over during the sermon—which just so happened to be about how God could flip your world upside down in an instant.

When Travis approached her after the service, Claire beamed and gave him a prolonged hug, smelling like a lemon tree. Her green eyes twinkled and her smile melted his insides. They talked a blue streak, laughing about school days and comparing notes about classmates. She was thin and looked light as a feather in her loose jeans and baggy sweater; she wore no makeup or wedding ring, or any other jewelry for that matter—and didn't need any of it to shine like a star.

Bo and LJ were pestering Travis from across the room to hurry up so they could beat the Baptists to Ryan's for the buffet. Meanwhile, an older woman approached Claire and whispered something.

"That's fine, you go on," Claire said. "I'll see you back at the house." She turned back to Travis. "That was my Aunt Genevieve. I brought her, but she's going to brunch with friends. Who'd you come with?"

Travis hated to have her even look over at LJ and Bo, who resembled two of the Three Stooges, all hot and bothered about how long he was taking to join them for lunch.

"I'm with my dad and my brother and LJ's boy, Bo."

*

Claire gave LJ and Bo a wave and asked about Travis's mother, whom she remembered from their youth. Travis told her she had passed, and Claire seemed genuinely sorry.

Uh oh. LJ was making his way over.

"Excuse me, miss." He towered over Claire, wearing his best black eye patch. He leaned into Travis. "Come on! You're takin' longer than Daddy, for Pete's sake. You know how crowded it's gonna be."

He steamrolled out of there, grabbing Daddy and Bo on his way.

"I'm afraid I've got to go. We're going to lunch. That was LJ—"

"I think I remember him, except for the eye patch."

"Yeah, that's a relatively new look for him."

Claire smiled. "Well, it sure has been amazing seeing you."

"I wish I'd have driven separately. I could talk to you all day."

She laughed. "Wouldn't you miss your lunch? I mean, I could take you home if you want to talk some more."

Travis got chill bumps head to toe. "Are you serious?"

"Sure. We could get coffee or something."

Travis just about went to the moon and back.

"Have you tried the Jittery Joe's that went in over on Brubaker?" he said. "It's my treat, okay?" He motioned for her to stay right there while he hurried off to tell the boys. He called back over his shoulder, "We can go wherever you like, wherever you like . . . coffee, lunch, brunch . . . it's up to you. Don't you move now."

He had turned his excitement into a joke, and Claire Fontaine had gotten it.

She was laughing.

And Travis was thinking that was the best sermon he'd ever heard.

• • •

Derrick was deep in thought as he sat on the couch in his loft apartment that frigid Sunday night in Trenton City. He'd just hung up with a distraught Jenness Brinkman. She and Tatum had been at Trenton City police headquarters, where they were informed that their father's car had been found that afternoon, abandoned beneath a bridge near the interstate. Spivey Brinkman was officially a missing person.

Derrick had planned on questioning Jenness and Tatum when he finally met up with Spivey, but now that was on hold indefinitely.

His phone rang. It was Jack. He and his family—and the mother-in-law—were back from the funeral in Cleveland. Pam had taken Jack to the Randalls' place to pick up his car, and he was driving home.

"I got a call today from Leonard Bendickson's personal assistant," Jack said. "He needs to move our interview up to tomorrow at three, at his office. Can you do it?"

Derrick hesitated. "I think so. I'm sure not going to tell Cecil."

"I'm not sure if the son is going to be there or not; they won't give me a straight answer."

"Dude, is this thing starting to freak you out at all?"

"How do you mean?"

"All that's happened to the Randalls? Now Spivey's missing. What if Demler-Vargus really is behind this?"

"Then we need to stop them! That's what I've been trying to get across to the Randalls. I think they're in more danger than they realize."

"You think it's safe for us to do this interview . . . with Bendickson?"

Jack chuckled. "Well, they aren't going to murder us in broad daylight at their own offices!"

Derrick didn't laugh.

"It'll be fine, man," said Jack. "We're going to find out the truth. Who knows? Maybe Demler-Vargus is completely innocent."

"You don't believe that."

"No, I don't, but right now we've got nothing solid on them."

Derrick checked his laptop while Jack talked about some of the things he planned to ask Bendickson.

"Hold up, Jack. I got a new Facebook message from Amy Sheets's brother Brendon . . . It says *Accept my friend request. Go to online chat.*"

"Dude, score! You better hurry up and do it."

Derrick accepted the request. "I've never done online chat . . ."

"It's a column on the right, I think. At the bottom you click 'go online.' You see it?"

"Yeah, I'm doing it."

"If he's there you'll see a little green light. Click it and start chatting."

Derrick scanned the names in the chat column and there it was, Brendon Sheets, with a green dot next to it. "Bingo. All right, I'm gonna send him a message, I'll let you know what happens."

They hung up and Derrick clicked Brendon's name. A box and blinking cursor popped up. He typed.

Brendon, this is Derrick Whittaker, are you there?

Derrick waited. The answer from Brendon came quickly.

Yes.

Thanks for getting back to me. Am I correct that you are the brother of Amy Sheets, former reporter for the Trenton City Dispatch?

Yes.

Brendon, we are trying to reach Amy about a story she worked on at the Dispatch. Can you give me her phone number or e-mail address?

We don't speak.

I'm sorry to hear that. Do you know where she lives?

Don't be sorry. It was my choice.

We've heard she moved to Columbus, but can't find any listing for her there.

Derrick waited and waited, but got no response. He tried again.

Can you tell me where Amy lives?

It took awhile, but the screen finally showed *"Brendon is typing . . ."*

She does not want to be found.

Derrick was not about to tell Brendon that he knew about Amy's pregnancy. He racked his brain for a different way to phrase the same question.

We heard Amy moved to be closer to your parents . . .

That's the story.

Story? So, she is or is not in the Columbus area?

Have you contacted my parents?

I contacted Rebekah Sheets via FB; assuming she is your mother. She said they don't know where Amy is.

Lie.

Brendon, can we talk by phone? It would be easier. I can call you right now if you give me your number.

Why is this so urgent?

Can I call you to discuss this?

NO and I don't want you to contact me ANY MORE after this.

We're working on an investigative piece. Amy did some interviews before she left. We think what she learned will help us immensely in the story we're working on now.

I knew this day was coming.

Okay, be his psychologist. Just get on the train and ride with the guy . . .

You mean you knew someone from the Dispatch would be trying to find Amy?

I warned them. There are no shortcuts in life.

Warned who?

My family.

About what?

Exactly what's happening right this second.

Brendon, all I want to do is talk to Amy by phone. It will take ten minutes and we'll be done. I won't contact either of you again.

I can't. She couldn't tell you the truth anyway.

Why?

Too great a risk. Please leave us alone. Find your information elsewhere. Talk to the same people Amy talked to. You'll find what you need.

Brendon, do you know what this is about?

What I know is that if you continue to pursue Amy you will put her and my parents at great risk. Do you understand?

No, I don't.

Amy made mistakes, but she is not the real criminal. You know who it is. Keep going after THEM and you will have the dirty party. You're on the right track.

Who is THEM?

I'm signing off. Please don't attempt to contact me again.

Wait Brendon, please don't get off yet.

If you have any mercy, you will STOP trying to contact Amy. That's it.

Derrick tried several more times to type back to Brendon, but he was gone. Quickly, Derrick highlighted all the text from their conversation, copied it, pasted it onto a blank page, and printed it, just to make sure he had a hard copy. Next he e-mailed it to Jack. Then he went back to Facebook, typed in Brendon's name, and found what he suspected—Brendon had already removed him as a friend. His status had flipped back to private.

Derrick reviewed the facts from the conversation: Brendon did not speak to Amy; Amy did not want to be found; Brendon called it a "story" that Amy supposedly moved to the Columbus area to be closer to her parents; he called it a lie that her parents did not know where she was; Amy could not tell the truth if they did find her, because it would put her at risk; Amy had made mistakes.

Derrick organized his notes around the laptop.

What had Amy found out about Demler-Vargus?

He went to Google and entered Amy's name for the hundredth time.

Why hadn't she written about what she discovered?

Derrick was determined to find any thread that would lead them to Amy Sheets.

Was she really pregnant, or was there another reason she had moved away from Trenton City? Had she really moved away at all?

15

It was Sunday night. Everyone was tired from the funeral and the three-hour drive back to Trenton City. Rebecca and Faye were in bed, asleep, Jack hoped. He and Pam were sorting through the mail in the kitchen. They'd had no time to talk in private since the fiasco at the funeral, when Margaret thought she saw Granger.

"It's starting." He nodded toward Pam's mother. Hunched slightly with her hair pulled back and cold cream on her cheeks, wearing a beige robe and slippers, Margaret was going from door to door, checking the locks, and window to window, closing the blinds.

Pam pretended to faint and they chuckled softly.

"You know it's going to be like that," she said. "You better get used to it."

"What do you think happened at the funeral?"

Pam shook her head. "She hasn't slept hardly at all since Daddy died. She's frazzled. She's barely eaten anything . . ."

But she has found a way to drink, Jack thought.

Pam looked around the corner for her mom.

"I think I heard her go upstairs," Jack said.

"Thanks for helping me get her room made up. She usually has a light on all night. She reads or watches TV. She's afraid to go to sleep."

"It's sad."

"I've talked to her about God. She says, 'Oh, I know, I pray . . .' But there's nothing beyond that. I've encouraged her to take comfort in the Bible, she just never does. It's right there for her . . ."

"Hey." Jack covered Pam's hand in his. "You never know what kind of impact you're having on her. She knows what you've been through, and she sees you shining through it. She knows where you get your peace. You just keep being you."

Pam put her other hand on top of Jack's. "Thanks."

He nodded. "I don't deserve you. I'm so thankful you're the mother of my girls. They wouldn't be anything like they are, without you."

They examined each other.

The kitchen was quiet.

"I love you so much, Pam."

They reached for each other.

Jack embraced her, looked down into her beautiful face, and kissed her warmly, deeply.

Pam pulled back and looked into his eyes. "I have something to tell you."

Jack raised his eyebrows. "Yes?"

"It's a good something, if you ask me."

Jack heard footsteps upstairs, one of the girls running.

"Daddy, Mommy!" It was Rebecca, flying down the stairs in her nightgown.

"What is it, baby?" They knelt to greet her in the kitchen.

"MawMaw came in my room and did something to my window. She said something about strangers. Is that Granger man coming back? She scared me." Rebecca threw herself into Jack's arms. "Now she's in Faye's room . . ."

They found Margaret peering out the blinds in Faye's room, and Jack escorted her back to her room, where the smell of alcohol was heavy in the air. He made sure she got in bed and turned out all the lights but one. Then he and Pam checked on the girls again and went to bed.

In Jack's dream, there were only three people in the enormous white room: Evan McDaniel, wearing black, seated behind a glass desk; Granger Meade, wearing white, seated in a wood chair to Evan's left; and Jack, dressed in red, strapped to an electric chair to Evan's right.

Although Jack could sense that the room was freezing, he was sweating profusely and his neck hurt from craning to see Evan and Granger from the ominous electric chair. His arms and legs were numb, the circulation cut off by the thick leather belts that pinned him down.

"I never like these cases," Evan sighed. "They really are backward." His voice echoed crisply off the fifty-foot ceiling, and he spoke with great emotion. "But when you think about it, Christ's case was backward. All he did was come to pardon our transgressions. Oh . . . but we didn't want to admit we had any! We loved our own appetites. And what did we do instead of accepting his gift? Spit. Mock. Whip. Curse. Bruise. And what did he do in

return? Extended his arms and legs to take the nails. Said, 'Forgive them. They don't realize what they are doing.'"

Granger's head was bowed.

"Forgive your enemies." Evan threw an arm toward Granger. "Forgive them, seventy times seven. Give them a gift and a prayer instead. Trust God with their judgment. But that is not normal, is it? That is not natural."

Guilt engulfed Jack as he sat pinned in the electric chair, the hard, black bowl jiggling against his sweaty head.

"You know who didn't get the message about forgiveness?" Evan stood, came around and sat on the front of the glass desk with his arms crossed. "It was the proud, self-righteous hypocrites who decided they were too good to forgive."

He turned his back and walked slowly toward Granger. "The extent to which you forgive others, that is the extent to which you will be forgiven." He rounded behind Granger, stopped, put his hands on the man's massive shoulders, and locked eyes on Jack. "People through the ages have forgiven much more heinous crimes than those committed against your wife, Mr. Crittendon. They may not have wanted to, but they did it—by faith, because that's what God's children do. But not you! Not you . . ."

Evan inhaled deeply through flared nostrils and exhaled in silence. He shook his head. "No, I never like these cases. They are a shame. A shame because good people like you, Mr. Crittendon, squelch your fruitfulness. You're like salt that's lost its flavor. What are you good for? Nothing more than to be thrown out and trampled underfoot. Why? Because you chose to be the judge. You chose to be the holder of the keys."

"Didn't this man come to you—more than once?" Evan slapped Granger hard on the shoulders with both hands. "Attempting to undo the bad things he'd done?" He slapped Granger's shoulders again. "To give back what he took?" Slap. "To plead your forgiveness?" Slap. "Well, Mr. Crittendon, you made the wrong move when you decided to play gatekeeper over God."

Evan walked to the wall behind the glass desk and stopped next to a large lever that was painted white and blended in with the wall; Jack hadn't noticed it before. The second Evan put his hand on the lever, Jack's stomach imploded and his entire body felt as if was being devoured by burning worms.

"I am sorry, Jack . . ." Evan shook his head, pursed his lips, and began to throw the switch.

"No!" Jack ripped out of bed, drenched in sweat.

Pam was out of bed in an instant. "Jack, what is it? What is it, honey?"

He stood frozen in the dark, holding sheets and blankets, heart pounding. He couldn't speak, trying to get his bearings.

"Was it a bad dream?"

He nodded, feeling like a scared animal. His arms and legs were numb.

"It's okay," Pam assured him. "Everything's fine. We're all here. Everyone's safe."

Pam guided him toward the bed, one hand on the back of his perspiration-soaked T-shirt.

"Sit here, let me get you another shirt." She went to his dresser. He dropped his head, wide awake, the dream blazing in his mind.

The floor squeaked in the hallway.

"Mom?" Pam left the room. "What are you doing?"

Jack had probably startled her when he woke up.

He opened and closed his fingers and shook his hands, trying to get the circulation going.

Pam returned quietly, offered him a shirt, and sat next to him on the bed.

"Is she okay?" Jack mumbled.

"Yes, what about you?"

He looked at Pam's silhouette in the dark. He peeled off the soaked shirt, threw it in the corner, and stood to go wash his face.

"I'm fine. Just a really bad dream."

"What about?"

"I'll tell you in the morning. Go back to sleep. I'll be there in a minute."

He shut the door of the bathroom, turned on the light, and leaned over the sink. His hair was a mess, his eyes bloodshot.

The extent to which you forgive others, that is the extent to which you will be forgiven.

He turned on the cold water and splashed his face over and over, trying to wash away the white room and the electric chair.

• • •

Pamela got up early Monday morning, turned up the heat, made a cup of tea, and snuggled up with her Bible before Jack and the girls came down. She knew her mom never got any fitful sleep until the first light of day; then she would finally let her guard down and snooze for an hour or two.

As she reviewed several passages their pastor had read Sunday, Pamela determined she would use the upcoming days to make up for lost time with her mother. She had long harbored bitterness toward Margaret for her chronic paranoia, and how it had threatened to rub off on Pamela. But having been kidnapped herself, Pamela was now better able to understand Margaret's fears, to overlook her issues and simply offer mercy and hope.

As she stood in the kitchen cooking eggs and slicing fruit onto plates for everyone, Pamela still couldn't face the reality that her dad was gone. No more hugs, no more talks, no more knowing he was always there—her safety net. He would never get to see the baby that she was almost certain she was carrying.

She still hadn't been able to tell Jack about missing her period. That was a clear indicator of the precarious state of their relationship; she used to be able to approach him about anything, any time. She'd picked up a home pregnancy test kit a few days before and was hoping they could be together that morning when she tested, after the girls went to school.

Before she knew it the kitchen was teeming with activity as the girls scurried about gathering books, sweaters, and backpacks. Jack lumbered directly to the coffeemaker. They exchanged a kiss, as always.

"What was that dream about?" Pamela said.

Jack loaded the filter and began scooping coffee. "Oh wow, I forgot about that."

"You jumped out of bed; it scared me to death. Remember?"

"Yeah, kind of . . ."

"Did you dream you heard something?"

"No." He made sure the girls were out of earshot. "Granger and Evan were in it."

"Oh boy."

"Yeah." He filled the carafe with water.

"Well, what happened?"

He rubbed his eye with the heel of his hand. "We were in this huge white room. It was so weird . . ."

"Was I in it?"

"No."

"The girls?"

"No. Just me, Evan, and him." He poured the water into the coffeemaker and switched it on. "It was some kind of trial. Evan was the judge . . . I can't remember much. I'm sure it'll come back to me. Any sign of your mom this morning?"

Maybe he just didn't want to talk about it.

"Not yet."

"What was she doing up—when I had the dream?"

Pamela recalled the thick smell of alcohol on her mom's breath in the hallway. "She couldn't sleep. She was going downstairs to read."

"Mommy, have you seen my language book?" Rebecca asked.

"It was on the table in the living room last I saw it."

"Thank you."

Jack leaned with his back to the counter and thumb-scrolled through his phone.

Pamela planned to address the drinking with her mom when they were alone that morning. She didn't know exactly what she was going to say, but thought it best to get it out in the open and talk about some house ground rules.

"I almost forgot." Jack put the phone to his ear. "I gotta call Derrick. He texted me like ten times really late last night."

"Breakfast is almost ready . . ."

"Okay." He headed out of the room.

It seemed like he was constantly checking his e-mails, texts, and whatever else he did on that phone.

"Mommy, did you forget Pop-Tarts?" Faye stared up at her.

"Did you put them on the list when you finished the last box?"

"Yes, I sure did. You want me to show you?"

"Well, I guess I forgot them. Those are too much sugar first thing in the morning, anyway. There're bagels in the fridge."

The smell of the eggs made a wave of nausea linger at the base of Pamela's throat. Suddenly, the acidity of the fruit didn't appeal either. "Come on, girls, time to eat." She put a piece of bread in the toaster and went to the table. "Daddy's on the phone. Faye, would you pray for our day?"

Faye bowed her head and began to pray.

Pamela closed her eyes, but was preoccupied with the notion that Jack was going to be in a hurry, that there would be no time to share the news budding within her.

16

At Derrick's instruction, Jack quickly opened his laptop and read the Facebook conversation from the night before between Derrick and Brendon Sheets. Then he called Derrick back.

"Dude, what did he mean, Amy's made mistakes?" Jack said. "It sounds like they're covering something up—more than her pregnancy."

"Hold up, hold up, dude," Derrick said. "After I talked to Brendon, I got online and really did some digging. Get this: Amy's parents recently moved from a $140,000 house to a $260,000 dollar house; I found the real estate transaction."

"When?"

"Seven months ago. From what I can tell, Amy's dad does the same thing he's always done, heating and air; blue collar all the way. I don't think the mom works."

"There was a windfall."

"Apparently . . . Who knows, he may have hit the lotto, but I didn't see anything about it online. I kept reading my chat with Brendon over and over. That part where he said he knew this day was coming, that he warned the family there were no shortcuts? It sounds like he was against something the family did. He and Amy don't speak."

"By his choice."

"It sounds like there was something he didn't approve of. He de-friended me right after we chatted."

"He said it was a lie that the parents don't know where Amy is. Is she with them, do you think?"

"Don't know."

"Too bad we can't just drive over there and confront them," Jack said.

"It's only an hour. We could knock it out in a morning or afternoon."

"Cecil would never go for it. We're not even supposed to be pursuing Amy."

"I was thinking maybe one of us could go," Derrick said. "Call in sick one day."

"Brendon said you know who the real criminal is . . ."

"I know, dog! Right? He sounded like a mind reader, like he knew we were investigating Demler-Vargus."

Jack buried his head in his hands. The girls were calling him to come to breakfast; he didn't want to miss them. Yet the gears were clicking, clicking, clicking in his head.

"I mean, let's just brainstorm," Derrick said. "What if Amy found some heavy dirt on Demler-Vargus? Let's say she told her family . . ."

"Daaa-dy." Faye came around the corner. She reached out and tugged Jack's hand. "Eggs are ready. Mommy says hurry up, we have to leave soon or we'll miss the bus and then you'll have to drive us."

He didn't have time for that. "Derrick, hold that thought. Keep running with it." Jack went with Faye. "I've got to see the kids off. I'll get back to you."

They hung up and Jack and Faye took their seats at the kitchen table. Pamela and the girls were almost finished eating. "Sorry about that," Jack said. "Derrick found some new info he had to share." Jack dug into the eggs.

"Daddy, you didn't pray," Faye said.

Rebecca stared at him. Pamela flashed one of her patented forced smiles that always made him feel like a terrible husband, father, and human being.

He closed his eyes and bowed his head, but all he could think about was Amy Sheets. *God, thanks for everything. Help Derrick and me figure this thing out.* "Amen!" he said.

"Excuse me." Rebecca cleared her dishes. Pam did the same. Faye gave him a sympathetic frown and followed suit.

Jack ate quickly, finishing on the way to the sink.

He always tried to keep things light and fun before school. "Now I want you girls to have a wonderful day," he said, as they got on their heavy winter coats. "Be alert. Pay attention. Stay on top of your game."

Like a well-oiled machine, Jack handed them lunches and water bottles from the fridge. Pam was acting cold toward him, probably because he had taken the call from Derrick and missed breakfast.

Jack checked the thermometer outside the kitchen window. "Thirty-four degrees," he announced. "Hats and gloves. Scarves and mittens." He clapped his hands. "Bundle up. It's gonna be coldy, coldy."

• • •

Jack was so moody. Pamela longed for the consistency and stability they once had. Yes, he was funny now, but what about ten minutes from now, or ten hours? Couldn't that call with Derrick have waited until he got to work? She threw on her winter coat. "Let's go, girls."

She appreciated what a hard worker Jack was, but it certainly hadn't helped lately, as emotionally detached as they were. Rebecca helped hoist Faye's pack onto her back and the girls quietly followed Pamela to the front door. Jack had disappeared again.

"We're leaving," Pamela yelled.

After the Granger episode, she had phoned the school district and requested that the girls' bus stop be moved from around the corner, out of sight of the house, to the end of the street, where she could see them. After much ado, the request had been granted. But ever since they found out Granger had been released from prison, Pamela and Jack walked the girls to the bus stop.

Before heading out the front door, Pamela took one last glance at the top of the steps and froze; the girls bumped into her from behind. Jack was bending over, adjusting the gun and ankle holster. Their eyes met. "Coming." He stood and shook his leg. "Coming, coming, coming."

Pamela unlatched the bolt lock and headed into the cold, hoping the girls hadn't seen the gun. "I don't think we're going to see much sunshine today," she said to them. "It's going to stay pretty cold and we might get some more snow."

"Mommy, Maggie Hebert just wears a skimpy little pink windbreaker, even on cold days like this," Rebecca said, as they walked down the sidewalk toward the end of the street. "Maybe we could give her one of our coats."

"Maybe she's just warmblooded," Pamela said, looking back for Jack, who was just opening the front door.

"No, she's always freezing. Her teeth click together all the time."

"Hey, wait for me, you crazy kids!" Jack jogged toward them.

"Well," Pamela said, "why don't we look tonight and see if we have one we don't want. Is she your size?"

"She's a bit plump," Faye said.

"Faye, that's not nice," Rebecca said. "She's just big-boned. But I have that one green coat with the fur collar-hoody thingy that I never wear. I've never liked it very much, and it's toasty warm."

Jack caught up with them, huffing and puffing to be funny. "Whew, you guys move fast."

"You're right we do," Faye said. "We've got a bus to catch, mister."

Jack laughed and looked at Pamela, who just shook her head.

Pamela could hear the bus chugging up the main road. "We're going to be just in time."

"Here." Jack stopped and knelt. "Give us a hug. We'll watch from here."

"Good idea," said Rebecca, who was feeling too old to be walked to the bus stop.

They all hugged and kissed, and Rebecca led the way down the rest of the street, with Faye right beside her.

The school bus rambled up the street and squeaked to a halt, its red and orange lights flashing. Pamela scanned the neighborhood. The bus let out a burst, its doors opened, and the girls climbed aboard. It was one of the newer buses with the tinted windows, so they couldn't see where the girls sat. Pamela and Jack waved anyway. Jack turned to walk back toward the house, but Pamela watched until it was almost out of sight, and gave one last wave.

It was damp and cold to the core, like Pamela felt inside.

Jack had waited for her. "What are your plans for the day?" he said.

Pamela told him she would go to the library and Target, and pick up some groceries; all the while she was wondering if she should mention the pregnancy test. She didn't even feel like taking it now.

"There's a lot happening with this Demler-Vargus story. We're supposed to interview the CEO and his son today."

"Didn't you just interview him?"

"Yeah, but that was a feature story. This is for an investigative piece."

Pamela knew him so well. Just the way he looked down at the road and up into the sky. He was already at the newspaper in his mind.

"Oh boy," he said. "Don't look now. We're being watched."

It scared her for a second, but when she looked at Jack, he was grinning and scratching his forehead to cover his eyes.

Pamela glanced up at the house. The blinds in the guestroom were awkwardly spread open about three inches, and her mom was peering out.

"She never misses a trick," Pamela said.

Jack chuckled. "Hey, at least we'll know right away if you-know-who shows up again."

Just walk, Pamela thought. *Don't say a word. It's not even worth it.*

They reached the end of the driveway. She removed a magnet sticker from the mailbox advertising a snowplow service. She was so frustrated. Nothing was working for them. Everything was off.

Jack picked up the copy of the *Dispatch* that had been thrown there in the wee hours of the morning. He took it out of the plastic bag, opened it, and examined the front page as they walked up the driveway to the front door.

Pamela glanced up at her mom's window one last time; the blind dropped shut.

They got inside, and Jack tossed the paper on the steps. "I'm gonna get ready and get into work. Big day ahead."

She lifted her head to acknowledge him.

He took several stairs and stopped. "Hey, what was that exciting news you were going to tell me?"

She stared blankly. No words came.

"Can't remember?" he said.

She shook her head.

"Okay." He took the steps fast. "Let me know if you think of it."

He was gone.

She stood there; the house quiet.

She was surprised she didn't burst into tears. But she wasn't even close. And that scared her . . . more than Granger Meade ever had.

17

Travis could barely keep his mind on the new muffler hanging over his head. Claire Fontaine had lit up his life like a Roman candle. She was funny and kind, sensitive and pretty—shoot, she had it all. Was it too soon to say she was the best thing that had ever happened to him? They'd spent the whole tooting day together Sunday, went their separate ways for a few hours, then met back up for chocolate cheesecake at Tiffany's on the square.

All he wanted was to be with her again.

"Trav, you done yet?" LJ called from beneath a Ford Fusion in the adjoining bay. "We're backin' up here. You been on that Mustang the whole dern morning."

"Almost," Travis called.

"Look, it's Monday, I'm tired, I'm ill. Don't make me go off on you."

Travis laughed. "What the holy fire is wrong with you? Didn't you get enough of Daddy's grits this mornin'?"

"That Mercury's next. He needs it by three. Man, since when am I the traffic coordinator 'round here? We need to get Daddy back out here."

"I'm goin' to lunch when I'm done with this'un."

LJ rolled out from beneath the Fusion, squinting with his one eye. "Lunch? What're you talkin' about?"

"Claire's pickin' me up. We're goin' for pizza."

LJ rolled back under the car, mumbling and grumbling.

Travis snickered and tightened the last few bolts on the new muffler.

There was a knock at the side door.

He tossed the socket wrench, grabbed the dirty towel from his shoulder, and wiped his greasy hands on the way to the door.

Ralston Coon stepped in from the cold in his fancy black lawyer coat.

"I hope to goodness you come bearing good news." Travis called for LJ to come out.

LJ took his time wheeling out, wiping his hands on his navy coveralls, grunting and groaning his way over. Coon held his pudgy hands up, not wanting to shake with either of the Randalls.

"Do you mind?" The lawyer moved over, rubbing his hands beneath the glowing orange space heater that hung in the corner. "I can't get warm today."

"Watchya got, Mr. Coon?" LJ said. "We run a busy shop here."

Coon took off his silver glasses, pulled a little cleaning cloth from his pocket, and rubbed the lenses. "Gentlemen, I have some very encouraging news. Should we go inside where your father can hear?"

"Just lay it on us. We'll tell Daddy," said LJ.

"All right then. First of all, our friends at Demler-Vargus admit absolutely no wrongdoing whatsoever—"

"Give me a big fat break." LJ spit toward the corner.

"Wait." Coon held up a hand. "Just wait. To a corporate giant like this, the amount they are offering to pay you is a mere pittance, if they can keep their name out of the news and squelch any bad press."

"How much?" LJ said.

"Let me finish . . . They require each of you, and your father, to sign an affidavit stating that you know of no wrongdoing on their behalf, and that you are accusing them of no wrongdoing, and will not do so in the future."

Travis began to protest, but the lawyer spoke louder. ". . . *And* that you will talk to no one, absolutely no one, about Demler-Vargus ever again."

Travis dropped his head. The biggest bully on the block would get its way, and would be able to continue hurting people.

"How much?" LJ squeezed the back of his long neck.

Coon evened his gaze with LJ, then Travis. "A cool two-point-five million."

LJ and Travis went limp at the same time.

They would be taken care of.

Travis felt tears welling in his eyes. Anything Daddy needed, they could afford.

"Have 'em round it up to three and that'll be a million each," LJ said.

"LJ." Travis gave him a nasty frown.

"Shall we run it by Galen?" Coon said. "If all three of you agree, we need to pick an afternoon this week to meet with them. They're ready to be done with it."

"Oh, now they're in a hurry." LJ stomped over to one of the red tool chests.

"Well, they're gonna git their way." Travis headed for the door. "Pay us what amounts to a drop in the bucket for them, and keep on killin' people."

LJ and Coon stared at him.

"Isn't there a way we could cripple them more? Stop what happened to Momma from happening to other folks round here?"

LJ looked at Coon now too.

"Gentlemen, if . . . if you want me to ask for a bit more money, I'll consider it. But if you're talking about seeking some astronomical figure that you think is going to somehow impair this mega manufacturing giant or somehow pay them back for your mother's death—that is not what I signed up for."

The boys exchanged glances, but said nothing.

"Now I suggest we go lay this out for your father and come to a decision," Coon said. "I've been working diligently on this for weeks, and the iron is red hot. We need to *strike.*"

The house was toasty warm when Travis and LJ brought Coon inside. Travis made everybody take their shoes off, to the lawyer's clear discomfort, and they pulled up chairs to the kitchen table. He rousted his father, who was snoozing in his recliner with his radio on.

Daddy poured himself a glass of prune juice and joined the others at the table.

Bo was poking around in the fridge, and Coon nodded toward him and addressed LJ. "Do you mind? This is just between the four of us."

"Bo, take a hike for a few," LJ said, but he gave Coon a nasty look.

Bo shrugged and wandered off.

It only took a minute for the lawyer to outline the offer. Travis followed up with his concerns.

Galen sat silently with his hands resting on the kitchen table.

"Well?" said Coon. "Are we going to do this deal? I can't believe I even have to ask that question. I thought this was what you wanted. It *is* what you wanted."

Galen cleared his throat. "You've done a fine job, Mr. Coon. We appreciate it." He looked down at his hands and interlocked fingers. "I understand Travis's points. By making us an offer, they are admitting their guilt—"

"But remember—"

"I understand about signing the affidavit, Mr. Coon. But we all know they're guilty as the day is long. And if we accept this offer . . . well, let's just say we're not helping anybody but ourselves."

Coon took in an enormous breath.

LJ crossed his arms. Travis waited.

"As much as I'd like to have a hand in bringin' Demler-Vargus to its knees, and somehow get revenge for your mother's death . . . that's God's doing." Galen's old eyes blinked toward Travis, then LJ. "I've got to think about you boys and your future. This'll make your lives much better. You can keep right on doin' what you're doin' out in the shop, there just won't be as much pressure."

"Then it's settled." Coon stood. "I'll set the meeting up for one afternoon this week, the first available for them, if that suits you gentlemen?"

Without looking at Coon, Galen gave a nod and downed the remainder of his juice.

Travis and LJ got up and saw the lawyer to the door. He was on his way out when Bo spoke from the living room doorway. "Don't forget your hat."

Coon gave him a glare, grabbed his hat, and made his exit.

Travis kept his eye out for Claire as he scrubbed the grime off his hands at the kitchen sink. LJ was back at work in the shop and had put Bo on an oil change and lube job.

She rolled into the parking lot like a stockcar driver in her little blue Fiat, right on time. She was out in an instant, all carefree and looking around for which door to go to.

Travis opened the back door and stepped into the cold, his heart racing like a high school kid with a crush. "Hey, Claire," he called.

She smiled, dodged several patches of snow with her leather bag swaying on her hip, and bounced right on up the back steps. "Hey there!" She patted his arm. "Are you ready for the best pizza you've ever tasted?" Her eyes twinkled beneath her white knit cap, and she gave her matching scarf a tug.

"Come in for a second." Travis held the door. "You can say hey to Daddy and I'll grab my coat."

Travis wished he'd had more time to spruce up. The kitchen looked like a pack of vagrants had been living there. Anyway, it didn't seem to matter to Claire. She blew in like a summer breeze.

Daddy's eyes lit up when she entered the TV room and Travis introduced them. They hit it right off, so Travis excused himself and hustled upstairs. He brushed his teeth, splashed on some Aqua Velva, and checked himself in the mirror. He'd shaved extra close that morning but acknowledged again that he needed a haircut.

By the time he got downstairs, Daddy had managed to lure Claire into his web. They were sitting in straight-back chairs over by the window. His father was rambling on about his rare coins, and Claire was examining one with his enormous magnifying glass.

Travis managed to roust them out of there, and Claire insisted on driving. She knew the east side as well as he did, taking turns and shortcuts to an old two-story house on Winston Avenue that had been converted into an Italian restaurant, Savelli's. Travis had seen the place for years, but never considered eating there.

The place was a true find. They sat across from each other in a cushy booth. The dark wood table featured a mini jukebox and a candle in an old Italian wine bottle, with dry wax dripped down the sides. Mr. Savelli himself waited on them, and Claire assured Travis that one slice would be enough. She was right; it was the size of the plate and mouthwatering.

They couldn't talk enough, about the old days, the neighborhood, the people and places they shared in common, and about her experiences in social work. Travis told her about his family and his work, and when he finally got around to detailing the crazy events of the past week, Claire was shocked.

"Travis, your dad was poisoned. Your house was wrecked. That man was following you. Now, all of a sudden, they're going to pay you two-point-five million dollars and leave you alone?" Claire shook her head. "I don't believe it for a minute."

"We don't know for sure that Demler-Vargus was behind all that stuff."

Claire shrugged. "Who else would it be? All they took from your house was your dad's notes. They wanted that evidence."

She was confronting him with things none of his family wanted to admit, because there was a pot of gold at the end of the rainbow. Her sober observations made him feel ignorant and greedy—and frightened about what Demler-Vargus might really be up to.

"What are the police doing?" she said.

He explained that they were trying to track down the silver Toyota, but that they didn't have the time, interest, or resources to investigate a corporate giant. His ultimate hope was that Jack and Derrick would expose the harm and corruption spewing from Demler-Vargus.

But when he told her that the reporters were having a difficult time tracking down Amy Sheets, and that Spivey Brinkman was missing, Claire about went through Savelli's roof.

"Travis, this is nothing to be taken lightly. You and LJ need to protect your dad. You need to talk to an investigator. This is dangerous."

Travis glanced at Claire's watch and did a double take. More than two hours had flown past. LJ would be having a cow. Claire asked Mr. Savelli for a to-go box and insisted on picking up the tab. "After all, I invited you!" she said.

As she zipped them toward his home in the Fiat, Travis told her about the various leads Jack and Derrick were pursuing. When he mentioned that Amy Sheets had interviewed Emmett and Barb Doyle, Claire's knee jerked off the gas and Travis bucked forward.

She swerved to the side of the road, slammed to a stop, and turned the car off.

"What is it?" he said.

Claire turned to face him. Her face was chalk white, washing away the color of her lips and freckles.

"Are you sick?"

She nodded once and rocketed from the car into some weeds at the edge of the woods. Travis rushed to her, but stayed back several feet as she ripped off her hat, bent over, and vomited. He dashed back to the car and grabbed the napkins from the carryout bag. "Here."

She reached back and took them, steam rising from the wet weeds beneath her. She wiped her mouth with the napkins, then retched again.

She turned slightly and stuck the hat out. Travis grabbed it. Then she bent over and rested both hands on her knees.

After a moment, Travis bent down with her. "Take deep breaths."

She did, wiping her mouth again. Then she stood, eyes locked on his. "My mom . . . our family . . . we were close friends with Barb and Emmett . . . they moved to Charleston . . ."

"Claire, take it easy." He rested a hand on her back. "We'll talk about it later—"

"No." She shook her head. "You don't understand . . ."

She was shaking badly. She stood up and grabbed both elbows to stop shivering. "This can't be . . . it just can't be." She staggered and shot a fist to her mouth, and Travis thought she was going to be sick again. She swallowed hard and took a deep breath, her eyes searching him frantically. "My mom just heard, Barb and Emmett are dead . . ."

18

"M is for Monday and M is for meatloaf!" Derrick had been going on about the lunch special at the Sparta ever since he and Jack met up at the paper that morning, so at lunchtime the duo hurried in to grab a bite. The crowded place was a throwback, with a long yellow Formica counter and barstools, several yellow booths, and a window that ran the length of the place, allowing diners to observe downtown Trenton City and passersby.

They got a booth on the window. "It is meatloaf and mashed day, right?" Derrick said. "I didn't see it on the board."

"Calm down, dude. I'm sure it hasn't changed," Jack said.

"They season it so good. Best deal in town for four ninety-nine. Is Pam a good cook?"

Hearing Pam's name reminded Jack of the friction between them that had been bothering him all day. He'd called her midmorning to say hello and gotten a cold response. All he knew to do was to continue to put one step in front of the other.

"Pretty good," he answered. "She's calorie conscious, though."

"Zenia buys those budget TV dinners. I don't think she knows what a spatula is."

They laughed as a waitress in the standard Sparta uniform of yellow dress and white apron brought waters in clear plastic glasses. Her name tag said Marleen.

"I've got a craving for a grilled cheese and fries," Jack told her.

"Well, you know what I'm here for, Marleen," Derrick said. "I'll have the healthiest portion of the meatloaf and mashed taters that you can scare up."

Two men stood at the busy counter, waiting to pay for their meal. Jack recognized one, then the other—and his stomach turned inside out.

"Shoot." His face flushed. "Don't look now." He quickly glanced out the window, hoping they hadn't seen him.

"Who is it?" Derrick said.

"I'll tell you in a minute. Just don't look."

Jack tried to find the men in the reflection of the glass. Yes, it was Granger, getting his coat on. Couldn't miss him, the guy was so tall.

"Hello, Jack."

Ugh.

Jack turned to find Evan McDaniel standing over them. "It's been awhile."

Jack shook hands with Evan and re-introduced him to Derrick.

"Hey, any chance we can talk for a second?" Evan said.

Derrick slid out. "I need to use the boys' room anyway, before the food gets here. You guys go ahead."

The bell at the door jingled, and Granger meandered out to the street.

Good.

Holding his coat, Evan slid in across from Jack. He looked less gaunt and his face had much better color than the last time Jack saw him.

"How's Wendy?" Jack liked Evan's wife, whom he had befriended when Evan disappeared a year and a half ago, with the intent of taking his own life.

"She's wonderful, especially now that she's out from under the pressure of being a pastor's wife. Thanks for asking."

"And the boys?"

"All fine. Growing up too fast." Evan glanced around, then leaned over the table. "Look, Jack, here's what I want to say. I've been meeting with Granger ever since he was arrested. We've become friends."

Jack cleared his throat and looked back out the window. Granger loitered in the cold with his hands stuffed in his coat pockets like a kid waiting for his mom.

"When he wanted to apologize to you and Pam, well, it wasn't supposed to happen like it did."

Jack stared at Evan, trying not to look sour, just wanting him to go.

"I was going to call you and Pam, go with Granger when he went to talk to you—and not at your house. We'd discussed that, but . . . well, he decided he couldn't wait."

Jack could only muster a slight nod. He was concentrating hard on keeping his mouth shut, knowing if he spoke it would be toxic.

"I'm sorry about the way it unfolded. Granger is too."

Jack forced a smile and nodded again.

Evan closed his eyes, sighed, and slid out of the booth. He quietly put on his coat. "I hope you guys are healing from what happened. We're all trying."

When Jack said nothing, Evan nodded and walked away.

Derrick slid back into the booth. "What was that all about?"

Jack inhaled deeply and set his shoulders back. "He apologized for Granger's visit the other night. Said he'd wanted to set up a meeting with us together, not at the house."

Derrick shrugged.

Marleen arrived and set their plates before them.

"Now that's what I'm talkin' about," Derrick said. "Beautiful, Marleen, beautiful."

"Can I get you anything else?" she said.

Jack shook his head.

"We're good, we're good." Derrick was already cutting his meatloaf.

"Gentlemen." With a smile, the waitress smoothly slid a black receipt holder onto the table. "Your meal and tip have been taken care of today."

Jack knew, instantly, but Derrick sat back, crazy-eyed. "By who?"

Marleen nodded toward the door. "It wasn't the man who was just over here talking to you, but the one he was with. The tall redheaded gentleman. It's your lucky day . . ."

• • •

It was a gloomy afternoon, a mix of rain and snow swirling. The meatloaf and mashed potatoes weren't sitting well with Derrick. He reached across Jack for a Tums in the glove compartment. Derrick was driving them to Spivey Brinkman's place to interview Jenness and Tatum.

Where could Spivey be in this weather?

Jack had been talking with Travis on his phone. He turned it off and looked at Derrick. "We gotta change plans."

Derrick slowed down. "What's up?"

"Travis has news about Barb and Emmett Doyle, he wouldn't say what. He's having a big powwow at the house. We need to be there."

"Right now?"

"Yep."

Since Brinkman's place was right around the corner from Randalls', Derrick phoned Jenness to tell her they would be late. "Don't forget, we got Bendickson today," Derrick said.

"We should make it. Let's find out what's going on with the Randalls and take it from there."

They arrived at the Randalls' place in minutes. Travis asked them to take their shoes off and walked them into the TV room, sockfooted. LJ was seated backwards on a straight-back chair, tipping forward as he watched Dr. Phil. Galen reclined in his favorite chair, his frown increasing more with each new guest that arrived. Bo was at the very end of the couch, shaved head down, thumbing away at his handheld. Ralston Coon was seated on the middle of the couch, overdressed as usual, with a notepad opened on the coffee table in front of him, drumming a pen on the table.

"Everybody"—Travis stood at the center of the room—"this is an old friend of mine from the neighborhood, Claire Fontaine." He extended his hand toward a cute, fair-skinned redhead who gave a nod and a smile as she sat in the corner with her arms and legs crossed, bobbing a foot up and down.

LJ's ex, Roxanne, swept into the room in a black ZZ Top T-shirt, tight jeans, and cowboy boots. "What can I get everybody to drink?" she said.

"LJ, turn that dern TV off." Travis closed his eyes, as if to tell himself to calm down. "I'm sure we're all fine, Roxanne."

"Do you have any Alka-Seltzer?" Derrick whispered to Roxanne.

She leaned in close, smelling of cigarettes. "No, but Galen swears by ginger ale, and we got them little eight-ounce bottles in the fridge. Can I get you one?"

Derrick nodded and Roxanne headed for the kitchen. A green-and-black butterfly tattoo peeked above the waist of her low-rider jeans.

"Okay, listen up, folks." Travis turned to LJ. "Would you tell your son to take that dadgum headset off?"

LJ stomped loudly. Bo looked up. LJ squinted like Clint Eastwood and tapped his own ear one time. Bo removed the headphones.

"We got a ton a work to do in the garage," Travis said. "But I wanted us to put our heads together. Claire here shared some news with me about Barb and Emmett Doyle. It's . . . it's a darn shame—and it's troubling. See, her family and Barb and Emmett go way back. As it turns out, the Doyles moved to Charleston, South Carolina, because the doctors said the warmer climate would be good for Barb. She was having the breathing issues and skin trouble—"

"Same as Momma," LJ chimed in. "Same dern thing."

Roxanne returned with the ginger ale for Derrick, then plunked down on the floor next to LJ, who ignored her.

"Anyways . . ." Travis scratched his head and looked down at the floor. "Claire's momma learned from a neighbor of the Doyles in Charleston that they had a house fire. Both of 'em perished, I'm sorry to say."

Galen pulled the lever on the side of his chair and sat up. "I didn't hear nothin' about it on the radio."

LJ stopped tipping his chair, huffed, and covered his mouth with a greasy hand.

"You'll recall the Doyles went to Demler-Vargus asking for money to help with their medical bills." Travis walked slowly about the TV room pointing from one finger to the next, as if counting. "When they didn't pay, the Doyles went to the *Dispatch* reporter, Amy Sheets." He swung around to face Derrick and Jack.

Derrick felt a patch of sweat break out on his forehead. He looked at Jack, whose mouth was sealed and whose head was shaking ever so slightly. Derrick's stomach churned.

"We've got some news about Amy Sheets." Jack motioned to Derrick, who told the group about his online chat with Amy's brother, and how Amy's parents had moved to an expensive home and might be lying about Amy's whereabouts.

"It's time to get the police more heavily involved," Jack said. "I know an officer with the Trenton City PD, Dennis DeVry. He'll know what to do."

"Folks, we can't do that." Ralston Coon tossed his pen onto the coffee table and watched it slide off the edge. Roxanne snatched it and put it right back. "You have an agreement with Demler-Vargus that's going to be signed Thursday afternoon at two o'clock. It's my job to get you the funds you deserve, and so help me, I'm going to do it. Until then, this thing stays under wraps. And you guys know this is off the record."

Derrick's face was red hot. "What about their safety?" he waved at Galen, LJ, and Travis. "These aren't coincidences. Someone poisoned Galen and broke in here. Spivey Brinkman is *gone*. The Doyles are *dead*."

Claire nodded, and so did Jack.

"Honestly, if I were you, I wouldn't stay here right now," Jack said, addressing the Randalls. "Go to some relatives or get a hotel—"

"Son," Galen interrupted. "I know you mean well, but we ain't goin' nowheres. Boys, load them guns up and keep 'em handy. I'll be darned if the crooks who killed Betty Jo is gonna run us out of our own home. By golly, they ain't comin' in my house agin." He pointed at Coon. "You tell 'em to bring it on."

"Cool down, Daddy," Travis said. "Everybody cool down."

"Look," Jack said, "the thing is, even if you do get the police involved now, today, they're not going to go busting down the doors at Demler-Vargus anytime soon. It's going to take time. An investigation. My advice to you is, get that started now."

"Thank you very much, Mr. Crittendon," Coon said sarcastically. "We'll take your advice into consideration."

"I agree with Jack." Claire's words came as a surprise from her quiet corner.

"By the way, Mr. Coon," Derrick said, "I just want to clarify, we *are* going to write about this. The Doyles were residents of Trenton City; their death is local news. Spivey Brinkman's disappearance is news—"

Coon stood. "We agreed you would leave the Randalls out of this. And I am assuming you're going to keep your word, or there will be legal ramifications."

Derrick and Jack looked at each other.

"I just wish you were more concerned about the Randalls' well-being than about the paycheck they're going to bring you," Jack said.

"If anything happens to them—" Derrick said.

"If anything happens, it'll be our own fault," Galen said. "I'm the stubborn coot who says we're stayin', and I think the boys agree . . ."

"Darn right." LJ stood.

Travis eyed Claire, who pleaded at him with her eyes. But he said nothing.

19

Pamela's morning did not go as planned. Margaret awoke in pain soon after Jack and the girls left. She was certain it was one of her frequent urinary tract infections, so Pamela made an appointment for her to see their family doctor. The pregnancy test and talk with her mother about her drinking would have to wait.

Margaret was moving slowly, and by the time they got out of the doctor's office, stopped at the pharmacy to get her meds, and grabbed some salads in town, it was well into the afternoon and getting colder.

"Be careful, it might be slippery." Pamela held an umbrella over her mom as they walked from Tiffany's along the wet sidewalk to her red Accord. This was the first time Pamela had ever felt the need to reach out and steady her mom, and she waited for Margaret to protest, but the older woman said nothing. The years and Benjamin's death were taking their toll.

"This foul weather makes my arthritis so bad," Margaret said. "I belong in a nursing home, I swear."

"We'll get you home and you can get your afternoon nap." Pamela unlocked with the remote and walked her mom to the passenger door as the rain came harder, tapping the umbrella like sleet.

"I'm nothing but a burden," Margaret said.

"Mom, you are not a burden. Just sit tight." Pamela shut the door and walked gingerly around to her side. She noticed a man in a black overcoat seated in the driver's seat of the car next to hers, reading a newspaper, and chastised herself inwardly for feeling suspicious. She'd been hypersensitive to everyone around her since Granger had invaded their lives.

It took forever to back out in the traffic. Once around the city square and heading toward home, the car got warm—and quiet.

Now was as good a time as any.

"Mom, can we talk about your drinking?"

Margaret turned and stared out the passenger window at the dark afternoon. "Here we go…"

"Well, I smelled it on your breath last night."

Margaret wiped her nose with a wadded-up tissue. "It helps me sleep."

"Mom, I'm concerned about you, and I'm concerned about the girls seeing you drink."

"It was in the middle of the night. They were sound asleep."

"Okay, I'm not bringing it up to argue. We just need to have some kind of ground rules while you're with us."

"Pamela, you make me sound like a child."

She didn't dare say what she was thinking: that her mom was exactly like a spoiled, self-centered child.

"I don't mean to hurt your feelings, Mom. Look, why can't you keep the bottle in the kitchen or in the pantry and just have a drink in the evening? You're an adult. Jack and I are adults. There's no reason to hide it. If the girls ask what it is, we'll tell them you like your adult beverage in the evening."

"You're so religious . . . I didn't think you'd want that."

"Well, if you need to drink while you're here, that might—"

"Let's get something straight. I don't *need* to drink. I enjoy it. It helps me relax. I look forward to it . . . You wouldn't understand."

Pamela drove in silence, debating whether she had said enough.

"Well, what would be wrong with doing it like I said? Have an evening drink and be done with it?"

"I can't believe we're talking about this."

"Mom, I'm thinking about Rebecca and Faye. If you drink, you drink— do it in front of them."

"What am I going to do, turn them into alcoholics?"

"You could have too much and say something, or do something . . ."

Margaret huffed. "I knew this wasn't going to work. I told you that."

"Okay, let's put it out there, Mom. How much do you drink in a day? Is it more than one drink? Is that the problem? Is it three? Is it five? If it is, you need to get help."

There, she'd said it.

"Pamela Anne . . . you have no right to speak to me like that. Your father wouldn't want you to address me with such disrespect."

"He told me you went to AA once. We could do that here. I can go with you."

"It was a farce. That's why I never went back. Those people were weak. Just pitiful . . ." Her voice trailed off.

"Mom, listen to yourself. Everyone else has the problem—everyone but you."

Pamela knew she'd gone too far. Now she'd get the silent treatment. The only sounds were the windshield wipers and the rain and sleet drizzling on the roof.

Pamela maneuvered the car through a series of sharp curves near the sprawling water treatment plant where Jack had covered stories before, and then opened up onto the four-lane road that would lead them to Merriman Woods.

She took another glance at the small, silver car that had been behind her most of the trip. The driver, a man, sat low in the driver's seat.

"I started drinking after the . . . after the man broke into my dorm room that night." Margaret looked straight ahead, as if in a trance. "I never told your dad what happened. Never told anyone." Her head dropped and her frail shoulders shook. She cried.

Pamela was surprised her mom hadn't shut her off. Maybe they could make some progress after all.

Margaret took a breath and held it, forcing herself to keep going. "Anyway, after it happened, I couldn't sleep. I just could—not—sleep. I was more awake in the night than in the day." She sniffled. "I'd never drunk before. The first time, some of the girls in my dorm were going out. It was a weeknight, and they invited me to go. The place had dime beers, of all things. I got drunk. I got sick. But I slept!" She spoke those last words with such intensity, such victory.

"I slept the whole night through for the first time in a month. That next afternoon, I asked a friend to buy me some wine. I wasn't going to drink alone. I was going to keep the wine on hand, just in case. But that night, I lay in bed like an owl. I was living in utter terror."

"So you drank to be able to sleep."

Margaret whimpered and nodded. "Yes . . . yes."

Pamela had never felt such compassion for her mom as she did at that moment.

She checked the rearview. Good. The man in the silver car was gone.

"What is he doing?" Margaret looked with furrowed brow directly past Pamela, out the driver's side window. Pamela's eyes followed hers . . .

It was him!

The man in the black coat who had parked next to them on the square! He was riding right next to them, staring in at them unabashedly.

He'd been following the whole way . . .

Pamela looked ahead. She had a car in front of her and couldn't speed up, so she took her foot off the gas. But the man slowed too, staying directly beside her.

"What on earth is he doing?" Margaret pleaded. "Do you know him?"

"No!"

"What is he saying?"

They could see the stranger talking brashly, wagging his head. Of course they couldn't hear him. Pamela tried to read his lips while watching the road, too.

"Get away from him," Margaret said. "Oh dear . . . do something!"

"Mom, I'm trying—"

There was a gap ahead, and Pamela sped up, but it was as if his car was affixed to hers. He stayed right there, even with her.

She knew there were exits ahead; she would drive off the next one.

"Get my phone from my purse," Pamela ordered.

Her mom snatched the purse from the floor and dug in. "Where is it? There's so much junk in here . . ."

"Stay calm, Mom, it's in there."

The man would not budge from her side.

A sign showed the next exit in one mile.

"Got it!" Margaret handed the phone to Pamela.

The man was shaking his head, forming what she guessed were exaggerated cuss words with his sick mouth

What he didn't realize was that Pamela was not unfamiliar with terror.

"You see this?" She shook the phone at him. "Nine. One. One. You ever heard of that?"

"Pamela, stop!" Margaret grabbed her arm. "You don't mess with a freak like that. Oh my word. He'll kill us!"

"Be quiet, Mom." Holding the phone above the steering wheel where the man could see it, she punched in one number at a time, exaggeratedly, like a child pecking initials on a keyboard: nine, one, one. "You see what I did?" She talked sarcastically to the man, holding up the phone, though she knew he couldn't hear her. "Po-lice. Po-lice. You understand?"

"You are crazy," Margaret said. "There's an exit coming."

"I know, we're taking it. Hold on."

The exit ramp was within sight.

Suddenly, the silver car swerved toward them.

Pamela dropped the phone and ripped the wheel right.

Margaret screamed.

The car jolted and bumped off the road, vibrating loudly against speed bumps and into the cinders as Pamela tried to correct.

She couldn't stop or he would be on them.

Keep going!

She straightened the car, looking desperately in front and in back for a way out.

But the man's car was there, sticking to them like a Doberman.

He was laughing.

"Get the phone," Pamela said. "Tell them where we are."

The exit was there.

Pamela drove fast in her lane, as if going past the exit.

"Hello?" Her mom had picked up the phone.

The white lines for the exit formed a V, with a huge sign pole right in the middle.

"Mom, hold on tight."

At the last millisecond Pamela jerked hard right, flying over the white lines.

Margaret squealed as their bodies slammed left.

The car just missed the sign pole and blew down the ramp.

Silence.

"Is he back there?" Pamela asked.

Margaret put an arm on the seat and craned back, out of breath. "No! Keep going. You did good, you did good. You're so brave . . ."

Pamela turned right and gunned it up a four-lane road, but slowed when she hit traffic. It was a congested retail area she usually avoided.

Margaret handed her the phone. "I don't think the call went through."

Pamela continued to check her rearview.

No sign of him.

Who was he?

Was there some connection with Granger?

Why had he picked them?

20

It was Monday night in the *Dispatch* newsroom. Jack and Derrick were on and off their phones, frantically scribbling notes, fingers flying over keyboards in their side-by-side cubicles. Pam was home safe with the girls and Margaret, thank God. Although she wasn't able to get the tag numbers from the car that followed her, her description lined up identically with the man in black who had been harassing the Randalls—right down to his cleft lip.

What did the stranger want with Pam? Was it a warning for Jack to lay off the story? Jack had postponed the interviews with the Brinkman girls and Leonard Bendickson and dashed home to meet Pam and Margaret that afternoon. They'd agreed not to tell Rebecca and Faye about the incident. Margaret, who was badly shaken, was not shy about pouring herself a healthy Scotch on the rocks while they waited for the girls to get home from school. Pam's hands were clammy and the color in her face was off slightly, but Jack could tell she was determined to be the calming influence her own mother had never been.

As Jack and Derrick exchanged notes and talked back and forth at their desks, he became more convinced they were getting closer and closer to blowing the lid off the corruption at Demler-Vargus—and what he believed was a deadly cover-up exploding all around them.

The evening deadline at the *Dispatch* had passed and only a few employees remained in the dark newsroom. Cecil's office, however, was a hotbed of activity. His lights were burning brightly, and Nigel and Pete were in there with him. Soon Jack and Derrick were expected to report to them with an update on the Demler-Vargus story.

"Dude," Derrick called over the partition, "the Doyle fire was in the Colonial Lake section of Charleston. That part of town is high cotton."

"How do Barb and Emmett move from the poor east side of Trenton City to a prestigious neighborhood within a chip shot of Broad Street in Charleston?"

"The same way Amy's parents moved to that big house in Columbus."

An e-mail popped up on Jack's computer from the reporter he had contacted at Live5News TV in Charleston, asking for details about the Doyle fire. He read it and chills swept over him.

"Dude, you're not gonna believe this." He read it aloud for Derrick:

Jack,

I can help you, but this is all OFF THE RECORD until we go live with it (I'll let you know when—likely tomorrow). Barb and Emmett Doyle didn't know what hit them. They were found in the master bedroom, middle floor of the three-story house. Autopsies show both died of smoke inhalation; they never made it out of bed. Fire marshal believes accelerant was used to start fire in kitchen and mud room on first floor. Sign of break-in through carport below building. AGAIN, THIS IS FOR YOUR EYES ONLY for now . . .

Good luck,
Patrick Roe

Derrick was in Jack's cubicle by the time he finished reading it. "Dude, is this for real?" His eyes were huge.

"I'm afraid so," Jack said. "The Randalls aren't safe."

"Are *we*?"

Derrick was saying what Jack was thinking.

"Seriously. This is starting to freak me out," Derrick said.

The last thing Jack needed was for Derrick to unravel. "Keep cool. We've gotta go over our questions for Bendickson."

"Cecil wants us in there." Derrick looked toward the editor's office.

"I know." Jack looked too.

"What did the Doyles know about Demler-Vargus?" Derrick said. "It was something they found out working in the plant."

"What does Amy know?" Jack said. "She's the one we have to get to."

"And the Brinkman girls."

"We'll find out tomorrow."

"Are they safe?"

When Jack looked through the big window to Cecil's office again he saw his boss glaring at him. Cecil threw up his hands and yelled something.

"We'd better get in there," Jack said. "Bring your notes."

Cecil sat behind his huge desk with his fingers locked behind his head, and Pete and Nigel sat along the front edge of the desk, as if on barstools. Over the next ten minutes, Jack and Derrick spilled everything they knew about the Demler-Vargus investigation. The more they talked, the higher Jack's hopes got that the editors would turn him and Derrick loose on the story full-time.

"Okay, look." Cecil sat up and pulled at his stringy hair. "I know you think you've got a big story here, and you might, you very well might. But right now, in reality, we've got very little hard news, if any."

"And obviously," Nigel said, "you guys have spent a lot more time on this than we gave you. Derrick, I wish you were this committed to the other news on that side of town."

"I don't like that," Cecil said.

"Look, we've already covered the Spivey Brinkman disappearance," Nigel said. "But there's no tie to Demler-Vargus."

"He's an alcoholic with an up-and-down past," Cecil added, waving it off. "Until he turns up and officially blows the whistle with some concrete evidence, that's a non-lead."

Jack had told Derrick before they went in to remain calm. The editors were a rough bunch. Sometimes things worked themselves out by simply letting them talk till they were blue in the face.

"If the Doyle thing is arson, that's of interest," Pete said.

"Yeah, but again, what's the connect to Demler-Vargus besides their former employment there?" Cecil said. "We got nothing to fit the pieces together—unless there's something you haven't told us."

"We need time," Jack pleaded. "We've gotta dig deeper. We'll find evidence."

"What about all the crazy stuff going down with the Randalls?" Derrick said. "That's news!"

"You've said yourself most of that is off the record, because they're still trying to make a deal with Demler-Vargus," Nigel said. "All we have is a bunch of opinions and accusations. By now, you guys should know what's news and what's not. It sounds to me like this thing needs to play out longer before it deserves any more of our attention."

"But if you give us time, we'll find the smoking gun at Demler-Vargus," Jack said. "Cecil, this is an exclusive. No one else is onto this."

Nigel pursed his lips and examined his watch. Pete stood with his arms crossed. Everyone was waiting on Cecil, who rocked back and combed his fingers through his hair.

Jack went around the desk and whispered to Cecil, "Amy Sheets is the answer. She has what we need."

Cecil shook his head and sat up. "No, Jack. That's still not an option and never will be. Forget it."

Jack wondered if Cecil would be that loyal to him if he ever had to disappear. The thought crossed his mind that Cecil may have been romantically involved with Amy, and that's why he was covering up her whereabouts—but that was not only unrealistic, it was laughable.

"Here's the deal," Cecil said. "Derrick, you keep tabs on the Randalls. That might turn into something. But I'm going to tell you both right now—and listen to me good—the last thing this paper needs is a lawsuit, especially from a monster like Demler-Vargus. And believe me, they could bring it. They would destroy us. We're running on a shoestring as it is, and all the pressure stops right here." He pounded his desk.

"Cecil, I can't believe you. This is major scandal." Jack searched the editors' faces. "People are missing. People are dead! My wife was run off the road. We've got to stay on this. I guarantee it'll pay off."

"Man, ya'll, if this ain't news I don't know what is," Derrick said.

"You've made that clear." Nigel smirked.

In the back of his mind Jack knew Cecil had a point. They needed hard evidence before they could print anything negative about Demler-Vargus. They needed Any Sheets and Spivey Brinkman. They needed the Brinkman girls to talk. He wondered if the Bendickson interview was even worth their time.

"Jack." Cecil stood, flapped his tie, and came around the desk. "There's a new Farley's Home Store in Pell Town. It got robbed this afternoon."

Jack wilted.

"There's surveillance video. Two-man job." Cecil wasn't making eye contact; Jack knew what was coming. "It's the second Farley's to get held up in the metro, and I want you to cover it. No more time on Demler-Vargus until we've got a real story."

Jack dropped his head and exhaled loudly.

Nigel opened the door and stood there.

"I know you understand, Jack." Cecil stuck his fists on his waist. "Demler-Vargus just isn't worth it right now. We'll know when it is, if it is—and if that happens, you and Derrick will cover it."

There was an awkward silence.

"Derrick," Cecil said, "you've got one hour a day to follow up your leads on Demler-Vargus. That's it. No more. Or you're gonna be looking for a job at the *Auto Trader*."

Nigel cleared his throat and raised his eyebrows, holding the door open with one arm.

Jack and Derrick looked at each other and headed out.

• • •

They walked through the dark newsroom. "I need something." Jack turned into the break room and Derrick followed.

"You know Cecil better than I do," Derrick said. "What gives? Why's he holding back on this?"

Jack shrugged and put his money into a machine. "You heard him. He's scared silly. He'd rather ignore it altogether than take a chance of getting sued."

"But we'd just be conveying the facts."

"I know." Jack hit some buttons, and a bag of Chex Mix dropped. "And we need more time to get the facts. You're right—it isn't like him. I think Nigel's paranoid. He's been against this from the beginning, and Cecil listens to him for some reason."

Derrick grabbed a bottle of water from the mini fridge on the counter and tossed one to Jack.

"I wasn't about to tell him about our interview with Bendickson." Jack headed for his cubicle.

"We gonna go through with it?" Derrick followed.

"It was already scheduled."

Derrick was apprehensive about disobeying Cecil and Nigel any further. The last thing he needed was to get fired with his wedding coming up.

"What about talking to Spivey Brinkman's girls?" Derrick said.

"Same with that," Jack said. "Cecil and Nigel won't know, don't worry."

What paper would hire Derrick if he were fired for going against his editors? How would he make a living? How would he support Zenia?

"Dude, that isn't like you," Derrick said. "You're usually straight by the book."

They got to their cubicles and squared up.

"I'm gonna call Dennis DeVry, too," Jack said.

"Police? You heard what Coon said—"

"I don't care. I couldn't live with myself if something happened to the Randalls and I hadn't done everything I could. Too many weird things have gone down."

21

It was a frigid night. The girls were in bed and Pamela sat bundled up in gray sweats, an Ohio State hoody, and warm socks, with her feet curled beneath her in the family room. The library book she leaned toward the lamp was called *The Well*, about getting your needs met by God instead of people.

Jack had phoned earlier to tell her he would be working late. He wanted to make sure all the doors were locked; they'd both chuckled, knowing Margaret would have taken care of that already. The pregnancy test was still in the cupboard in the bathroom; maybe tomorrow morning Jack would have time.

The doorknob jiggled in the kitchen, and Pamela sat straight up. Then the shutters clacked shut and she relaxed.

"Are the floodlights on?" Margaret came around the corner in her robe and slippers, hair pulled back, cold cream on her cheeks.

"Mom, those keep the girls awake, remember?"

"Oh . . . I keep forgetting." She rattled the bolt lock on the front door.

"It's all locked up, Mom."

"Just checking." She peeked out one of the vertical windows alongside the front door. "You really should get some of those little sheer blinds on here, honey, or those mini blinds. People can see right in—especially at night."

"Mom, do you know how many times you've said that since you've been here?"

"Well, it's a good idea." Margaret shuffled over, turned on a lamp, and sat at one end of the couch. She shook her head. "I'm just thinking of the girls, that's all."

"Those vertical windows are three inches wide. No one's going to see anything through those from the street."

Her mom stared at her for the longest time, then tilted her head. "I'm proud of you, Pamela. You are a brave young woman."

Pamela's whole body went limp. A compliment from her mother was a rare thing. "Thank you."

"The girls are . . . amazing. So confident."

Pamela smiled.

"I realize what I'm like." Margaret looked down at her frail hands and rubbed in her lotion some more. "I don't know how your father put up with me all those years."

"He knew that what happened to you in college changed your life," Pamela said. "He understood."

Margaret nodded. "But how do you do it? How can you stay in this house after what happened?"

Pamela took a deep breath. Walls were coming down. "We love this place, this neighborhood—"

"No . . . I mean, you never seem worried. I don't see you looking over your shoulder."

"I do look over my shoulder, Mom, but I don't want to worry the girls—"

"The way I worried you?"

"I realize that what happened to you was terrifying. And you've not been able to let it go."

She tapped her head. "His face is seared in here."

"Mom, Jack is going through the same thing you are, but with Granger."

Margaret squinted. "I don't follow."

"He can't forgive Granger."

"After what that maniac did? I don't blame him."

"You asked me how I live in this house, in this town, with Granger free, after what he did. Do you want to hear my answer or not?"

Margaret's mouth sealed into a frown and she crossed her arms.

"It's forgiveness, Mom." Pamela spoke quietly. "It set me free. I had a lot of your tendencies, even before Granger came into our lives. It was paranoia."

Margaret jerked as if someone had poked her in the side with a stick.

"Jesus set an example of forgiveness," Pamela said. "We forgive like he did and it sets us free."

Margaret examined Pamela as if looking into her soul.

"Free, Mom," Pamela whispered. "Those two words go together: forgiveness and freedom."

"You're saying I should forgive the man who raped me . . ."

"Yes, I am. Forgive him and let it go. It will change your life."

"And just how would I do that even if I wanted to? He never said he was sorry. I don't know where he is."

"You do it alone with God. And you mean it."

Margaret pursed her lips and eyed Pamela as if considering a business deal.

Pamela knew her advice had sunk in. Having got that far, she sensed that her mother wouldn't want to hear another word about it, so she changed the subject.

"Hey, you want to see something?" She hopped up and held out her hand. "Come on, I've been waiting to do this forever, and I'm done waiting."

"Do what?" Margaret took her hand and followed Pamela down the hall to the bathroom.

"This!" Pamela opened the cabinet, found the pregnancy kit, and presented it to her mom.

Margaret's mouth dropped open and her eyes ballooned.

Pamela nodded excitedly. "I think number three is on the way!"

They hugged.

And the embrace turned into rocking.

And the rocking turned into tears.

The tears of life.

• • •

After they'd exhausted all of their energy and brainpower, Jack and Derrick went their separate ways into the freezing night. On his drive home, Jack called Officer DeVry and told him everything he knew about Demler-Vargus and all the people involved with it.

When he finally pulled into the driveway, he was spent. Pam greeted him with a smile and a peck on the cheek. Jack grabbed a slice of pizza from the fridge and filled her in on the night's events as they stood at the kitchen counter. The house was quiet; Jack wondered if Margaret was actually asleep or tiptoeing around, eavesdropping.

"I think Derrick's scared," Jack said.

Pamela's eyes got big.

"What?" he said.

"Aren't you scared? I mean, are we safe—Mom and the girls and me?"

Jack was so tired, he couldn't think of anything to say.

"Whoever is behind all this obviously wants you and Derrick to quit digging around. I think they made that clear today, don't you?"

"I know, but I feel like if we don't keep going, who's gonna stop this? Not the police—"

"You've got to think of your family first, Jack. Besides, Cecil told you you're off it. The last thing you want to do is get yourself fired."

"He wouldn't do that."

"Jack, it's not your call. He's your boss. Maybe he knows something you don't."

He wiped his mouth with a napkin, not about to tell her he planned to go forward with the interview the next day with Bendickson and his son.

"What about OSHA or the EPA?" Pam said. "Can't you tell them what you know and just turn it over to them?"

"That's just it; we aren't there yet. We don't have enough solid evidence."

Pam crossed her arms and put her head down.

"We're so close," he said.

It was quiet for a moment. Jack thought he heard a creak in the floor upstairs. Probably Margaret drifting about.

"Why does this mean so much to you?" Pam eyed him.

"Honey, I have no doubt in my mind, Demler-Vargus is killing people. They think they can trample on those families with no consequences. Now they're trying to cover it up with scare tactics."

"More than scare tactics, Jack! Spivey Brinkman is more than scared, he's missing. The Doyles aren't scared, they're dead!"

He crossed to the sink and threw his napkin in the trash. "You know what?" he said. "Ever since Granger Meade came into our lives, you've been different. You've treated me differently."

"What are you talking about?"

"You used to trust me. Anything I said or did, you got behind me. It's not like that anymore."

"I don't know where this is coming from." She shook her head. "What are you talking about?"

"It's a lack of trust. You think that because I haven't forgiven Granger, I'm somehow not right with God, or that God isn't going to have favor on us anymore."

"Jack, I was not thinking that just now. It's all in your head."

"But you have thought it. You said yourself I don't read the Bible like I used to. Let's get it out on the table."

"Okay, fine, let's get it out. You know what upsets me?" Pam's eyes filled with tears. "I'm shocked about your lack of concern for Mom and me today. That guy could've put us in the hospital!"

"I came back to check on you. You both seemed fine. I didn't think it was any big deal."

"I was trying to be strong for Mom so she wouldn't freak out, but it scared me to death, Jack. And then you turn around and go back to work and don't come home till now?" She threw her hands up. "You know how that makes me feel?"

"I'm sorry, Pam. You just seemed to take it so well—"

"This isn't you, Jack. If that'd happened two years ago, you would not have left my side. Seriously. You have changed. You used to cherish me . . . so much."

He looked down.

Staring at the counter.

Silence.

It was true. She was right. What had happened to him? To them?

"And if you want my opinion, yes, I really believe your unwillingness to forgive Granger is causing collateral damage. You want more proof? I've been trying to get five minutes alone with you for days, to do a pregnancy test with me . . ."

Pregnancy test?

Jack instantly felt dizzy. His ears buzzed. "You think you're pregnant?"

Pam crossed her arms. Her bottom lip quivered, and the tears broke loose. She nodded. "We *are* pregnant."

He reached out for her, but she kept her arms folded and didn't turn toward him.

He was a stupid idiot! She was right.

He put his hands atop her shoulders from behind. "I'm sorry, honey."

She dropped her head and cried.

"That's wonderful news," he whispered.

She flinched, as if it was too late for his attention.

Jack cursed himself.

He'd blown it again.

22

The clock at Travis's bedside read 4:48 AM. He shoved the covers aside and rolled onto his back. He'd been half awake the whole night, listening for intruders, worrying about Daddy's health, daydreaming about Claire, fretting about Demler-Vargus.

If they could just fast-forward to Thursday afternoon, 2.5 million bucks would be theirs. He and LJ could give their father everything he needed, and they could live comfortably while keeping the shop going. Travis could even provide for Claire . . .

Wait up.

Who was he kidding?

Did he really expect Claire Fontaine to fall in love with a middle-aged grease monkey like him? Lord, she was beautiful; way out of his league. Being with her was like being in the winner's circle at Talladega. Nothing topped it.

Claire was something special. She was always so interested in Travis, in everybody. Her life was like a bonfire. She wasn't ashamed about how much she loved God, but wore it right on her sleeve. She brought God up in conversations naturally, the way Travis would mention Daddy or NASCAR.

Travis smiled. He could see himself taking Claire to church every Sunday for the rest of their lives.

Holy smokes . . . You're getting way too far ahead of yourself.

Claire had been upset with Travis after everyone left the night before. She was worried about his family's safety and begged him to get the police more deeply involved. She didn't think Demler-Vargus was going to pay them and simply walk away.

It might seem weird to most folks, but Travis had a strange feeling Claire got insights directly from God. She had a wisdom about her that he trusted.

That's what was keeping him awake.

Even if the payoff did happen as planned, Travis wrestled with accepting it, keeping mum, and letting his neighbors continue to suffer.

He was counting heavily on the stories Jack and Derrick would write to expose Demler-Vargus for their wrongdoing—after his family got their payment, of course.

He heard a noise.

In the house?

Yes.

Travis got up and felt for the small flashlight by the clock. He turned it on and headed down the hall.

Yes, it was coming from Daddy's room.

He went in, partially covering the flashlight, but his father wasn't in his bed.

The sound of coughing, bad coughing, more like heaving, came from the bathroom.

Travis's heart broke. He stood for a second, debating whether to go in. Daddy was proud. He wouldn't want any help for a coughing spell.

But this was more than a cough. Daddy was retching.

Travis stood there a second longer, took a deep breath, and went in. The nightlight revealed his father on his knees at the toilet in his flannel pj's. He looked so fragile. One arm lay across the tank, and his head against that.

"Daddy," Travis whispered, not wanting to scare him. "You okay?"

His father flushed the toilet.

Something dark swirled in the bowl and disappeared.

"Was that blood?" Travis said.

"Hand me a towel."

Travis grabbed one and gave it to him, and his father wiped his mouth, his forehead.

"You want some water?"

"I'll git it." Daddy worked his way to his feet and crossed to the sink. He ran water, took a swig, swished, and spit. It wasn't clear. And there was blood on the towel. "This happens." He leaned on the sink with both hands. "I'm all right. Comes with the territory."

"Daddy, we need to take you to the hospital." Travis began readjusting his day, thinking which cars could wait a day, which ones he could give to Bo.

His father shook his head and leaned over the sink on his forearms. He coughed violently, his old frame teetering, his pajamas looking three sizes too large.

Travis noticed a smattering of blood in the sink, just before his father turned on the water and splashed it away.

"I'm okay. Give me a minute."

"I'm afraid you might have what Momma had," Travis whispered. "You need to get looked at."

"They would've spotted it when I was just in," Daddy said. "I know something's wrong. Heck, nobody lives forever—not down here, at least."

The thing was, his father despised hospitals. He was afraid that once he went in he'd never come out. He was old-fashioned to the core—a typical codger who'd rather live richly on his own land for a day and die with his greasy coveralls on than live for a month trapped in some hospital, being kept alive by medicine and machines.

He turned on the water, leaned over the sink, and splashed water on his face, then patted it with a towel.

"I know you don't want to go," Travis said. "But I want you to. Will you let me take you if I promise not to let them keep you?"

Daddy looked Travis in the eye and put a hand on his shoulder. "Have I ever told you what a fine son you've been, Travis?"

It hit him like a two-by-four. Travis's nose tingled and tears filled his eyes. It was one of those talks that could only happen in the dreamy pre-dawn hours. "Thank you." He dropped his head, not wanting his father to see his tears.

"It's okay, son." Daddy patted his shoulder. "We've had a darn good life, haven't we?"

Travis nodded, still looking down.

"God's been good, all these years."

Travis looked up at him. "We still got time."

Daddy nodded. "Sure we do. And when my time runs out, that's just down here. I'll be alive and well, just somewhere else, on another shore . . ."

"Somewhere good."

"That's right." Daddy patted him again. "Somewhere far better than here."

"Will you let me take you in?"

"I like Claire. She reminds me a yer momma."

Travis laughed, and a few more tears snuck out.

Daddy chuckled. "I'll go, under one condition."

"What's that?"

"You won't let them keep me overnight."

"Only if it's an absolute emergency."

Daddy stared at him. "All right."

"How 'bout you get dressed. We'll get in there early. In and out."

"Now you're talkin'."

"Good." Travis started to leave. "Then you can buy me a biscuit and gravy."

"Travis."

Travis stopped and turned around.

Daddy extended his arms. "I love you, son."

His father felt so light and slender in Travis's arms. And he never talked like this.

Did he know his time was coming?

Travis held the embrace, even after his father relaxed.

"I couldn't have a better father," Travis said. "I love you too, Daddy."

It was barely starting to get light outside when Claire showed up at the hospital with three cups of Dunkin' Donuts coffee and a bag of plain and powdered doughnuts. They'd put Daddy in a room on the fourth floor, and he'd been in and out for tests since Travis got him there.

He was gone for more tests now, and Travis and Claire stood at the window in his room, watching a light snow fall on the silhouetted landscape below.

"You're quiet," she said.

"He's getting weak." Travis shook his head. "It hurts. I know it must bother him to feel so frail."

Claire covered one of Travis's hands with hers. "He still seems strong. And he gets around really well, for his age."

"Nothin's ever gotten him down. He's like an old Ford. Low maintenance. Just keeps truckin'. You just expect him to start up ever mornin'."

There was a soft knock at the door.

"Come in," Travis said.

"Good morning." A short, thin doctor in a white lab coat walked in clutching a clipboard. He introduced himself as Dr. Richard Beezenhour.

Of course Claire offered him a doughnut, which he kindly refused.

"I just wanted to give you an update on your father's condition," the doctor said. "And I was hoping to ask you a few questions."

"Sure, fire away," Travis said.

"I see from his records he's been in and out quite a bit lately."

Travis explained the background, which Beezenhour cut short.

"How long has he been coughing up blood?"

Travis looked at Claire and back at him. "Golly, I've only known him to do it a couple times. 'Course, he might be keepin' it from us. He told me this morning it does happen from time to time."

"Well, the good news is, I think the blood your father brought up this morning was simply an irritation of the throat, caused by the violent coughing."

"Thank God for that," Travis said.

"What concerns me, however, is what's causing that cough." Beezenhour adjusted his stethoscope.

"He's been coughing more lately," Travis said.

"That was my next question. His recent CAT scan was clear. He's got some minor blockage in his arteries, but his blood flow is adequate and, at his age, it's nothing I would be concerned with."

"That's all good," Travis said.

"Now, I saw in the records from his initial visit that your family was concerned about the effects of living near the Demler-Vargus plant."

Travis and Claire nodded, and Travis told the doctor about his mother's symptoms and passing. He started off on a rabbit trail, but Dr. Beezenhour corraled him.

"The reason I ask is because I've done extensive research on the dangers of synthetic chemicals used in manufacturing," the doctor said. "I've had some papers published; it's kind of a hobby for me. I've been studying it for years. Your father told me he's experienced some headaches lately, a bit of dizziness, some confusion."

"'Course he don't say nothin'," Travis said. "We've noticed he's slowed down. You know he's had breathing issues. He gets tired real easy. There have been a few instances of short-term memory loss."

"Right now I'm checking his kidney enzyme functions and doing some more blood work." Beezenhour had a habit of blinking repeatedly. "We're also checking his urine, because it can tell us if there is something present in his system called Fenarene. That's actually a synthetic chemical used extensively in the manufacturing of resins, plastics, fiberglass, and such. If it is present, these tests will tell how his body is breaking it down."

"Thank you for being on top of this," Claire said. "It's wonderful we've found you."

"Yes, indeed," Travis said. "Now . . . I kind of promised Daddy if he came to the hospital, I'd make sure he didn't have to stay the night or anything. When do you think he can go home?"

"Sometimes Fenarene effects the central nervous system, so I want to keep an eye on him for a little while at least, do some observation. Let me get some more of the tests back and we'll talk then."

"This Fenarene, Doc, does it kill you?"

Beezenhour hugged the clipboard to his chest and grimaced. "I wish definitive proof existed one way or the other. Some epidemiologic studies suggest there is an association between Fenarene exposure and an increased risk of leukemia and lymphoma."

"Momma died of lymphoma!" Travis said.

"Yes, I read that in your father's history."

"She didn't even work in the plant. Daddy either."

"Don't have to. Ambient air in urban locations can contain Fenarene." Beezenhour scratched his thinning brown hair. "Of course, indoor air is the principal route of exposure, but your folks have lived near that plant so long . . . it makes me wonder."

"Well, you keep wonderin', Doc, 'cause we sure could use some proof."

They shook hands, and Dr. Beezenhour headed for the door. "We'll have your father back here in a few minutes. I'll follow up after I've reviewed everything. Shouldn't take too much longer."

"Doc."

Beezenhour stopped and turned to face them.

"What if you do find this Fenarene in Daddy? What then?"

"Then we see what it's doing to him, and how his body is handling it—or not."

23

Jack sat numb in his car early Tuesday morning outside Farley's Home Store in Pell Town, watching quarter-sized snowflakes blanket the empty parking lot while he waited for the manager to arrive. His mind was on overload. He was going to be a father, and he wasn't right with God—or Granger Meade. He and Pam were at odds, and she and the girls could be in danger. Yet he knew Demler-Vargus was dirty and that he was probably the one person who could stop them from unleashing further damage.

He started the car, turned the heat up, and hit the wipers. The snow blurred the windshield and was getting so thick in the air it looked like a massive pillow fight with feathers galore. He had to set his priorities and attack one thing at a time. His plan was to knock out the robbery story Cecil had given him so he could finish preparing for his interview with the CEO of Demler-Vargus.

His phone rang. It was Claire. Travis had asked her to call Jack to give him an update on Galen and the tests a Dr. Beezenhour was running to find any trace in him of a synthetic chemical called Fenarene. Although Jack hated that Galen was back in the hospital, he considered that Dr. Beezenhour just might be the godsend for which they'd been waiting.

An old brown Mazda with no hubcaps silently glided across the vast parking lot like a sleigh floating across a field.

"Claire, I've got to run. Give Galen my best, and tell Travis I'll be in touch. We're getting closer."

The car slightly skidded to a halt. Jack finished scribbling some notes as a tall bald man with black glasses got out.

Jack grabbed his notebook and met the manager, Ray Brucks, on his way into Farley's. Ray greeted Jack kindly and ushered him into his office, where the two men took off their coats and set their stuff down.

"If you don't mind, I'm going to put on a pot of coffee. Why don't you come with me, and we can talk as I do that."

The break room was right around the corner. Ray grabbed a trash can and went along the counter throwing away used paper plates, Styrofoam cups, dirty napkins, and a variety of wrappers from vending machine items.

"People are so messy," he said. "Do they do this at home? Some of them, probably." He threw away the old filter and coffee grounds, rinsed the old coffee from the pot and filled it with tap water.

Jack asked Ray to give him an overview of the robbery.

"I can show you the surveillance video," Ray said. "It was a two-man job. Same as the other Farley's robbery in Wilkesburg. Had to have been the same guys."

He turned on the coffeemaker and sighed. "Come on, I'll show you what we have."

They went back to his office. Ray pushed piles of papers aside so he could get to his mouse, and punched up the video of the robbery on his computer. There were four split-screens.

"Top right is the parking lot," he said. "See the green conversion van sitting there? He was in a fire lane about thirty or forty feet from the entrance; same place he parked at the job in Wilkesburg. Can't see much of the driver. Looks white, dark beard, dark ski cap. Here now, you see the passenger getting out?"

It was blurry footage, and authorities couldn't get a license number, Ray said. But once the armed man entered Farley's, the quality of the video improved on one of the different cameras. "Here he comes." Ray pointed to the bottom right screen. "He loitered for a few minutes at the jewelry counter." He fast-forwarded the tape and hit play. "Now, see, he goes to the checkout. See, here he is." He tapped a different screen. "He actually got in line behind this guy with the cart full of toilet tissue and paper towels."

The robber's right hand hovered over his stomach, where Jack assumed he had the gun. He swayed like an anxious child about to step onto a roller coaster. And he looked around nervously, waiting for the man in front of him to check out. "The guy in front of him had a ton of coupons for paper products, so we get a good look at the robber here as he waits."

The man was older, perhaps fifty-five or sixty. He had dark, curly hair—possibly dyed—and a shadow of grayish beard. He wore a leather bomber jacket, loose fitting dark corduroy pants, and white tennis shoes.

"Here it comes," Ray said. "The guy in front of him wheels his cart away and right here, the guy draws his gun."

The young female clerk jumped back two feet and her hands locked over her mouth. The robber waved the menacing gun at the cash register, then at her face, then back at the register.

To scare someone like that was so low. So stinking low.

"I felt so badly for Jenny, my checkout girl," Ray said. "She really was afraid she was going to take a bullet. You can see she's leaning back away from him as far as she can while she gets the money from her drawer. She's shaking horribly. You can see there was no way she could've hit her alarm, he's all over her."

"Can you e-mail a still shot of this guy?" Jack said.

"Sure."

"We can probably run it. Give me as much of a close-up as you can. Don't show Jenny, though."

The idiot yelled something at Jenny, who tipped over the metal bag rack while getting a plastic bag. Her hands were trembling so badly, she could barely make them do what she wanted. The thief ripped the bag from her and jabbed his gun to the right. Jenny crossed her arms in an X over her chest and hurried to where he pointed. He hurdled the counter, dumped the money in the bag, and bolted, leaving Jenny dropping to the floor in tears.

"Back to the outside camera." Ray pointed to the top right screen. "Here he comes, running now. They take off . . . Just another pleasant day of shopping at your local Farley's Home Store."

24

Back at the *Dispatch* later that morning, Jack hammered away at the story on the Farley's robbery from his freezing cubicle. A small space heater hummed away at his feet. Derrick's cubicle was still dark.

When Jack was under pressure, he wrote extremely fast. He was ahead of where he'd wanted to be on the robbery piece, so he saved the story, hit the restroom, and headed for the break room to get more coffee.

"Crittendon." It was Cecil waving him over from the city desk.

Jack headed that way, hoping Cecil wasn't going to pile any more work on him.

"Derrick's not coming in," Cecil said. "Sick."

"Really?" The reporter in Jack immediately wondered if Demler-Vargus had gotten to his colleague.

"Really. Pete's reassigning a few of his stories. No big deal. How's the robbery story coming?"

"I'm on it."

"Good." Cecil started to walk away.

"If I wrap that piece up soon, can I work on Demler-Vargus for a little bit?"

Cecil shook his head impatiently, threw his hands up, his eyes darting about. "Nothing's changed since we talked about this last night."

"Precisely why we need more time."

"Jack, we've got hard news to cover. When the police make an arrest, then it'll be news. We're not going down this path until we have more. We've been through this."

Jack lowered his voice so no one else could hear. "You're scared, Cecil, and I've never seen you scared in all the years we've worked together."

"Huh." Cecil shook his head with a sour frown. "The problem is, you don't understand the big picture of the business. You don't have to worry about getting sued or telling all these people they're out of jobs because we printed something we should have left alone. You're a reporter, Jack. I'm the commander. I don't blame you for wanting to dig into this can of worms, but you have got to start respecting my point of view. I'm thinking about eight gazillion things that never enter your radar."

"It's just not like you." Jack looked away. "This isn't the newsman I know."

Cecil took a step closer to Jack. "The publisher is watching me like a hawk." He spoke quietly and evenly, just below boiling. "There're a thousand details you don't know—and don't need to know. You need to trust me on this. Just do what Nigel and I told you last night. If and when Demler-Vargus becomes a concrete story, you'll be the first one we turn loose."

"Cecil, my gosh, this thing has gotten personal! Who the heck do you think is doing all this stuff? All that's gone down with the Randalls? The Doyles? The guy who followed Pam. Come on—"

"That's enough." Cecil jabbed an outstretched hand toward Jack's chest. "You think you can just run around and play Woodward and Bernstein all day and answer to no one. You live in a dream world. I've got a business to keep afloat and people to answer to. You know nothing of that stuff and I've asked you to respect that—but you keep pushing. Stop it, Crittendon. I mean it. Get off my back—or we're going to have a real problem."

Cecil walked off in a huff.

That was a threat. Jack didn't know whether Cecil would suspend him, fire him, or what, but for the first time in their working history, Jack felt his boss was prepared to cut him loose if he continued to pester him about Demler-Vargus.

The rift made Jack's stomach ache. That was all he needed, another fractured relationship.

No longer feeling like coffee, he returned to his cubicle. Still standing, he dialed Derrick.

"Hey, Jack."

"Where are you?"

"Not feeling good. Just gonna hang low. Have a fire. Watch some movies."

"Dude, what's happened since last night?"

"I don't know, man. This whole thing has got me so stressed out."

"Are you scared?"

Long pause.

"I'm worried for Zenia. Scared? Kind of, yeah. Aren't you?"

"Yeah, I'm scared, but we can't stop now."

"Dude, it might be different if Cecil wanted us covering this thing, but he doesn't. That's number one. Number two, I don't have any personal stake in this, so I don't need to be sticking Z's neck or my neck out on the line. Besides, I can't afford to be losing my job when I'm about to get hitched—"

"Derrick, come on, man. I need you—"

"Jack . . . Jack, stop! You're such a bullhead. Just stop a minute. Think about what they did to Pam. That is *not* okay. No one else wants to pursue this except you—"

"I thought you did."

"Let the Randalls get their money and be done with it. That's it. You need to know when to give up, man."

"What about Spivey Brinkman? What about what they did to the Doyles?"

"We don't know that."

"Come on, man, don't stick your head in the sand. If we don't keep on this, Demler-Vargus keeps steamrolling people."

"Jack, you know what? It happens. This is the world we live in. I just think I'm done with it. Ask Cecil for my hour a day."

Derrick's mind was made up.

Was Jack a stubborn idiot to keep pursuing it? Maybe he should just quit too. That would be the easy way. Maybe Derrick was right. Sometimes the bad guys just won.

"I think I found a way to find Amy Sheets," Derrick said. "I'll send you the link. It's some white pages source; they claim they can find anybody. You have to pay like fifteen bucks. But I found a profile in there that matches her. You pay the money, it gives you her address and contact info—bam. I just sent it to you."

"I'll take a look."

"Interview with the Bendicksons still on?"

"I don't know . . . Maybe you're right. I think the rest of my life has been so screwed up, I've used this whole Demler-Vargus thing as some kind of escape."

"Call it quits, Jack. It isn't worth your career—or your marriage."

Jack's countenance fell.

"I don't like to leave you hanging," Derrick said.

"Don't worry about it. Call me if you change your mind."

Jack sank into his chair and looked out at the white day.

He wasn't right with God, so he was going to be righteous another way. By playing the good guy, the superhero. By bringing down the bad guy—Demler-Vargus.

He leaned over, arms on knees, exhaled, and tried to relax.

Maybe it was time to give up. Cancel the Bendickson interview.

It would be so much easier.

Just do the safe work.

Maybe even forgive Granger Meade.

Invest in Pam and the girls—and the new baby.

He picked up the phone and dialed Pam.

"Hello," she answered.

"Hey, it's me."

"Hi. Everything okay?"

"Yeah. I just wanted to tell you I'm sorry . . ." Jack was cut short by a stab of emotion.

He took a deep breath and composed himself.

"I haven't been myself for a long time, I know. You've been so patient. I want things to be right between us."

He thought he heard a hitch in Pam's breathing.

It felt good to confess, to apologize.

"I've been in denial about a lot of things," he said. "I just want things to be back to normal."

"What happened, Jack?"

He leaned back in his chair, instinctively moving the mouse on his desk.

"Just something with Derrick. I'll tell you tonight. I just wanted you to know I love you. I love our new baby. I even love your mom . . ."

They both laughed.

Jack noticed a new e-mail from Derrick.

"Maybe we could leave the girls with your mom and go out for a romantic dinner."

"We'll see." Pam hesitated. "I'm thawing pork chops . . ."

Jack guessed she was concerned about the man who had followed her, and that she wanted to stick close to home.

"Well, just think about it. I'm looking forward to spending the evening with you."

"Thanks, Jack. Thanks for calling. It means a lot."

Jack opened the e-mail from Derrick and clicked the link to the white pages website.

As Derrick instructed, Jack typed in Amy Sheets's name, approximate date of birth, mother's name, brothers' names, and possible location of Columbus, Ohio. He clicked "Find This Person," and a screen came up requesting a fifteen-dollar payment.

Jack sat back and swiveled in his chair.

He and Amy had been good friends. He was convinced, if he could find her she would tell him what she knew about Demler-Vargus.

He stopped and stared at the glowing screen and the blue button enticing him to pay the fee to find Amy Sheets.

But if he was giving up on this whole thing, why even bother?

It just ticked him off that Demler-Vargus was such a dirty bully; that they could do what they'd done to old Galen and his boys and get away with it; that they could continue poisoning people in the name of making a profit and not be stopped; that they could use scare tactics on women, as they'd done to Pam and Margaret; that they might actually be the first-degree murderers who killed Barb and Emmett Doyle. And who knows what role they may have played in Spivey Brinkman's disappearance?

Why not?

He leaned forward and clicked the blue button. He whipped out his wallet and entered the credit card information before he could change his mind. Account number—tap, tap, tap, tap . . . He would try to talk to Amy. If he couldn't reach her, that would be his sign to drop the whole thing.

A pink and white bar showed the search was 25 percent complete, 50 percent, 80 percent . . . at 95 percent it seemed to stall out.

Great, the one person it can't find . . .

Jack began planning how he would contact the company to try to get his money back. But at that moment, a new screen folded down, populated with information.

Amy Sheets

3351 Applegate Plaza, Suite 882
Columbus, Ohio 43203
Home phone: unknown
Cell phone: (614) 498-2552
E-mail: unknown
Facebook: unknown
Twitter: unknown

Jack Googled Amy's address, clicked satellite view, and quickly determined that she lived in some kind of high-rise condo or apartment in downtown Columbus. He clicked for directions. She was forty-one miles away, a fifty-four-minute drive.

Jack's heart raced. He knelt down and turned off the space heater.

He opened a clean Word doc, put on his headset, and got his thoughts together. He should probably take five or ten minutes to jot down specific questions, but the anticipation was too much. He dialed Amy's number and prayed it was right.

The phone rang once, twice, three times, four times.

Someone picked up.

A long pause.

"Hello." The female voice was meek, apprehensive, but it was Amy.

"Amy? It's Jack, from the *Dispatch*."

Silence.

"Amy? Hello?"

Jack's face flushed. He immediately thought he'd made a huge mistake. Amy really was pregnant. She'd not wanted to be found. He'd gone against Cecil's wishes to protect her privacy.

"How'd you find me?" Her voice was robotic.

"On the Internet. We've been searching for you for days."

"We?"

"Me and Derrick Whittaker. You remember him."

"I figured my brother told you—or Cecil."

"Cecil wouldn't give me your contact information, for some reason. Neither would your brother."

"I see. What do you want?"

"I'm calling about Demler-Vargus."

She said nothing. Jack listened hard for a baby in the background, but heard only silence.

"I know you interviewed Galen Randall, and Barb and Emmett Doyle."

"Stop. We can't talk about this. Not on the phone."

"Why not? What's wrong?"

"I can't . . . You wouldn't understand. Just, just—"

"Yes I would, Amy. Yes I would. That's why I'm calling. All kinds of weird stuff is happening—to the Randalls, the Doyles. I know Demler-Vargus is behind it—"

"Don't say any more! Please, just leave this alone."

"Amy, Demler-Vargus is hurting people. Galen Randall was poisoned. Their house was ransacked. The Doyles are *dead*—"

"No! No, they're not! Don't say that. Don't do that. This is . . . is this a trick?"

"Their house in Charleston burned down. It was arson."

"Shut up, Jack! This phone could be tapped. I'm hanging up . . ."

"Spivey Brinkman is missing. Did you interview him?"

The line went dead.

25

Pamela made up her mind. She put the pork chops back in the freezer. It had been a long time since Jack had suggested they go on a date, and she wasn't about to let fear, or routine, or her mother, or some creep on Demler-Vargus's payroll ruin an opportunity to get her marriage back on track.

Where would they go, someplace fancy? Remington's on the square was one of her favorites, especially in the winter; they always had a real fire crackling and soft music playing. It was dark and candlelit and romantic. Maybe she could convince Jack to splurge.

She checked the kitchen clock. If she hurried, she could make it to Marshalls or TJ Maxx before the girls got home from school. She'd been wanting a new winter outfit to wear with her brown boots anyway.

"I'm going to stop." Margaret came around the corner carrying a bottle by the neck in her left hand and another in her right. She clanked them on the counter, opened one, and turned it upside down over the sink.

As the clear liquid gurgled down the drain, the harsh aroma of hard liquor permeated the kitchen.

When Margaret was finished pouring, she examined the gold label on the bottle as if she were admiring a cherished family photograph. She sniffed the bottle top and extended it toward Pamela. "Where do you want that, recycle?"

Pamela took it. "Sure . . . I'll get rid of it."

The next bottle to go was vodka, with a blue and silver label.

"Thirty-six bucks a pop." Margaret poured it away like water.

"Wow, I didn't know it was that expensive."

"Not all of it; just the good stuff." Margaret forced a smile and watched in a daze as the vodka disappeared.

"Why are you doing this?"

"I'm not making any promises. Just saying I'm going to give it a go." She sealed the second bottle and handed it to Pamela. "You helped me realize I need it too much. I'm not myself. I don't even know who 'myself' is anymore, because of that stuff. But I'm ready to find out . . . I think."

"Well, I'm proud of you. Dad would be proud."

"Don't be proud yet. It's all talk at this point. I thought about not even telling you, but you'll know something is up. I'm sure there'll be some sort of side effects."

Pamela immediately thought of Rebecca and Faye. Would Mom's withdrawal symptoms frighten them? Endanger them?

"I've done some research," Margaret said. "There's a clinic in Columbus. If I can't handle it alone, you and Jack can get me checked in."

"I don't know what to say, Mom. This is fantastic."

Margaret took a step toward Pamela. "You are a light to me, Pamela. A shining example of a strong, confident woman. You're truly fearless."

Pamela chuckled. "I put on a pretty good front, I guess."

Margaret shook her head. "It's no front. I wouldn't fall for that. In many ways, you're a lot like your father, you know that? I look back . . ." Her head dropped. "I put him through a lot of hard stuff."

"But he loved you, Mom. He understood."

Margaret nodded. "He did. So patient."

"I think about him a lot," Pamela said. "He was such a good guy."

"More than I deserved. We've been lucky, Pam."

"Hey, speaking of lucky, Jack wants to take me on a date tonight."

"It's about time."

"I was thinking we could hang around until the girls eat and get baths. All you'd have to do is read them some bedtime stories and put them down."

Normally Pamela would worry about her mom's paranoia and drinking around the girls, but Pamela wasn't going there that night. She was trusting that the date with Jack was meant to be and that God would take care of the details.

"Consider it done," Margaret said.

"You'll be all right?"

"Of course. Do you know what you're going to wear?"

"Actually, I was thinking of looking for a new outfit real quick, before the girls get home."

Margaret was in motion. "I'm coming with you—and I'm buying."

"Really? Wow."

"Yep, let's hurry up."

They headed in separate directions to get their things.

"Hey," Margaret called, "maybe we can even look for those sheers for the windows by the front door while we're out."

"Mom, we won't have time for all that."

"Okay, never mind. Sorry. You know me . . ."

Pamela smiled, and a deep sense of relief filled her. Perhaps, just perhaps, things were finally coming around.

• • •

Jack quickly finished the story on the robbery at the Farley's Home Store in Pell Town, did a spell check, printed it out, and edited the hard copy with a red pen. He input those edits, spellchecked again and, instead of e-mailing the story to the copy desk, sat on it. Cecil would assume he was still working on it.

Instead, he called up the questions he'd written for Leonard Bendickson III and his son, Devon. He read them over, tweaking and adding new questions based on his conversation with Claire—questions about the dangers of synthetic chemicals used in manufacturing, specifically Fenarene.

His phone rang. "Crittendon," he answered.

"I'm calling from a pay phone." Jack sat to attention. It was Amy Sheets. "I think my other phones are bugged, or they're listening somehow."

"Who's they?"

"Everything I'm about to tell you is off the record for now. Just . . . we have to start that way." Amy spoke fast. "I'm going to tell you what's happened, and we'll decide what to do from there."

"Okay." Jack opened a clean document and typed Amy's name, half wondering if she had gone off the deep end.

"The only reason I'm doing this is because I know you're a Christian— and I can trust you."

Jack recalled talking with Amy about his faith at an office party one time. She had never attended church, but seemed interested.

"Thank you, Amy. Now tell me what's going on."

"I've made some terrible mistakes, Jack. Stupid, stupid mistakes."

Jack typed, then prompted her. "One thing I know is that you interviewed Barb and Emmett Doyle. Want to start there?"

"Are they really dead?"

"I'm afraid so. It was arson at their house in Charleston. Expensive place, which is suspicious."

"They called me," Amy said. "They'd gone to Demler-Vargus requesting help paying their medical bills." Her voice was breaking up. "They threatened to contact the *Dispatch* if Demler-Vargus didn't help. They were ignored. They called me. I interviewed them at their house."

"What'd you find out?"

"They worked in the plant. They both had terrible symptoms. Dizziness. Shortness of breath. Bad eye problems. Chronic rashes."

"I was told they led you to Galen Randall."

"His wife had the same symptoms. You said earlier Spivey Brinkman is missing…"

"Four or five days now. Did you have contact with him?"

"Yes, Galen told me about him. He was leading the charge to shut Demler-Vargus down…This cannot be happening."

"I know. And I can't get Cecil to let me spend any time on it. He's afraid Demler-Vargus is going to sue the *Dispatch*. It's not like him—"

"Look, Jack, here's the Holy Grail. At various times, often in the middle of the night, Demler-Vargus produces a certain type of fiberglass that is in extremely high demand; it's bought by companies that make expensive products with it. The thing is, when Demler-Vargus switches into that manufacturing mode, to produce that type of fiberglass, the plant releases certain toxins and pollutants that are making people sick."

Jack typed as fast as he could.

"Those carcinogens are in the air in the plant and outside—in the neighborhood. They're deadly. It's illegal to do what they're doing."

"Is one of those pollutants Fenarene?" Jack said.

"I don't know."

"Is there a name for this expensive fiberglass they produce?"

"The Doyles called it Streamflex. I'm not sure that's what Demler-Vargus calls it. It comes in long sheets, one inch thick; the sheets are three feet by twelve feet."

"How'd you find this out?"

"The Doyles. Spivey Brinkman. People in the plant know, or at least there are rumors about the dangers associated with it."

"What about OSHA and the EPA—don't they know about it?"

"Let's just keep going. I can't talk about that."

"Hmm. Are they still producing it?"

"I doubt it. They know you're onto them, obviously."

"Oh yeah. My wife was followed and nearly run off the road."

"I can't believe this. Is Mr. Randall okay? You said he was poisoned."

"He's okay for now.That's the thing, Amy; I'm the only one crying foul! More people are going to get hurt, but not if we can stop them. Do you have notes from your interviews? How much of this can I tell Cecil? This is what he needs to hear—"

"Jack, hold up."

Amy hadn't told him about her mistakes yet, but he had a feeling that's what was coming.

"When you approached Cecil about contacting me, what did he say?"

"It was confidential; that you left for personal reasons, to be back near your folks."

"I'm not pregnant. I never was."

What? "You lied to Cecil? Why? I don't follow."

Her silence made his mind reel.

Then it hit him.

"Wait. Did Cecil know you weren't pregnant?"

"Cecil came up with that lie!"

"What? Why?"

She must be nuts.

"So no one would contact me and find out what I know about Demler-Vargus. He forced me into this; made it so attractive. I should have blown the whistle on him right then!"

"You're saying *Cecil* is in on this—with Demler-Vargus . . ."

"You said yourself it's not like him to ignore a story like this."

The gears in Jack's head spun out of control. Cecil, on the take? Impossible! They'd worked together for years. Amy must have her facts wrong.

"This is all about money, Jack. Or at least it was. It's changed now. It's become dangerous—just like my brother warned us."

"Who's us?"

Silence. Jack heard a car whiz by in the background.

"I've got to go," Amy said. "Someone's been following me."

"Who?"

"Two guys. I don't know who. They've been watching me."

"Amy, what part of this is on the record?"

"You don't get it, do you, Jack? Cecil's in on this! He's not going to run anything."

"Why did you tell me all this if I can't use any of it?"

"Shoot. I've gotta go . . . I told you because I'm in trouble. I just know you're a good man. I'm gone—"

The phone rattled and went dead.

Breathlessly Jack tried to recall every word Amy had said, typing as fast as his fingers would fly. When he'd gotten it all down, he dropped back in his chair and closed his eyes.

God, please, protect Amy right now . . .

26

For a city boy, Derrick was proud of the decent fire he had blazing in the fireplace at his apartment. He had bought one of those packages of precut firewood and a lighter at the gas station around the corner. Lying on the couch in sweats and thick socks near the crackling blaze, he scrolled through the movie choices on the TV screen, and finally realized he just wanted quiet.

He clicked off the TV and stared at the ceiling.

Most everyone in his complex was at work, so it was peaceful, still.

He was embarrassed that his fears were holding him back from helping Jack. He'd let his best friend down—hard. And Jack needed him.

But Derrick was protecting his job and his future marriage.

And to be honest, he was scared of what Demler-Vargus might do to him if he pursued the story.

He thought of Galen, Travis, and LJ; of Spivey Brinkman and his girls; of all the poor residents on the east side.

The phone rang.

It could wait.

He went over and tossed another log on, determined to enjoy the rest of his day off.

The answering machine picked up, gave his brief message, then the tone.

"Mr. Whittaker, this is Jenness Brinkman, Spivey's daughter . . ."

Derrick crossed to the answering machine and leaned over it.

"We're desperate. My dad's still missing. We're racking our brains, trying everything we know to find him. There was something I didn't tell you that day you were here. I won't leave it on the machine, but if you want, you can reach me at—"

Derrick picked up. "Jenness, it's Derrick. Sorry about that. I'm off today. What was it you wanted to tell me?"

"Oh, hi, Mr. Whittaker. Thank you for taking my call."

"Gladly. I'm sorry to hear your dad hasn't turned up."

"Thank you. I'll get right to the point. You might have noticed that day you were over, with my sister Tatum, it got kind of awkward . . ."

"Yeah, it did. I got the impression you two were dancing around something. In fact, I meant to get back to you, but I haven't found time."

"Well, what I thought you should know is this," Jenness said. "My dad went to the editor of your paper a number of times with solid information about Demler-Vargus, and nothing happened. Nothing ever got printed."

"Are you talking about Cecil Barton?"

"Yes."

Something pricked Derrick's mind. "What kind of information, specifically?" He opened the drawer, got out a pen and paper, and sat down.

"Well, there was a man who worked in the plant for like thirty years. Merv Geddy was his name. He died of lymphoma."

Derrick was listening, but half his mind was focused on Cecil—why had the editor with the nose for hard news not turned Derrick and Jack loose on Demler-Vargus?

"My dad found out that Merv had a son, Oliver, who happened to be an attorney from Idaho. I don't know all the details, but Oliver believed Demler-Vargus was responsible for his dad's cancer and said he had medical evidence to prove it."

It was starting to make sense. Why else would Cecil have stonewalled them when they were trying to connect Demler-Vargus with the arson at the Doyles', Spivey Brinkman's disappearance, and all that was happening to the Randalls?

"So what happened?"

"Oliver was in the process of filing a lawsuit against Demler-Vargus when he went down in a plane crash in Sawtooth National Forest, not too far from his home in Boise."

Derrick got chills.

"He was the pilot and the only one on board," Jenness said. "He owned a little Cessna four-seater. They called it pilot error."

Derrick's stomach flipped. "Jenness, what are you saying?"

"That's just one example. My dad knows a lot of people on the east side, people who've worked at Demler-Vargus for a long time and have lived in this neighborhood forever. It's become pretty clear that Cecil Barton has no intention of running negative stories about Demler-Vargus. In fact, Dad said if the interview with you didn't get anywhere, he was going to WDUC radio and the big newspaper in Columbus, for starters."

"This makes so much sense," Derrick said.

"Since my dad . . . isn't here, I wanted to let you know. But I'm sorry to be the one to say that about your own boss or whatever."

"It's good you did."

"And I don't know that my dad has proof. It's just what he's come to believe."

"I'm grateful, Jenness. Thank you for calling. I'm hoping to God your dad turns up alive and well, very soon."

They hung up, and Derrick went over and knelt by the fire. He rubbed his freezing hands and reached them toward the heat.

He had a hollow feeling inside . . . and a decision to make.

Could he do this? Did he have the guts to pursue Demler-Vargus? He could get killed. Was Cecil really involved? How would he handle that? Jack would know what to do.

But Derrick could quietly ignore all of this. Act like he'd never talked to Jenness. Not mention any of it to Jack. Go about his job. He'd be safe, and so would Zenia.

He inched closer to the comforting heat, staring at the flames.

He admired Jack so much. The guy would not back down; Derrick knew that at his core. Jack would stand up and speak out for the truth, for the victims, even though he had Pam and the girls to worry about. Jack trusted God and steamrolled ahead. He did what was right.

What had Derrick accomplished? What had he really done with his life?

He had an opportunity to help people—the Randalls; the Brinkman girls and their dad; and all those other poor people on the east side who had no voice, who were being taken advantage of and made ill, all for the sake of big corporate dollars.

Staying silent, forgetting the whole thing, would be so easy—so *safe*.

That's what Derrick had always done.

He stared at the fire, feeling something akin to it burning inside him.

It was time to fish or cut bait.

• • •

When the nurses wheeled Galen back to his hospital room, he was grumpier than a grizzly and couldn't sit still in the bed. "I feel like a dern pin cushion," he said. "Son, you got me into this, now you can git me out." Travis tried to calm him and comb his hair, but his father pushed his hand away. "I'm fine. I just wanna go home. That was the deal."

"Here, Daddy, you'll feel better with your glasses on." Travis put the glasses on him, but they were miserably crooked.

Galen ripped them off and glared at Travis. "Son, your bedside manner is atrocious."

Claire had found a microwave and brought Daddy his coffee, along with a big powdered doughnut. She pulled a chair right up next to him, sat, and served him.

"Now that's more like it, right there." He took a bite and smiled at Claire, who patted away the white powder that drifted down to the front of his light blue nightgown.

"I told Travis you remind me of his momma," Daddy said.

Claire lit up. "Well, that is a compliment. I remember Mrs. Randall."

"Ya do?" Galen's head tilted.

"Yes, sir. One time I saw her at our school—I think she was dropping something off—"

"I probably forgot my lunch." Travis snickered.

"Don't interrupt, son."

"Sorry, Claire."

Claire gave Travis a slow nod, agreeing with Galen.

Travis chuckled.

"Anyway," she said, "this huge kid, Freddy Sikorski, was picking on a younger boy, calling him names. And right when Mrs. Randall came down the sidewalk, Freddy shoved the younger boy down to the pavement."

"No," Daddy said.

Claire bit her bottom lip and nodded. "Yes! She got one look at what was going on, and she grabbed Freddy by the wrist and dragged him inside. My friends and I followed them, and she took him straight to the principal's office. That was back when they still paddled kids, and I think he got it good from Mr. Tanker."

Daddy shook his head. "That's my girl."

"I can't believe you remember that," Travis said. "I can just imagine Momma doin' that."

Claire handed Galen his coffee. He took it with shaking hands and managed to get a sip. He wouldn't have taken it from Travis. Daddy really liked her.

"How are the boys doin' at the shop?" Daddy asked. "Have you talked to 'em?"

"LJ called a couple hours ago to see how you was doin'. Things sounded okay. But he was still waitin' for Bo to drag his lazy bones out of bed."

"Dadgummit. When is he gonna make that boy grow up?"

"Well, I'm assumin' they're on top a' things now."

"You should know by now not to assume anything when it comes to yer brother."

"I'll give him a ring." Travis went for the phone next to the bed, but it rang just as he got to it.

"Trav, LJ. How's Daddy?"

"Cranky as all get out, but good. Waitin' for the doctor. Hopin' to get outta here soon. How 'bout you boys? Bo rise from the dead yet?"

"Yeah, I got him on that Dodge; he's in his glory workin' on that thing. He's got a couple cars he's supposed to be detailin'—"

"They's gonna have to wait, LJ. We need him on our stuff first."

"I know, I'll have to break it to him."

Travis rolled his eyes. "Anything else new?"

"No, and I'm hopin' nothin' else shows up. You better git your skinny buns back here."

"Doin' my best."

"Thanks for takin' him, by the way," LJ said.

"Sure thing. Good to have Claire here, too. She brightens it up."

"Hey, I forgot to tell you, Coon dropped by."

"What now?"

"Our meeting with Demler-Vargus got moved up. It's tomorrow afternoon, two o'clock, instead of Thursday."

"Did he say why?"

"Nope, and I didn't ask. Sooner we do this deal, the better. It's time we git this monkey off our backs."

Travis turned and looked out the window, staring at all the cars in the snow-covered parking lot below.

Another gray day. The lot was a slushy mess.

"Yeah." LJ laughed. "Old Coon didn't look too good."

"Really? What was wrong with him?"

"Said he fell down some stairs. Had a big bandage on his forehead, one on his chin, bad bruise on his cheek."

Fell down some stairs? Or got the pulp beat out of him?

"This thing ain't sittin' right with me," Travis said.

The thought of receiving a check from Demler-Vargus made him feel filthy, just like the grimy, salt-covered cars below.

"Oh, come on, Trav. This is what we've been waitin' for. Come about this time tomorrow, you're gonna be a wealthy man, and all this junk will be history. I was thinkin' maybe we could even get Daddy outta here for a spell, maybe take him on one a them fancy cruises to the Tropics."

At the very core of his being, Travis felt like a traitor a man about to sell his soul at the expense of others.

They said good-bye and Travis put the phone down.

"Everything okay at the shop?" Daddy said.

Travis nodded. "Yep." He crossed his arms. "Ralston Coon stopped in. Our meeting with Demler-Vargus got moved up. Tomorrow at two."

He took a deep breath and turned his gaze to Claire. Her mouth was reduced to a slit and her green eyes burned into him.

"Well," Daddy said, "I suppose that's good news. At least we'll finally get a little payback from old Goliath. That'll be something anyway."

Travis nodded and managed a smile.

But Claire didn't say a word.

She didn't have to.

Every fiber of her being shouted *danger.*

27

Tension filled the small space between Jack and Derrick at a lamplit table for two at Ella's, the hip coffee shop on the square in Trenton City. Derrick had phoned Jack an hour earlier, insisting they meet, which gave Jack a second wind. Now they sat with their heavy coats draped over the backs of their chairs, sweater sleeves rolled up, sipping coffees, comparing notes, and staring at each other in disbelief.

"First things first." Jack looked at his watch. "I'm gonna do this interview with Bendicksons, and I'm gonna confront them about everything we have."

Derrick craned toward Jack, his eyes huge. "But what are we gonna do with all this info? Cecil's dirty; Jenness and Amy confirmed it. He's not printing anything about Demler-Vargus."

"I know. Now it's him we've got to get dirt on. It'll come, it'll come; we just need to keep moving forward a step at a time. The key is getting evidence on all this stuff; once we've got that, we can take it anywhere."

Derrick took in a deep breath.

"In my mind," Jack said, "the biggest thing is we've got to get Amy, on the record. And the only way that's gonna happen is in person. There's no way she's gonna talk on the phone anymore. She's scared stiff."

Derrick looked at his watch. "I've got the rest of the day off. I could be there in an hour."

Jack nodded excitedly. "I was thinking that, but never thought you'd go for it."

"I told you, I'm in."

Jack wished Derrick's body language lined up with his words; he looked apprehensive.

"We need everything she says on record. You got a recorder?"

Derrick nodded.

"We need her to say it was Cecil's idea to cover up all the leads on Demler-Vargus . . . Better write all this down."

Derrick was already in motion.

"We need her to say the whole pregnancy story was Cecil's idea. Who paid Amy to keep quiet, and how much? Did the payments come from Cecil?

From someone at Demler-Vargus? Who? And who paid off the Doyles? How much?"

"Slow down." Derrick scribbled furiously.

"It looks to me like Demler-Vargus started this cover-up by trying to pay people to keep quiet: Cecil, Amy, the Doyles—"

"I wonder if anyone else at the paper is on the take. Nigel?"

"Good question. Ask Amy."

Derrick continued writing.

"At first they weren't hurting people," Jack said.

"But then it started to get away from them."

"Exactly. I don't know if they tried to pay Spivey or not; if they did, I'm assuming he didn't take it. But I think he's the one who forced them to take it to the next level, because of all he knows."

"By next level, you mean . . ."

"Murder. The Doyles. Maybe Spivey? That's why I've been so afraid for Galen and the boys."

"Yeah," Derrick said. "And now they got us in their sights."

"Not to mention Amy. Whoever knows about Demler-Vargus and isn't on their side is getting silenced."

Derrick shook his head and blew out a breath.

"What?" Jack said.

"I've never been in on anything even close to this big."

"I know, me neither."

"I wanna know if Amy knows anything about Merv Geddy and his son," Derrick said. "Did she know Oliver was filing a lawsuit? Did she cover up that lead . . . his plane crash?"

"Write it down," Jack nodded.

Derrick did.

"We also need her, on the record, talking about the production of Streamflex. That might be the biggest thing. Why hasn't OSHA or the EPA caught it? Could they be in on the cover-up?"

Derrick was writing so fast and in such sloppy handwriting that Jack wondered if he could possibly decipher it later. He bent down to tighten his ankle holster. The tile floor had puddled where the snow had melted off their shoes.

"I got an e-mail from Patrick, that Live5 reporter in Charleston," Jack said.

"And . . ."

"Police found a fire safe hidden in the Doyles' house. There are some DVDs in there, and one is labeled Demler-Vargus."

"You're kidding me."

"Uh-uh. Police have it, but Patrick is trying to get his hands on it, and some other stuff. He'll let me know if and when they do."

"Has his station officially called it arson yet?"

"Tonight at eleven."

"Wonder what Cecil will think of to not cover that story . . ."

There was so much swirling around in Jack's mind, he felt blotchy. He started throwing his things into his leather shoulder bag. "Look, I gotta make my way over to Demler-Vargus." He took an enormous breath. His heart raced.

"This is big, dog," Derrick said.

"Tell me about it." Jack stood, put his satchel in the chair, and got his coat on. Derrick arose and did the same.

"You got Amy's address, right?" Jack said.

"Yeah. Why don't you call me when you're done there. I'll still be on the road, probably."

"Sounds like a plan." Jack hoisted the satchel over his shoulder. "Maybe we should meet up later tonight when you get back, if it's not too late. Compare notes. By then I'm thinking we're going to have one heck of a story."

Derrick blew into a fist. "Sounds good. If I get going now, spend an hour or two with her, I should be back by ten or eleven."

Derrick looked tense; perhaps even scared. Jack was feeling the same way. They were at a turning point. The remaining hours of the day would be critical. Jack looked around at the crowded room. "Sit down for a sec. Let's pray."

Derrick hesitated, but when Jack sat on the edge of his chair, Derrick did the same.

Jack put his head down, not waiting for Derrick's response. "Father, Derrick and I need you now," he said quietly. "Please keep us and our girls safe. Give us wisdom, discretion, understanding. Put your angels around us.

Help us get the information we need, and help us know what to do with it. Amen."

They stood.

It was the first time Derrick had smiled since they'd met up, and Jack wasn't sure why. Was he making fun of Jack's prayer, or did he approve?

Jack led the way out of Ella's.

They stood beneath the large brown awning, immediately able to see their breaths. Cars streaked by in a blurry haze of rain and snow.

It was time.

They shook hands, patted shoulders.

"Good luck," Jack said.

"Good luck, dog."

They jogged into the rain in separate directions, unsure what the rest of the day, and night, would bring.

28

Pamela hadn't felt so excited in weeks, perhaps months. She tried on dresses and shoes and even new coats at Marshalls, and her mom insisted on picking up the tab for a rust-colored sweater dress for her date with Jack. They looked at perfume and makeup at the Ulta store in Trenton City, then bundled up and dashed several doors down to the neighborhood Starbucks.

"You needed a few hours out on the town." Margaret sipped her caramel macchiato.

"Did I ever," Pamela said. "Thanks, Mom. I mean it, this has been fun."

"It's done me wonders too."

The place was hopping. Nearby were two women talking intimately over a small table, several people tapping away at laptops, and others reading and listening to music. It was the ideal place to cuddle up on a blustery afternoon.

"How are you feeling?" Margaret smiled and eyed Pamela's tummy. "Any symptoms?"

"I feel fantastic." Pamela took the lid off her Zen tea to let it cool. "The first three months with Faye were awful, remember?"

"Oh yeah. Your dad felt so bad for you."

"Were you sick with me?"

Margaret's head tilted as she thought. "Not much. Maybe a little queasy over certain foods and smells."

"I'm so excited about tonight. I can't even remember the last time we went on a date."

"Don't you have a good babysitter in the neighborhood?"

"You remember Tommy and Darlene next door? They watch the girls every once in a while. They used to do it more."

Every time Pamela thought of Tommy Sweeney she was reminded of the day Granger broke into their house almost two years ago. She'd whisked the girls to the Sweeneys' house and barged right in seeking safety.

Margaret was talking, but Pamela was no longer listening.

She found herself searching the Starbucks for Granger . . . for the man who'd run them off the road the day before . . .

Her heart kicked up a notch.

Calm. Be calm.

She breathed in deeply, set her shoulders back, and exhaled without her mom noticing.

Every now and then, fear just ravaged her; shook her entire being.

It was usually just for a moment, like that.

And she was better.

She'd come a long way, but she had a long way to go.

But tonight, nothing was going to interfere with her date with Jack. They were going. And they were going to have fun, just like old times.

"Pam . . . did you hear me?" Margaret leaned toward her, snapping her fingers. "My goodness, you're in another world."

"Sorry." Pam chuckled. "I was daydreaming."

"I said, what time do we need to leave to be home for the girls? Isn't it about time—"

Startled, Pamela looked at her watch. "Oh! We've got to go! My gosh." She was on her feet, ready to run out with coat in hand.

"Honey, okay, calm down. Get your coat on." Margaret stood.

"What was I thinking? They'll be home in fifteen minutes." She threw her coat on and grabbed their bags. "Hurry, Mom."

"I'm coming." Margaret got her coat on. "Now, we're not going to fall on the ice or something. Just take it easy."

Look who was telling whom to take it easy.

• • •

"Finally!" Daddy got right on Dr. Beezenhour when he entered his hospital room. "Good golly, I thought you'd gone ice fishin'." It sounded funny, but his father's jaw was locked and his face was a deep shade of scarlet.

Travis had just about fallen asleep in the vinyl chair in the corner, and it looked like Claire had been helping Daddy with the crossword.

"I apologize for the delay, Mr. Randall." The doctor pulled up a chair, licked his fingers, and flipped through the pages on his handy clipboard. "We've had an influx of patients today. Forgive me."

"Yeah, yeah, so give me the good news and send me home," Daddy said.

Beezenhour was thoughtful before he spoke. "Mr. Randall, I want to keep you awhile longer—"

"Dadgummit." Daddy tugged the sheets up around his shoulders. "I knew this would happen. A person can't come in here without gettin' nickeled and dimed to death. What's wrong now? I feel good."

"I'm sorry you're agitated, sir." Beezenhour blinked relentlessly. "What's happened is, we did find some traces of the synthetic chemical Fenarene in your system."

Travis's heart sank.

Claire frowned and crossed her arms.

"Now, it's not an enormous amount by any stretch, but I want to know how well your body is getting rid of it, and to do that we need to do more tests."

"Now wait a minute, doc." Travis stood. "Is this necessary, or are you just wantin' to use Daddy as your guinea pig?"

"Travis!" Claire said.

"It's okay." Beezenhour held up a hand. "I told you of my interest in the chemicals used in manufacturing and how they affect the body, so it's a fair question. What I want to find out is this: is your father's body eliminating the Fenarene, or could that chemical be sticking around, possibly causing harm?"

"How long would Mr. Randall need to stay," Claire said, "and what would you do?"

Travis was sure glad she was there; otherwise he'd have blown a gasket.

The doctor nodded, as if to say at least there's someone in the room who has some sense. "He could probably go home by this evening; latest, tomorrow morning. It depends how fast I can get a neurologist here."

"Neurologist . . . a brain man?" Travis said.

Dr. Beezenhour nodded and blinked. "I want to put your father through a full neurological exam. It's not painful. But I believe it, and some other blood work and simple tests, will show us a lot more about what the Fenarene in his system is up to."

Travis paced, squeezing the back of his neck. They'd been there since before dawn. "What if we don't do it?" he said. "What if we just go home?"

The doctor's head swayed. "That is completely your prerogative. My concern is what we talked about before. Could this be making your father really sick? Could it be affecting his central nervous system? I will say, if it were my father I would want to know."

"May I ask," Claire said, "what if his body *isn't* getting rid of the Fenarene? Is there something you can do to help him get rid of it? And is that a necessity?"

"Good questions. Understand, this is all new ground," Beezenhour said. "We are at the cutting edge of studying this synthetic chemical in the system. There have been experiments—"

"I'm sorry, but I feel like this is exactly the case you've been waiting for and you're gonna milk it for all it's worth—"

"Travis." Claire glared at him. "Don't make assumptions like that. Please. Can we talk about it like adults?"

The cat had Travis's tongue. He wasn't used to having anyone around to put him in his place like that.

"If you've had enough for today, we can always schedule it for another day," Beezenhour said. "I just thought, while you were here, it would be a good idea to knock out these tests and try to get to the bottom of it."

Claire looked at Travis, then at Daddy. "What do you say, Mr. Randall?" she said. "It's your call."

Daddy stuck his jaw out and shook his head, not looking at any of them. "Dadgummit, Doc, I appreciate what you're doin', but I ain't up for no more today . . . especially not for waitin' around for some neurologist to get done with his four-hour lunch."

Beezenhour closed his eyes and nodded graciously, but it was clear he was disappointed.

"Can we schedule it for tomorrow?" Claire asked the doctor.

"Can't," Travis said. "We got the big thing tomorrow at two, remember?"

Claire's countenance fell. "What about the next day, Thursday. Would that work, Dr. Beezenhour?"

"Absolutely. You let me know what time works best, and we'll fit it in."

Travis faded out. He was dreading the meeting with Demler-Vargus the next day. Something about it wasn't sitting right. What did they call it, a premonition? Whatever it was, that's what he was having.

29

It was roasting in the plush chrome-and-glass conference room high above the Demler-Vargus plant, where a tall brunette secretary had led Jack in and asked him to have a seat to wait for CEO Leonard Bendickson III. Jack took off his winter coat and sweater, and was still burning up.

Why had he worn the gun in here? He should have left it in the car. Now he was afraid it might be showing. Looking through the glass wall leading to the reception area, he checked for onlookers. The secretary had her back to him. He bent down from the black swivel chair and shimmied the ankle holster higher up his calf and tightened it.

His notebook, pad, questions, mini recorder and tapes were all laid out on the thick glass table in front of him. He'd chosen the chair to the right of the head of the table, thinking Bendickson would want the place of honor.

He scribbled the date and *D-V* on his pad and wrote the names of the Bendicksons, then numbered them, 1 for the father, 2 for the son; he would write the number for each as he took notes, signifying who was talking.

Fifteen minutes passed.

These guys didn't care about making people wait.

Give me wisdom, Lord. Let me be relaxed and real. Help me get the truth. Help Derrick.

He stood and wandered to the floor-to-ceiling window. The carpet was cushy. They spared no expense on the glass, steel, and wood furniture, lamps, and opulent décor. He peered outside at the eerie, massive sculpture of metal apparatuses, scaffolding, storage tanks, pipes, and loading docks. The brilliant snow made everything look dirty, especially the yellow-gray smoke billowing from half a dozen towering smokestacks.

Jack put his hand on the window. Cold. Very cold.

The place gave him the creeps.

He was startled when a hidden door swung open in the middle of the paneled wall. Men in dark suits filed into the room. One, two, three, four, five—more than expected.

The heat of the situation pressed in on Jack.

"Good to see you again." Tan and dapper Leonard Bendickson III gave him a firm handshake. "Thanks for the feature story; we've had a lot of positive feedback."

That story was one of the reasons Bendickson had agreed to meet with Jack again; plus, they probably wanted to see how much he knew. They also likely felt safe about the meeting because Jack worked for Cecil Barton—who was apparently in their back pocket.

Bendickson, a towering man, stood behind the chair at the head of the table, gripping the top of it with his large, ruddy hands. He wore a black suit, yellow tie, crisp white shirt with shiny black and gold cufflinks, and a wide gold wedding band. "This is my son, Devon, our environmental liaison."

Jack could see the father-son resemblance as Devon smiled pleasantly and they shook hands.

One guy, the size of a building, crossed to the corner of the room, looked down at the floor as if he was positioning himself on a mark, then looked straight ahead to the opposite corner. His neck was the size of Jack's thigh, and he wore some sort of walkie-talkie earpiece. His large right hand gripped his left wrist in front of him.

Bendickson ignored the bodyguard and swept a hand toward the other two men, who were pulling out their chairs. "Harry Dorchester and Eli August, two of our attorneys." They barely nodded, but got busy opening their leather binders and getting situated. Eli clanked a tape recorder onto the table.

Bendickson apparently felt obligated to explain their presence. "Since we might be talking about some sensitive issues, we wanted to make sure we had legal counsel."

"That's fine." Jack hadn't expected the bodyguard, or the attorneys, or the recorder; he wiped the sweat from his forehead, wondering if anyone noticed how nervous he was. "I hope you don't mind if I record this as well. Just to make sure I get everything right."

Bendickson's dark eyes flicked to the attorneys.

"We'd rather you not," Dorchester said.

Jack swallowed hard, at a loss for words.

"Are you hot, Mr. Crittendon?" Bendickson said. "Devon, have Brenda turn down the heat, please."

Devon left the room.

"The purpose in my recording this is to make sure I get everything down accurately," Jack said. "It's really a benefit for you, to make sure I get the facts right."

Dorchester started to disagree.

"Oh, let him record it." Bendickson looked at the attorneys with his sharp brown eyes and perfect teeth. "We've nothing to hide. Just let me know when to shut up."

"Thank you." Again Jack wiped his forehead with his palm. The bodyguard stood like a statue, staring at the wall, mouth sealed. Devon reentered, set a bottle of water in front of Jack, and took his seat. Jack gave him a nod and thanked everyone for coming. He got the correct spelling of the attorneys' names and jotted numbers three and four next to them.

He'd put a lot of time into the questions before him, and had a strategy. He began with several simple questions about the company, its history, and products, just to get them relaxed and talking. Indeed, they seemed to be letting their guards down, thinking this wasn't going to be the interrogation they had anticipated.

"Now . . . you have had some violations in the past." Jack mentioned the specific citations, one in 2009, one in 2010, two each in 2011 and 2012. "Tell me about those. What went wrong and how did you correct those problems?"

Jack kept checking the bodyguard, who never flinched.

Devon explained the violations clearly, and his company's response sounded respectable. "You'll find those kinds of notices are quite normal with a manufacturing operation the size of ours," Devon said. "We actually embrace those red flags from OSHA and the EPA; we view them as opportunities for continuous improvement. With each, we've made the corrections requested and complied within the allotted timeframe. And we've developed new systems to make sure those mistakes don't happen again. They actually make us better."

Devon had a young, pink face, square jaw, and a pleasant demeanor that took Jack by surprise. He was cool and courteous, and seemed genuine in his desire to make Demler-Vargus an environmentally sound company. Could it be Devon didn't know about the bad stuff? Leonard was letting Devon do most of the talking. But as Devon rambled on with details about the specific violations, Jack wondered if he might be stonewalling, knowing they had only allotted one hour for the meeting.

He sipped his water as Devon talked about their green initiatives and how much the company was spending on safety measures for employees and air quality control measures. Could all that be true? Jack wanted to believe him.

Twenty-five minutes into the meeting, Jack realized he had to get down to the nitty-gritty. He plunged ahead. "I know you produce a ton of different products; what can you tell me about Streamflex?"

The bodyguard shifted his feet for the first time.

Dorchester's eyes flashed to Bendickson, then, as if he'd regretted it, fell back to his notepad; he looked like a child who'd just caught the glare of a fuming parent. The room fell silent. August didn't flinch, but stared right through Jack. Devon rocked back in his chair. Bendickson seemed frozen, with a thick, black eyebrow curled into an arch.

Devon rocked forward, steadied his chair, and spoke tentatively. "We have experimented with the production of Streamflex." He paused. "But we have not been able to find a way to produce it and remain within environmental guidelines."

The attorneys were now ramrod straight, looking as if they'd each had four shots of espresso.

"When was the last time you tried to produce it?" Jack said.

Devon's face scrunched up as if he smelled something rotten. "A year ago?" Nonchalantly, he rocked and waved a hand at his dad for confirmation.

Bendickson, who himself had developed a foul look on his face, only shrugged, as if the dialogue had just transgressed into meaningless chatter. He wasn't talking.

"I think it's been about a year," Devon said. "I know it was last winter some time, but I'm going to need to check on that for you."

Jack hated it when that happened—another loophole to follow up on, for which he would probably never get a straight answer.

His recorder clicked off. As calmly as he could, Jack ejected the micro-cassette. With trembling fingers he flipped the tape and hit record. Then he forged on. "Can you tell me, does your plant use, produce, or release the synthetic chemical Fenarene?"

August looked at his watch, pursed his lips, and glared at Jack.

"You want Devon to talk about that?" Bendickson addressed the attorneys.

"Let me try," Devon said, before the attorneys could answer. "A very high, high, high percentage of manufacturers like us—that produce plastics, rubbers, fiberglass, resins, and such—do use Fenarene. But we do so sparingly and within environmental guidelines. Twenty-five states, Puerto Rico and the Virgin Islands have OSHA-approved plans for the use of Fenarene. Ohio is one of those states, and we strictly adhere to their guidelines."

Man, this dude was killing Jack. It was all too neat, too perfect.

"Can you tell me if Fenarene is used to produce Streamflex?" he said.

August set one clenched fist on the table. "We don't need to get into that. We don't produce Streamflex, so it doesn't pertain."

The bodyguard turned his big head toward Jack, made stone-cold eye contact for three seconds, and turned back toward the wall.

Time was flying. Jack eyed his notes and looked at Devon. "Are you aware that some epidemiologic studies suggest there is an association between Fenarene exposure and an increased risk of leukemia and lymphoma?"

"No comment," Dorchester cut in before Devon could say anything. "Next question."

Devon sighed and chuckled, as if he would have preferred to answer.

The tension was palpable.

Jack swigged his water, hoping it would cool his system for the heated exchange he was about to ignite. "Are you familiar with a couple who worked in the plant named Barb and Emmett Doyle?"

In unison, the attorneys turned to Bendickson with eyes of apprehension.

The bodyguard's head dropped.

Bendickson laughed heartily. "Jack, do you have any idea how many people we employ?"

"Yes, I do."

"I'm sure I would recognize them if we went down on the floor."

Jack took a deep breath. "Can you confirm they came to you asking for compensation for their medical bills?"

Bendickson frowned sourly, shook his head and looked down, rubbing the leather binder in front of him—apparently a cue for the attorneys to do their jobs.

"We would have to look into that." Dorchester scribbled on his pad. "I can write down their names and do some research."

Another stall.

"The reason I ask is because a former reporter for the *Dispatch*, Amy Sheets, interviewed them. They said they came to you for compensation for medical issues and, getting none, they went to the media with their story."

The only sounds were pens tapping and chairs squeaking.

The bodyguard looked at Bendickson as if waiting for the order to boot Jack out on his can.

"Do any of you know Amy Sheets?" Jack probed.

Bendickson stuck his elbows on the table and craned his neck, as if his collar was too tight.

Devon spoke up. "Our PR people dealt with Miss Sheets on things like those minor infractions we talked about earlier. I don't know about the Doyles."

"What we learned," Jack said, "is that the Doyles told Amy Sheets about their issues with Demler-Vargus, but then they suddenly came into some money. They moved to a house in Charleston."

Bendickson sighed loudly. "Jack, what else do you want to talk about? Really. This is not what we want to do—"

"Let's leave it at that." Dorchester was leaning fully on the table now. "Time's about up."

August backed up his chair.

The bodyguard raised his eyebrows toward Bendickson, who leaned back and started to rise.

Jack remained seated like a spoiled child. "I would like to know if Demler-Vargus has ever paid anyone—the Doyles or anyone else—to help defray the costs of their illnesses?"

Bendickson stood, shooting daggers at Jack with his eyes. The others paused in their chairs, searching each other's faces.

Bad-dude August decided to be the fall guy. "No, we have not."

Before they could get up, Jack pushed on, reading directly from his notes, feeling as if the bodyguard might descend on him any second. "Can you confirm for me that Oliver Geddy, an attorney and the son of former Demler-Vargus employee Merv Geddy, was in the process of filing a lawsuit against your company for the wrongful death of his father? As you may know, Merv Geddy died of lymphoma . . ."

Jack was light-headed. The room spun for a second. He could feel his pulse in his temple.

The bodyguard glared at him directly now.

Devon rubbed his hands, his mouth sealed.

Bendickson raised his eyebrows at the attorneys as if to say *Speak up!*

"No, we can't confirm that." August stood. "Now we're done."

"Not yet." Arms straight out, Bendickson set both palms on the table. "Sit down, Eli. I want to hear what else Mr. Crittendon wants to know."

Right there, in that slow motion moment, something about Bendickson changed, as if huge tumblers shifted and slammed into place.

The towering man suddenly *looked* different.

What was it?

A callousness darkened his features.

"Go ahead." Bendickson playfully wound a hand toward Jack. "What else do you want to know, Mr. Crittendon?" His courtesy was gone.

Jack's stomach flopped, as if he'd just flown over the peak of a roller coaster.

He was dead meat.

Bendickson wanted to know all the dirt Jack had on Demler-Vargus; he wanted to know every person who was a leak—so he and his henchmen could snuff them.

But Jack had a secret weapon, a supernatural power, that he was certain Bendickson did *not* have. God was there, moving on his behalf, and Jack was convinced he could get one of the Demler-Vargus thugs to crack—on tape.

He checked the recorder to make sure it was still rolling.

"What happened to Spivey Brinkman?"

It looked like a small current went through Bendickson's body. His head dropped, then he glared stiffly out the window, gripping the top of the chair as if he was going to rip the stuffing out of it.

August's nostrils flared. "No. Comment."

The bodyguard sneered at Jack.

"Why did you poison Galen Randall and ransack his home?"

Bendickson shoved his chair and stomped to the window, looking out over his sinister empire. The bodyguard took several steps toward the CEO, who jabbed a hand at him, telling him to go back to his spot.

No one said a word, and their clenched jaws indicated they weren't going to.

Jack's heart banged. "Are you paying or have you ever paid Amy Sheets, and/or Cecil Barton, and/or anyone else at *The Dispatch,* to suppress negative stories about Demler-Vargus?"

All eyes turned to Bendickson, who remained frozen, staring out the window, arms crossed.

"Sir?" Dorchester looked as if he was about to cry or laugh or dash from the room.

"See. Him. *Out.*" Bendickson did not turn around.

The bodyguard came for Jack like a Rottweiler after meat. "You are so dead," he whispered.

August stood and leaned way over the table, a finger in Jack's face. "Whatever you're planning to do, you better get your facts right, because if you don't, we'll sue you for malice, libel, defamation . . . we'll sue you so hard it'll make your great-grandchildren hurt."

The bodyguard squeezed the back of Jack's neck like a vise, lifting him out of his chair.

When they got to the door, Bendickson shouted, "Wait."

The bodyguard jerked Jack around so he could see the CEO, whose black eyes burned through him like lasers.

"You made a big mistake coming here, sticking your nose into our business. Do your family a favor. Make sure your affairs are in order." Bendickson turned away, peering out at his empire again. "That's it. Get him away from here."

30

Pamela and Margaret arrived home from Trenton City just in time to get the car in the garage and walk down the driveway to greet Rebecca and Faye. The girls scampered home from the bus stop bundled up like Eskimos, eating snow and stomping in the slush.

After they changed out of their school clothes, the girls cozied up to the kitchen table for milk and cookies while they did their homework. Faye actually didn't have homework, but she liked to color and pretend she was a big girl like Rebecca.

Pamela checked the fridge, thinking about what she would serve the girls and Margaret for dinner while she and Jack went out. Margaret was from the old school, when meat and vegetables were a must at every meal.

She heard her mom humming away in another room. It had been a good decision for her to stay with them. The girls brought her a lot of joy and were a needed distraction from home and the memories of Benjamin.

But she wondered how Margaret would do without the alcohol. Would the withdrawal symptoms be nasty? Did she have a bottle hidden away somewhere?

"Honey?" Margaret called. "I've got an idea."

Pamela walked into the family room. Her mom was standing in the foyer. "I've got the measurements for these side windows."

Here we go again.

"Just a little sheer is all you need. I know just what I'm looking for— something thin, but thick enough that people can't see in; because right now, look, these side windows are wide open."

Patience.

"That's fine, Mom. We'll do it while you're here."

"Do you have Farley's down here?"

"Yeah, we do." Ironically, the closest one was next door to Crafts Galore, where Granger supposedly worked.

"They'll have exactly what I want; they even have the little brackets," Margaret said. "I was thinking, what if we were to run over there now and maybe bring home some dinner for the girls and me on the way? My treat."

Pamela sighed and checked the clock in the family room.

"We could get a pizza or something, and I could make a salad," Margaret said.

Jack wouldn't be home from work for another couple of hours, so it was a long time before their date. Going to Farley's would help make the evening come faster.

Pamela wandered into the kitchen. "Girls, are you about done with your homework?"

"I've got one, two, three more vocab words, and that'll be it," Rebecca said, with her arms up in the air.

"And I've got one, two, three more colors to add to this picture, and that'll be it," Faye said, and copied her sister's gesture.

"Okay, well, wrap it up. We're going to run to Farley's with MawMaw and then we're going to get a pizza to bring home for your supper while Mommy and Daddy go out. How does that sound?"

"Yay!" Rebecca said. "Campolo's? Campolo's?"

"Yeah, Campolo's!" said Faye. "But not the kitchen sink pizza."

"I believe Campolo's might just have a carry-out deal." Pamela got the coupon folder out of a drawer. "Yep, here it is. Monday through Thursday, large one-item pizza pie, ten bucks. Can't beat that."

The girls cheered.

"Hurry up and finish, Faye." Rebecca instructed her little sister every chance she got.

Margaret walked into the kitchen, rubbed Rebecca's head, kissed Faye, and came over to Pamela. "This has been a great day," she said. "Thanks. Thanks for having me. I don't know what I would have done without you."

Pamela looked into her mom's eyes. "You're welcome. I wouldn't want you anyplace else right now."

"Your home is so . . . light; it's so much fun," Margaret said. "I want to think our home was that way, but I know it wasn't." Her head dropped.

Pamela could only muster a broken smile.

"It must have been hard for you," Margaret said, "growing up with me like that."

It was! Pamela wanted to scream, it was so difficult. And it had been so very hard to overcome.

But that was simply how it was. It was the hand she'd been dealt.

But, with time, God had made it okay. He had restored Pamela.

And perhaps now he was at work in her mom.

Pamela smiled. "You gave Dad fits, I know that."

"Oh, tell me about it. That man had the patience of Job."

Pamela made sure the back door was locked and clapped her hands. "All right. As Daddy likes to say, let's get this show on the road!"

"Let's do it!" Rebecca pumped a fist in the air.

They all headed for their winter coats.

"Bundle up and pile in," Pamela called. "I'm going to leave a note for Daddy—just in case he gets home first."

• • •

By the time Travis and Claire got Galen from the hospital back to the house it was late afternoon, almost dark, and the temperature was dropping. The compressor moaned out in the garage and light shone from around the edge of the metal door; LJ and Bo were still at work. Snow flurries swirled as Claire took one of Galen's arms and Travis the other, and they guided him up the steps into the toasty house.

"What about it, Pops? You ready to head for the sack?" Travis helped him get his coat and hat off.

"Heck no, we ain't even had supper yet," Galen said. "Just help me into my chair for now."

"It's kinda early for supper, ain't it?"

"What would you like to eat, Mr. Randall?" said Claire, as they got him into the TV room.

Travis rolled his eyes at her.

"Young lady"—he dropped into the recliner—"you need to start callin' me Galen."

She laughed. "All righty, Galen, I'll do that. Is there something we can get you?"

"You ever have breakfast for dinner, Claire?"

"Yes, my mom and I have done that before, every once in a while."

"Well, I got some of the best sawmill gravy you're ever gonna taste. Travis, we got any of that sausage left over?"

Travis was on his way to the kitchen. "Sure do. I'll git it goin'. I guess I'm a bit hungry myself."

As Travis raided the fridge for leftovers, his heart warmed to hear Claire and Daddy going back and forth. He felt like the luckiest man alive. Having Claire around was . . . well, it was just beyond any feeling Travis had ever known. He ducked back into the TV room. "You guys want me to put some go-joe on?"

"I'd drink some coffee," Daddy said.

Claire was still kneeling beside him. "Won't that keep you awake?"

"Once I hit the hay, Claire, I usually don't flinch till the cock crows, unless one a them coughing spells rouses me."

The phone rang.

Travis headed for the wall phone in the kitchen, which had LJ's grimy fingerprints all over it, darn him.

"Yell-o," Travis answered, trying to be funny for Claire.

"Travis?"

"Yessir, speaking."

"It's Jack. Are you guys okay?"

"Sure. We just got Daddy home from the hospital. They wanted him to stay for more tests, but I promised—"

"Travis, listen to me." Jack sounded out of breath. "I just met with Bendickson and their attorneys. I think you're in trouble. I think we all are— everyone who's a threat to Demler-Vargus. Your family, mine, Derrick . . ."

Claire was eyeballing Travis from the TV room and must've seen the concern on his face, because she excused herself, handed Daddy his radio, and came into the kitchen. Travis covered the mouthpiece and leaned the earpiece down where she could listen.

"Where are you, Jack?" he said.

"Leaving Trenton City PD. Had to see Officer DeVry in person."

"Jack, I wish you hadn't gone to the police. We're supposed to meet with Demler-Vargus tomorrow afternoon for the big payoff!"

"Travis, forget about that! They're done paying people off. They're furious. They're going to be after me. I know way too much. We all do."

Claire gritted her teeth and shook her head. "I told you!"

She was right. The supposed deal with Demler-Vargus was foul—possibly had been from the start.

"Do you understand?" Jack said.

"Yeah, Jack, we hear you. Claire's on the line with me."

"This isn't just a news story anymore, it's a police case. Cecil's bad too—and who knows who else at the *Dispatch*. I can't go back there. Amy Sheets was getting paid off too. We tracked her down in Columbus; Derrick's there now trying to get her to go on the record with all she knows."

"Holy cow." Travis was trying to digest it all.

"If looks could kill, I'd be dead," Jack said. "Those guys are desperate. I'm afraid of what they're going to do."

"What are you gonna do now?" Travis said.

"Get home as fast as I can. Get the family and get out of there. I suggest you do the same."

Claire looked up at Travis. "We can go to my house," she whispered. Then she said it to Jack. "We can all go to my house, Jack! They don't know about me. It would be safe there."

Travis squeezed Claire's shoulder. "Daddy'll never leave; neither will LJ. Jack, you and your family can come here. We're armed. Between all of us, we can keep someone on guard for the night. How long's this gonna last?"

"DeVry is on this thing. He's got the captain involved, and they've got a team together. I'm hoping they raid Demler-Vargus. I told him if they want to find Spivey Brinkman, they need to get in there and get to the bottom of it."

"Well, you just come on over if you need a place to go," Travis said. "We got sleeping bags and plenty of grub."

"Let me think about it," he said. "We might take you up on it. Thanks, Travis."

"I'm gonna call Coon and tell him the meeting's off," Travis said. "He's gonna blow a gasket."

"He'll thank you later."

"You think he's in danger too?"

"Yeah, I do."

"He can join the party, then, if he wants."

"I need to call DeVry and tell him you guys are supposed to meet Demler-Vargus tomorrow," Jack said. "He needs to know about that."

"So much for our big payday," Travis whined.

"By the way, what did the doctors find out about your dad?" Jack said.

"They found Fenarene in his system."

"I had a feeling. I'm sorry."

"Yep. They want to do more tests, but he wasn't up to it today. We was in there before dawn."

"Galen?" Claire hurried into the TV room where Daddy had risen from his chair and was shuffling toward the kitchen, clutching his transistor radio.

"Maybe I should give the Brinkman girls a heads-up," Travis said. "They live right out back of us, ya know. You think they're in any danger?"

"You better do that," Jack said. "They knew Cecil was on the take. And they knew about another important piece of the puzzle I haven't told you about yet. You remember a guy named Merv Geddy?"

"Sure, he and Daddy was buddies. I know his son."

Daddy's eyes were like saucers and his mouth was hanging wide open as Claire led him to the doorway of the kitchen.

Jack was talking, but Travis wasn't listening anymore.

Daddy bashed the doorframe with his shoulder and leaned there, trembling, holding up his radio. "They just found Spivey Brinkman . . ." His head dropped. He shook it. Forced himself to look up, tears gushing over. "He hanged himself . . . from the bridge over the Lincolntown River."

31

Derrick hoped he hadn't made the hour drive to Columbus in vain. He rang the doorbell at Amy's high-rise condo for the fourth or fifth time, but heard nothing from inside.

He knocked again, louder. "Amy, it's Derrick Whittaker. Please open up. I just want to talk."

Derrick looked both ways, no one in sight. The quiet hallway of the eighth-floor condo was decked out with maroon, black, and white carpet, recessed lighting, large plants, and textured wallpaper. Amy was definitely in the high-rent district.

He finally got the nerve up to try the door, but it was locked. He got his phone out and redialed her cell. All he got was endless ringing, and he did not hear Amy's phone ringing within the unit.

He made his way back to the elevator and took it down to the lavish lobby. He crossed beneath massive chandeliers, across the white-and-black tiled floor, to a carpeted area with several sleek tables and black leather sofas and chairs.

He set his shoulder bag down. Amy had to go up that elevator or the steps to get to her place. He would wait. He took off his coat and took a seat on the edge of a chair. His phone vibrated in his pocket, and he pulled it out to see Jack's name in the caller ID.

"Hey, dude. What's up."

"You make it?"

"Yeah. Amy doesn't answer her door. I'm watching for her in the lobby. How'd it go with Bendickson?"

"I'll tell you in a second, but first you need to know something else . . . they found Spivey Brinkman—dead."

As Jack explained how they found Spivey hanging above the icy waters of the Lincolntown River, Derrick's heart melted for Jenness and Tatum— those poor girls.

"Initial reports said suicide, but DeVry says it may have been staged," Jack said. "Dude, this thing is real and it's happening fast—like right now. Demler-Vargus is scared and they're getting messy."

A wave of fear practically knocked Derrick from the chair. His face burned. He wanted to be home, close to Zenia, not in this strange, dark city.

Jack continued. "Bendickson's son, two lawyers, and a henchman were with him. I couldn't get them to admit anything, but they are so dirty, man. I thought they might not let me leave. They ended up throwing me out, threatening me. They're desperate."

"You told DeVry all this?"

"Yeah, the police are fully engaged."

"You think Zenia's safe?"

Jack hesitated. "I don't know if any of us are. You need to be careful. Amy said she thought someone was following her, and that makes sense; she's the key witness in this whole thing."

Derrick scanned the lobby. Several ladies were talking by a small fountain, and a man in winter garb was working on a laptop.

This was way more than he'd bargained for. He wasn't some superman. He was a reporter. And he was scared.

"I'm not going back to the paper," Jack said. "I'm going to get the family and go somewhere, a hotel or something. You and Z can come if you want, when you get back tonight."

"What are you saying, man?"

"I'm saying Demler-Vargus is out to stop every leak, right now, no matter what it takes. They're in crisis mode. They silenced Spivey and the Doyles. That leaves Amy and the Randalls, Coon, and Spivey's girls."

"And you and me!" Derrick said. "And Z and Pam . . . Shoot, this is nuts! I need to get back!"

"Derrick, hold on, man. We need Amy to talk. Can you hang in there a little longer?"

"Jack, I'm not cut out for this, man. I'm gonna call Z, make sure everything's okay . . ."

"I can go get her after I get my gang, if you want. She can come with us wherever we go."

Derrick didn't want to scare Zenia if there was no definite threat. But he wouldn't be able to live with himself if she was harmed and he had done nothing to protect her.

"I tried to get the Randalls to pack up and get out, but Travis said no way; LJ and Galen won't budge. They're getting their shotguns out." Jack chuckled, trying to lighten things. "Their place might be the safest spot in town!"

"I gotta think this through," Derrick said. "Let's wait one more hour and see where we are."

"You got it. Listen, watch your back. Of all the people involved in this thing, Amy might be the most dangerous to them."

"Dude, don't even say that . . ."

A rail-thin woman pushed with all her might to come through the circular doors. She stopped and looked back outside, the wind blowing her beige overcoat and scarf.

Derrick's heart leapt.

"Hold on, Jack."

Could that be Amy? She turned back around. Yes! But the belt around her waist was so tight . . . she'd become a skeleton.

"I see her." Amy's once shiny blond hair was dark and stringy. Her young face had aged fifteen years and was sickly pale.

Derrick stood. She noticed and turned toward him, like a scene from a movie, as if they'd planned to meet.

"I'll call you later." He put the phone in his pocket and walked toward her slowly, arms outstretched, like a trainer approaching a wild animal.

She shook her head. "No." Her sunken eyes came alive, darting about the lobby. "Why did you come here?"

"Amy, please." Derrick continued toward her, gingerly. "Can we go up to your place where it's quiet, and talk?"

"This was not a good idea." She scrubbed her forehead with her knuckles and ran the hand through her oily hair. Her lips were cracked. She looked as if she hadn't eaten in days.

"Amy, things are happening really fast." He scanned the room. "We need to talk in private."

She trembled like a frightened dog, unable to get another word out.

Derrick wanted to sympathize with her, but the warning signals were blaring in his head.

"Amy, listen to me! Spivey Brinkman is dead. We need you to tell the truth, on the record. It's time."

Her scared eyes fixed on Derrick's. "Spivey Brinkman? How?"

Derrick was approaching frantic. He sensed danger, sensed people watching. He needed Amy to snap out of it.

"He was hung from the Lincolntown Bridge. We don't think you're safe either."

"Of course I'm not safe! I told Jack they've been watching me for days! They know my routine. They know everything about me. And they're outside right now!"

Derrick wished he were anywhere else, but he was in the middle of it now; he needed to be calm—and smart.

"Look, Jack has the police involved." He looked around and told himself to keep his voice down. "What if you pack a bag and I drive us back to Trenton City right now?"

Amy stomped her foot and shook her head, on the verge of tears.

"Just tell the truth!" Derrick said. "Who knows, maybe you can do some sort of a plea deal? You spill your guts about Demler-Vargus in exchange for a lighter sentence—or no sentence; maybe just community service or something. I don't know, but I know we've got to move!"

"My brother was right." She peered up at Derrick with watery eyes, her chapped lips quivering. "Why didn't I listen to him? I'm such a fool."

Derrick found it odd that the man on the laptop was still bundled up in coat and hat, yet working away on his computer. Could he be one of Demler-Vargus's people?

"Greed." Amy's eyes were glazed, as if she was hypnotized. "That's all it was. And ever since the very second I agreed—it's been nothing but poison." As if a hypnotist snapped her out of it, she gave a humorless laugh and looked right at Derrick. "Poison. Just as bad as anything Demler-Vargus is churning out."

"Okay, look, Amy . . . I don't feel comfortable out here in the wide open—"

"You're right, you're right." Finally a tinge of color filled her cheeks. She sniffed and seemed to sober up. "If you help me, I'll tell you whatever you want."

"On the record."

"On the record." She began walking, fast. "Come on."

Derrick grabbed his coat and bag. He couldn't believe he was following this unstable, "wanted" woman up to her condo. He checked back. The sour-looking guy on the laptop was staring at them.

Hurry up, hurry up.

Derrick was revved up to the max. Part of him was anxious because the end of this nightmare was within reach. If he hurried and played it smart, he would be home soon. But part of him was so scared that he was actually shivering. People were *dying*. Amy was a prime target. And—if he dared to admit it—so was he.

32

"How are you holding up?" Pamela asked as she maneuvered the Accord into a space in the snowy parking lot outside of Farley's Home Store. She couldn't help but wonder if her mom was going to be able to make it without a drink.

"Pam, please, it's not like I'm some . . ." Margaret turned around to make sure the girls weren't listening, then whispered, ". . . *drunk* or something. I'm fine. I'll let you know if there's anything to be concerned about."

"Bundle up, girls." Pamela eyed the Crafts Galore store right next door to Farley's.

Granger could be working right now . . . literally within yards of you.

"Mommy, how long is this going to take?" Rebecca opened her door. "I'm starving."

"Not long at all, peaches. MawMaw knows just what she's looking for. Right, MawMaw?"

It was frigid outside. Pamela took Faye's hand and Margaret took Rebecca's as they hurried through the parking lot toward the front door.

"Now, why would someone park there?" Margaret nodded toward a grimy old conversion van, covered in salt, parked and running at the curb off to the right of the entrance. The only clean part of the van was where the windshield wipers swiped periodically. "Smell that, for criminy sakes. Not only is he parked in a fire lane, but he's trying to kill us with gas fumes."

That was precisely the type of comment Pamela wished the girls didn't have to hear—negative, negative, negative. Pamela had grown up with it. She didn't comment, but hurried them inside, out of the cold.

"Okay, where to, Mom? Let's make this quick."

"Well, at the one we have at home, the fabric is all the way in the back corner."

"Let's check it out." Pamela continued to hold Faye's hand and led the way through the bright store. She wanted to get this over with fast, get the pizza, and meet up with Jack.

In just seconds, Margaret and Rebecca were lagging way behind. Margaret could never just zip in and out of a store; she had to browse. Now, she and Rebecca were lingering in the candle aisle.

"We're going to keep going," Pamela called. "Meet us back there. Don't be long, Mom, we don't have a lot of time."

Margaret smiled and kept looking at the candles.

Pamela and Faye found the fabric section and asked a sales associate for help finding the material Margaret had in mind. Although a bit crabby and slow, the woman led them to a section with several dozen choices.

"Oh dear, Faye, I don't know where to begin," Pamela said.

"What's this for again?" Faye said.

"MawMaw is going to make neat little curtains to go on those long windows on each side of the front door."

"Oh. I like looking out those windows, Mommy. Will we be able to move the curtains and see out?"

"That's a good question, honey. I'm not exactly sure how she plans to hang them."

"Well, I like this one." Faye fingered a swatch of sheer beige material.

"I like that too. Let's run that one by MawMaw when she gets here. And how about this lacy one?"

Faye took the fabric, rubbed it on her cheek, then smelled it. "I like that one, too."

"Good. Let's see if there are any more we really like, to show MawMaw."

While they were looking over the cloth, Rebecca and MawMaw came around the corner holding hands. Pamela showed them what she and Faye had found.

"This one is perfect," Margaret said.

"I picked that one," Faye said.

"It is exactly what I had in mind, Faye. You have an excellent eye for interior design."

Margaret got the attendant busy cutting the fabric the size she wanted it.

"Mom," Rebecca said, "did you get the poster board for my Clara Barton project?"

"No, I didn't. Good girl to remember! You saved me a trip," Pamela said. "Mom, let us go get that while you get the fabric. We'll meet you up front."

It took Pamela and the girls a few minutes to track down the poster board. Then, of course, Rebecca had to decide which color she wanted. She ended up choosing light green. They made it to the spacious area at the front of the store. There was a line of cash registers and quite a few people checking out, especially for such a chilly weeknight.

Pamela glanced around. "Girls, do you see MawMaw anywhere?"

Rebecca and Faye looked.

"Maybe she's not up here yet," Pamela said. "I supposed we could just get in line."

"Oh, there she is. Row number six," Rebecca said.

Pamela spotted her. "Excellent. Let's go get in line."

The next step she took, Pamela froze; the girls bumped into her.

It was Granger. In the line next to Margaret's. Checking out.

She immediately looked down, turned away, her back to him, and put her arms around the girls. He was about forty or fifty feet away.

"What are we doing, Mommy?" Faye said.

Good question.

Pamela wanted to race to the car, but what about Margaret? Would she notice Granger?

"Let's just stand here another second." Pamela's voice broke.

Would the girls recognize him? She turned them so they were all facing the opposite side of the store.

"Mom, why are we standing out here in the middle of the store?" Rebecca said. "Let's check out."

Pamela had begun to tremble. She ran a hand through her hair. What to do?

She took another peek back. Granger was still in line. He hadn't seen them.

Good. Okay, just be calm, for the girls . . .

• • •

It had gotten dark early and was one of those crystal clear, arctic winter evenings. The roads appeared free of ice. Jack drove toward home at a good clip, drumming the steering wheel, forcing himself to try to relax his neck and shoulders, which were tight as a drum.

Whenever Jack faced trying circumstances, as he was in now, he got the unmistakable notion he needed to have a clear conscience before God. And right now he knew he did not, and would not, until he forgave Granger Meade. It was something he needed to do, in person. It could be short and sweet, but it was time. Pam would be relieved to hear it.

Jack hated postponing their date, but that had become the least of his concerns. Something about speaking with Officer DeVry had made the severity of the situation chillingly real. And now that they had learned Spivey was dead, Jack knew the police would be all over Demler-Vargus. It was only a matter of time.

Getting a hotel room would seem drastic, but Jack had the distinct impression he needed to get the family away from the house, at least for the night. There was no way he was going to risk putting them through any more distress. Once again he thought about calling Pam to explain things and give her a heads-up, but this was way too explosive to discuss over the phone; he wanted to do it face-to-face.

He wondered what was going on with Derrick and Amy. Was there really someone after her? Were they in danger?

His phone rang. He looked at the screen.

Cecil!

Jack's mind scrambled. Dare he answer?

When they'd last talked, Cecil had used the smokescreen about how the publisher was watching him, worried about lawsuits.

Had Bendickson or his cronies told Cecil about Jack's interview? Had Cecil found out what Derrick was doing?

Jack decided to find out.

"This is Crittendon."

"Jack . . . good, I'm glad I caught you," Cecil said. "It's not too late, you know."

"Too late for what, Cecil?"

"You know . . ."

"No, I don't." Jack got a distressed feeling in the pit of his stomach. "What are you talking about?"

"You can still get in on the action. You're not going to get anywhere with this. You realize that, don't you?"

Cecil knew! They'd told him Jack was on to him.

"It's not too late, Jack. I told them I could get you on our side. You can make some extra money. Keep your family safe. We keep things going at the paper, business as usual."

"I can't believe this." Jack pushed harder on the gas, now within a mile of home. "How could you do this? What's happened to you?"

"Don't give me that Boy Scout crap. You know what kind of money we make. I've given the *Dispatch* eight years of my life, working eleven-, twelve-, thirteen-hour days, weekends, holidays; what have I got to show for it? A broken marriage and messed-up kids. Don't give me your moral—"

"And you're gonna take Amy down with you. Who else? Nigel? Is he in on it? What about Pete?" Jack's whole body was trembling with fury.

"Where are you, Jack?"

He checked his rearview. Were they after him right now?

"Come in. Let's talk about it face-to-face," Cecil said.

"Yeah, right. What did Bendickson do, call you right after I left there?"

"Where's Derrick, Jack?"

"Sick."

"No . . . he's not sick."

Jack's heart thundered as he finally wheeled the Jetta into his neighborhood.

"Jack, you don't mess with these people."

"What do you mean by that?"

"Just what I said. They're not going to let this get out, period. They're too big and too powerful. They know there are leaks, and they're in the process of patching those leaks. I'm calling you because I'm your friend—"

"Oh right, Cecil. Some friend you turned out to be."

"That's right! I don't want to see anything happen to you—or Pam or the girls."

Jack's heads buzzed with alarm.

Could someone be at the house right now?

He should have called Pam!

He was almost there.

He touched the gun strapped to his ankle.

"You tell them if they come near any of us, they're dead." Jack flew around the corner onto his street, tires squealing.

Cecil laughed. "Jack, you're one man. This is a *machine*. Trust me. You don't want to keep going with this. Where are you gonna go? What's your plan?"

"None of your business." Jack floored the Jetta and it roared up the street. "But you're gonna go down."

"One more chance. This is it. Come in now, talk to me, we work out a deal, we get Derrick in on it—everyone's happy."

"You know what, Cecil? *Take a flying leap!*"

There were no strange cars parked near the house. *Good.*

There was a long pause on the phone as Jack's car bumped into the driveway. He hit the garage door opener.

"You just made the biggest mistake of your short life, my friend," Cecil said.

"I'm not your friend—"

The line went dead.

Fine. We need to get him before he gets us.

The garage door lifted.

Pam's car was gone!

His mind seared white.

Where would they be?

He flew into the center of the garage, jerked to a stop, got out, and ran for the door.

He had been sure they would all be there, getting ready for the big date night.

He unlocked the door and ran inside. "Hello?"

Reaching for his cell phone to call Pam, he found a note on the kitchen island:

> *Jack, we're at Farley's getting sheers, then picking up pizza for the girls' dinner. Looking forward to our date! Love, P*

Phew.

They were okay. Everything was okay.
But Farley's Home Store . . .

33

Standing with the girls in the middle of Farley's, Pamela nervously debated whether to let her mom finish checking out in the aisle next to Granger, or go corral her and make a beeline for the door.

"Why are we waiting?" Faye whined, leaning against Pamela.

Pamela did not want the girls to see Granger.

The muffled ring of her phone sounded, and she fumbled for it in her purse.

"MawMaw's almost done checking out," Rebecca said. "Are we getting the poster board or not?"

Pamela glanced at the phone and saw Jack's name.

"Jack," she whispered, looking up to see Granger staring directly at her—and the girls.

"Hey, honey, I just found your note," Jack said. "Listen, don't go to Farley's for those curtains. Try somewhere else, okay, like Lowe's or something?"

Screams rang out in the store.

People scattered like roaches.

"Everyone on the floor!" A man in a bomber jacket brandished a gun. In a flash, he had Margaret in a headlock!

Pamela's knees wobbled and she dropped to the ground, bringing the crying girls down with her.

Within seconds, the gunman and Margaret were the only two people still standing.

"Not you." The gunman pointed at the tall, pimply checkout boy. "Get up, open the drawer. *Now!*"

People were wailing, shouting God's name.

"Shut up and get down low! On the floor, now!"

"Pam?" Jack's voice chirped from the phone.

"We're at Farley's," she whispered. "A man with a gun has Mom." That was all she could say before the man blew a shot straight into the ceiling.

"No cell phones. No calls. No texting!"

The unshaven man pointed his gun at the checkout boy, who looked amazingly calm. "All the money in a bag—quick, quick."

Pamela dropped the phone in her purse without ending the call, thinking that might help, somehow.

Margaret fought and squirmed like a cat.

The man laughed nervously and locked her tighter in the crease of his elbow.

Along with everyone else, Granger had dropped to the floor, but he still towered over the bodies around him. He gave a solemn nod to Pamela. Did he recognize Margaret as her mother? He'd seen her in the courtroom during his trial.

Still seemingly unruffled, the checkout boy dumped the contents of his drawer into a large Farley's bag as if he was emptying cat litter.

Pamela held the girls tight. She could hear Jack yelling into the phone, and prayed that the sporadic moans and frantic outcries of the other patrons would drown out his tinny voice.

"Next one, next one!" The gunman pivoted with Margaret, dragging her several steps, pointing the gun at the register in the next line—Granger's line!

"Empty it, hurry, hurry, hurry."

The boy scurried like a lanky, kicked dog, dodging several people to get to the register next to Granger.

"Let go of me," Margaret yelled. "Let go!"

The gunman wrenched her neck. "Don't give me a hard time, lady, or I'll blow your head off."

A man in sweats on the floor twenty feet away had his phone out. He was trying to call—

Bang.

Blood spurted from his calf. His phone cracked to the floor and he cried out, clutching his leg.

The girls screamed and locked tighter to Pamela, whose heart was in her throat.

God, please, let him leave, let him leave . . .

"I said no phones!" The gunman scanned the store with his smoking weapon. "Next one dies."

Granger scowled and dropped his head.

Had anyone been able to sound a silent alarm? Pamela didn't think so.

With a sober stare, the checkout boy handed the bag to the gunman, but he didn't take it. Instead, he choked Margaret tighter, making her squeal, then he scanned the room, the exit, as if deciding what to do next.

He snatched the bag with his gun hand and jammed the weapon to the checkout boy's throat. "You need to get that bad-boy look off your face."

Margaret threw a backward elbow toward the gunman's stomach, letting out a groan as she did. But he only grunted, then cackled.

"All right, old girl." He shoved Margaret along with the strength of his legs. "You want to have some fun? You can come with me."

At the split second that the gunman's head turned to the exit, Granger sprang heavy onto his back, taking all three of them down. Margaret screamed and hit the floor hard. Realizing she was free, she slithered away fast on all fours.

"Mom!" Pamela screamed with outstretched arms, not wanting to take the girls a step in that direction. "Mom, come here!"

People scattered in all directions.

Margaret got to her feet and ran to Pamela and the girls.

The armed man still squeezed the gun, but Granger was squarely on top of him, bashing his wrist against the floor. Three other men dived into the mix, helping Granger, locking the gunman down.

The gun clattered away. The checkout boy dashed for it, grabbed it, and locked it in front of him, pointing right at the man's head.

In the distance Pamela heard sirens.

She and Margaret hugged. They drew Rebecca and Faye in with them. Together, the four of them stood breathless in a circle, arms tight around each other—crying, laughing, thanking God.

• • •

The Randalls had the old house locked up tight, and Bo had just lit a fire in the cast iron stove in the TV room. Travis and LJ were sprawled out on the floor, loading the shotguns and pistols. The mouthwatering smell of breakfast filled the room. Daddy looked on from his recliner with sunken eyes and a tired face full of gray beard stubble.

"Can I help?" Bo said.

LJ coughed. "There's a tad bit of smoke in here, son. You got the flue open?"

"Yessir."

"Sit on down here, then. Grab you some bullets," LJ said.

Travis felt sick. He and Claire had just had themselves a jim-dandy of an argument. When she heard Spivey had been found dead, she'd about had a conniption fit. She could not for the life of her understand how Travis and the boys could stay in that house one more night—especially after Jack had warned them Demler-Vargus was on the warpath.

She'd pleaded with them to go to her house. They would be safe there, until the cops wrangled up Bendickson and his cronies. Even Galen had seemed agreeable; Spivey's death seemed to have truly rattled the old codger.

LJ, however, was up in arms about staying home. The last thing that boy was going to do was give in to the enemy and go hide out somewhere.

Claire had stormed to the kitchen and was hustling around with the phone at her ear, trying to reach Spivey's daughters while scrounging up breakfast for supper.

Being at odds with her was giving Travis a headache to beat the band.

"I gotta get me some Goody's," he said.

"Bo, be a scout and get your Uncle Travis one of them headache powders from the medicine cabinet, would you?" LJ said.

"Sure." Bo scampered off.

"You nervous?" LJ said.

"No, I ain't nervous, but I don't feel like I should put Claire in danger, having her stay here."

"I didn't know she planned on stayin' here," LJ said.

"Well, we kind of wanted to stay close till this thing blows over, ya know."

"You two is gettin' close mighty fast, ain't ya."

Travis gave him the old stare-down. "I like her. Anything wrong with that?"

"Not a thing. I like her too."

"Well, good, 'cause she's the best thing to happen around here since Momma passed."

"I ain't sayin' she ain't—"

"Would you two quit bickering?" Daddy said. "Are them guns even clean? They ain't been shot in a coon's age."

"We cleaned 'em back in November for the turkey shoot," LJ said. "I just dare them buggers to set a toenail on our property."

Speaking of Coon, Ralston Coon had been livid when Travis told him the Randalls were not going though with the meeting at Demler-Vargus the next afternoon. He insisted on coming over to try to "talk some sense" into them. Even LJ was hot about it, hating to see 2.5 million slip through his greasy fingers.

"Okay." Claire came into the TV room, wiping her hands on a towel. "Biscuits, sausage and gravy are ready. You can help yourselves whenever you want. They should stay warm for Mr. Coon. And there's fresh coffee."

Bo took off for the kitchen.

If that were Travis's son, he would teach the boy some manners; let the elders go first. But not LJ; he sat there, holding up his Winchester, squinting through the sites with his one eye, sweeping it across the room.

"Well, I do declare. Thank you, young lady. I believe you've found the way to my heart with this meal," Daddy said.

"Well, don't thank me yet; you haven't tasted it," Claire said. "After your day at the hospital, I'm sure you must be famished."

"How are Spivey's girls holding up?" Travis said.

"They didn't answer. I see lights on over there. I think I'll run over," Claire said.

"You want me to come with you?" Travis said.

"Nope." She tossed the towel over her shoulder. "I'll be right back."

"You bundle up now, you hear?" Daddy said. "It's colder than a banker's heart out there." He laughed at his own joke.

Bo left the kitchen, licking his fingers, carrying a plate piled ridiculously high. Again, lack of parental training.

Travis helped Claire get her coat on and saw her to the door. He looked out the back window and flipped on the floodlights. There was snow on the ground and, just beyond a patch of trees, he could see the lights on at Spivey's house.

What was he thinking, letting her go out there alone?

"You know what? I'm coming with you."

Claire's smile told him she'd been waiting for that. They chuckled as he threw on his parka and she pulled on her hat.

Travis gave a yell to the boys. "We're going to see Spivey's girls. Be right back."

They headed into the night.

34

Only a few days ago Derrick had thought Jack was nuts for carrying a gun. Now, as he and Amy rode the quiet elevator up to her eighth-floor condo, he wished anything he was packing—even though he'd never fired a gun in his life.

He just kept telling himself he would be home soon.

"I'll pack a bag and go back to Trenton City, but I'm taking my own car," Amy said.

"Fine. I'll follow you. I'll talk to Jack on the way and find out what the plan is," said Derrick.

"I have notes, Demler-Vargus stuff, hidden up at my place; I'll bring it."

"Good."

"I've also got a gun." She stared at him coldly.

"Why is it everyone around here has a gun except me?"

She didn't see the humor.

The elevator dinged and came to a stop on eight. Amy led the way down the sleek, low-lit hallway. Walking several feet behind her, Derrick took in an enormous breath, arched his shoulders, and exhaled through an almost closed mouth.

Relax.

"I'll need to get gas." Amy glanced back at him.

"That's cool."

She kept walking, looking into her purse, and got her keys out. Derrick couldn't believe how thin she'd gotten.

Suddenly she stopped. The upper half of her body bent over. She was examining the door to her condo.

Her head snapped back to Derrick.

The door was open several inches. It had been splintered.

They reached for each other, holding each other's wrists.

Their wild eyes met.

"I was just up here," Derrick whispered. "It wasn't like this. They must be in there. Come on!"

They were unarmed, that's all he could think. Sitting ducks. He yanked her by the arm. "Let's go!"

Her hands went up, palms facing her, all ten fingers extended. "What about my stuff?"

There was a sound from inside the condo.

Derrick threw his head toward the elevator. "Forget it. Come on!"

Amy flew toward him and he grabbed her hand and ran.

As they sprinted for the elevator, he was sure he was going to hear gunshots and die right there in the hallway with a bullet in his spine.

He spotted the door for the stairway and burst through with Amy right behind.

"You ride with me." Derrick flew down the steps. "Forget your car."

"Okay." Her voice quavered. "Where're you parked?"

"Ground level."

"Me too. I've got another gun in my car. If we have time . . ."

Derrick's feet barely touched each step as he flew down, down, down—listening above for any sign of followers.

"Almost there." He worked the car keys out of his pocket as he ran.

He heard nothing above them.

He busted through the door and into the dimly lit parking garage.

"Hurry!" He headed in the direction of his car.

Amy headed in the opposite direction, down the ramp. "My car's down here . . . right over here."

"Forget it! Come *on!*"

"It'll just take a sec. We need a gun."

Derrick fumed as he hit his remote. The lights on his SUV blinked thirty feet from him. He would start the car, pull up, and be ready to go when she got there.

It was eerily quiet. No movement, except Amy. "Hurry up!"

Just then he heard something.

Static?

A quick burst of it, like someone pressing the button on a walkie-talkie, and releasing . . .

It wasn't right.

"Amy, stop!"

She turned around. "It's just over here."

"No! Come back." Alarm gripped him. "Now!"

If she went for her car, he was leaving.

Her shoulders slouched, as if she was fed up with him, but she turned around and started back toward him.

"Hurry!" he yelled, and trotted for his car.

Like a trick, the pavement beneath his feet disappeared.

The bomb was deafening.

He slammed to the pavement, unable to break his fall.

The building teetered.

The pain in his left shoulder and side of his head was immediate and excruciating.

His ears rang. Debris hit all around him.

Amy . . .

A fender flew past, smashing two cars.

Where Amy had been standing, a thick cloud of brown smoke billowed toward him like a scene from 9/11. Behind the smoke, flames licked the ceiling of the parking deck. He couldn't even see what had exploded, but knew it was Amy's car.

He waited a second longer, until he was certain no more car parts were coming his way. He grabbed his keys, which he'd dropped, and got to his knees. The pain in his shoulder took his breath away. Smoke and gas fumes engulfed him. He stood, hunched over, and started toward where Amy had been.

Were the people who tripped the bomb watching?

Would they run him over?

He saw her feet first, recognized one of her brown shoes sticking out behind the rear tire of a green car. She was facedown. The back of her overcoat looked as if it had been clawed by an animal, her white blouse too. Her back was bleeding.

"Amy." He gently gripped her shoulders. "Amy. Please, please, be okay."

She lifted her head slightly and opened her eyes.

Derrick's ears were ringing loudly, and he assumed hers were too. The smoky air was blazing hot.

"I'm okay," she said. "Sorry . . ." She laid her head back to the ground.

"Are your legs okay? Can you walk?"

With her eyes still shut, her right foot lifted straight up and back down, then her left.

"Good. I'll bring my car. Just sit tight." He got up and braced his aching shoulder, hoping there wouldn't be another explosion. "We're gonna make it." He started running for his car. "I'll be right back."

But he didn't believe his own words.

He knew he was being watched.

They were targets.

In truth, he wasn't sure he would even make it back to his car.

• • •

By the time Jack arrived at Farley's, police cars, ambulances, and a fire truck were parked at all angles around the front of the business. Amid snow flurries, police officers in heavy parkas, and flashing blue and red lights, he ran inside.

The blood on the white floor of the home store made Jack cringe. After explaining to a cop that his family was involved, Jack hurried to the manager's office, where the girls practically knocked him over with their hugs. Pam and Margaret were seated with blankets wrapped around their shoulders. He knelt and hugged each of them.

"So much for our date." Pam gave him a wry smile.

Jack squeezed the back of her neck. "We'll take a rain check."

They seemed in good spirits; in a giddy aftershock mode, Jack imagined. The manager had given the girls Hershey bars, and Margaret and Pam sipped bottled waters and talked over each other as they explained what had happened.

Jack was floored when he heard it was Granger who had courageously diffused the situation.

"If it hadn't been for Granger, that maniac would've gotten away, and taken me with him," Margaret said. "I just can't believe it. I owe him my life—yet, I wanted them to take his." She dropped her head. "I don't know what's what anymore. Life doesn't make sense."

Pam nodded and looked at Jack. "He took the guy down. It was amazing. Who knows what he would have done?"

"Where is Granger now?" Jack said.

"In there." Pam nodded to the room next to theirs. "Police are talking to him."

Jack cursed himself for not talking with Granger sooner; now it was going to look like he was forgiving him based on his heroics.

"How's the guy who got shot?" Jack said.

"Going to be fine," Pam said. "They got him out of here fast."

"They're still after the driver," Margaret said. "I gave them a full description of him, and the van." She pointed at Pam. "I told you that guy looked suspicious."

Pam nodded. "Everyone looks suspicious to you."

They all chuckled.

"I guess I'm just a senile old woman."

"You are not a senile old woman," Rebecca spoke up.

"Well, thank you, pumpkin."

Jack stood. "I'll be right back."

Pam nodded. "We've told the police everything, so we can go."

"Okay, give me a minute."

Jack took in a deep breath and peeked into the room around the corner. There sat Granger, in a chair in the corner of an empty white room, as big and real as ever. Jack pulled back and stood around the corner a second longer, composing his thoughts.

Now or never.

His heart beat hard and strong as he knocked and stepped into the doorway. "Granger," he said with a nod.

"Jack." Granger sat very still, clutching a big winter coat in his lap. He looked older, but was still a towering guy with short, messy red hair and ruddy cheeks.

"Do you have a second?"

Granger's red eyebrows went up and down. "He said he'd be right back. That was ten minutes ago."

Jack pulled up the other free chair and sat, facing Granger.

"You apologized, and I'm sorry I didn't accept it." Jack looked him square in his tiny eyes.

"It's not a problem," Granger said. "I don't blame you."

"My unforgiveness has been wrong; it's been poisoning me."

Granger gave a simple nod.

The moment was silent and awkward. Jack hated the man; that hadn't changed. But he had to let it go, for many reasons.

"I accept your apology."

Granger nodded again. "Cool."

"Thanks for what you did here tonight."

Granger shrugged. "God had me here, that's all . . ."

Jack contemplated Granger's words for what seemed like a minute. He debated what else he should say. Then he stood and stuck out a hand. "Good luck."

Granger's body straightened. He stared at the hand, gripped it, and looked up at Jack. "Thank you. You too."

Jack left the room, Granger Meade, and a thousand regrets behind him.

35

Derrick's back burned intensely from the heat of the car bomb as he got Amy to her feet and eased her into the front seat of the SUV. She gasped from the pain. He was totally unprepared for this kind of insanity and apologized for having no blanket or anything to put on Amy's bleeding back.

"Don't worry." Her head bobbed. "Just get us out of here."

He buckled her in, slammed the door, and sprinted around to his side.

Throwing it into reverse, he whizzed the Toyota backward up the ramp some forty feet, swung around, and headed for the exit.

Amy slumped low in the seat.

"You okay?" he said, out of breath.

She nodded. Her eyes were enormous, her face ashen.

"I'll get you some water once we get clear of here, okay?"

She simply waved her hand. "Go, go."

In his rearview Derrick saw a dark red sedan with black windows lurch out of its parking space just seconds after they passed it.

"Shoot. We got someone on our tail. I knew it."

Amy whimpered.

Derrick's whole body shook. His hands were numb.

He couldn't see inside the car behind him, but it was menacingly close to his rear bumper.

"Here." He handed his phone to Amy. "Call 911."

She didn't hesitate.

They got to the exit of the parking garage and stopped at the cashier.

Derrick dug out a ten and handed it to the older Asian woman in the booth. "Please, call the police," he said. "The car behind us . . . they're trying to kill us. Please, get their tag number, call the police."

Derrick wondered if she'd understood what he said. She was still holding the bill, staring at him, looking at the car behind them. Its engine roared.

"Keep the change. Please, just let us out."

The gate went up.

"Call the police!" Derrick hit the gas and bounced out onto the city street.

Before the gate closed, the dark sedan shot through, bouncing onto the street right behind him.

"Here." Amy stuffed the phone back in Derrick's hand. "Go . . . talk!"

"Hello?"

"Is this an emergency, sir?"

Derrick checked a street sign. The red sedan was approaching fast on his left.

"Yes, yes. We are in a Toyota FJ Cruiser, maroon, heading up East Long Street toward I-71 North."

The car was directly beside them now. Its windows were black, but Jack was certain the person inside could see him on the phone.

"They just blew up my friend's car in the parking deck . . . on East High Street and North Long. Now they're following us."

Crunch.

Derrick gasped and fought to keep the SUV on the road as the red car smashed them. It was riding right there, meshed with his car!

This cannot be happening.

He floored it, jerking his wheel to the right. The other car broke away, veering back into its lane. But it must've had a monstrous engine, because it kept up with him without hesitation.

Amy had retrieved the phone and handed it back to him.

"I'm getting on I-71 North, then 161 east," he told the operator. "Please, send officers. Hurry!"

"Is anyone with you, sir?" The tension in the operator's voice had ratcheted.

"One person, a woman."

"Who is driving the other car and what is the make and model?"

"I can't see in. It's a dark red sedan, the windows are black. BMW . . . it's a BMW."

"What is your tag number, please, sir?"

"Shoot, I don't even know. Look, I'm a reporter with the *Trenton City Dispatch.* The Trenton City PD knows all about this—Officer Dennis DeVry."

Derrick's car got rammed so hard, Amy's feather-light frame slammed into the door. She groaned as Derrick swerved, banging onto the sidewalk and ramming a trash can and bench before he could maneuver the SUV back onto the street.

Amy's eyes were scrunched closed and she was biting her bottom lip.

The other car was weaving, as if playing cat and mouse.

That's *it.*

Derrick checked his rearview, saw no one, and told Amy to hang on. He jammed on his brakes and screeched sideways to a halt, facing the other lane. Amy grunted. The red car flew past by about thirty feet before skidding to a stop, then squealed backwards, tires smoking.

"Hold on, we're gonna ram him."

Amy cried, "You'll kill us!"

"Just hold on!"

As Derrick had hoped, the BMW barreled straight backwards and, when it got equal with the front of Derrick's SUV, Derrick locked his hands to the steering wheel, braced his arms straight out, and floored it. He didn't take his eyes off the BMW's right front quarter panel until he smashed it to smithereens.

"Take *that,* bad boy."

The BMW spun in the opposite direction.

Amy moaned.

Derrick whipped his car right, scraped a lamppost, and got it back on track. When he checked his rearview, the BMW was turning around slowly, steam rising from beneath its hood.

"We're going home," he said. "No matter what it takes."

• • •

"Pam, hold up," Jack called at the exit of Farley's.

Pamela had bundled Rebecca and Faye up and was about to head for her car, with Margaret in tow.

"I'll see you at home," she said. "You *are* coming home . . . ?"

Jack approached her. "Hon, listen, this Demler-Vargus thing is getting really dangerous. I had an interview over there today. They know how much I know. There's a lot going on right now that I haven't even had a chance to tell you."

"Well, we can talk about it at home. The girls are wiped out, and so is Mom. We're ready to call it a night."

"That's what I'm saying. I don't want to take any chances."

"What do you mean?"

"I was thinking maybe we should get a hotel room—just for tonight."

Pamela tilted her head and glared at him. "What do you know that you haven't told me?"

"For one, Spivey Brinkman is dead. They found him hanged today."

Pamela's head whirled. Her earlier anticipation about the date with Jack seemed a million miles away.

"Amy Sheets is being followed. Derrick's in Columbus now, trying to get her to go on record about Demler-Vargus's crimes."

Jack's phone rang, and Pamela's heart rate climbed with the sound of it. "A hotel's going to scare the girls, not to mention my mom," she said.

He looked at his phone. "It's DeVry. Let me grab this."

Jack answered, then listened. "You. Are. Kidding me." He arched his shoulders and looked straight up.

Pamela's anxiety intensified.

"Are they okay?" Jack said. "Is that the last you heard?" He nodded and told Dennis to hold on. "Derrick and Amy are being chased," he told Pamela. "They got run off the road on the way out of Columbus. They're trying to get back here."

"I'm back." Jack listened again. "Okay. When are you going to be there?"

Jack looked at his watch, then eyed Pamela. "Tell you what, I'll meet you there. Then my family and I need to decide what we're going to do for the night."

Pamela was numb.

Jack hung up. "Dennis is heading to Randalls' place right now. They're supposed to meet with Demler-Vargus tomorrow for a settlement. Dennis wants to wire them and do a sting operation."

Pamela dropped her head. She was beyond overload.

"You follow me to the Randalls' place and we'll decide what to do from there."

"Jack, I am not taking the girls and my mom to the Randalls' at this time of night! They've been through enough!"

"Believe me, it's the safest place in town right now—"

"If we have to go, we'll wait in my car."

"Okay, fine. I'm just trying to do what's best for everybody."

"I know. I just don't want to upset the girls anymore."

Jack nodded. "I understand. Look, follow me over there. I'll run in and get DeVry's advice on what we should do."

"Fine." Pamela just gave in. "Mom . . . girls, let's go." She looked at Jack. "I don't know how to get there, so go slow."

"I will. Come on, I'll get you guys in the car." Jack reached for Pamela's hand. "We *are* going on that date. Soon—I promise."

She sighed and did her best to manage a smile.

But she was not smiling on the inside.

On the inside, she was doing her best just to breathe—and keep going.

36

Derrick's left headlight wasn't working and he was quite certain the left front of his car was badly smashed, but those were the least of his worries. His main concern was the single headlight several hundred yards back. After the fray in Columbus and maneuvering on and off several different highways, he'd lost track of the BMW and couldn't tell if that was it back there or not.

Derrick's right headlight lit up snowflakes and a long, black stretch of Interstate 161, which would get them back to Trenton City within thirty minutes. He'd seen no cops or flashing lights, maybe because he had gone outside of the Columbus police district? If that *was* the BMW back there, why weren't they coming after Derrick and Amy with all they had?

What are they waiting for?

Amy was sitting up and looking dead ahead with glassy eyes and arms crossed.

Tension filled the car.

"You holding up okay?" he asked.

"Yes."

"Warm enough?"

"Yes."

"In much pain?"

"I'll live."

It was a weeknight in the dead of winter. There weren't many cars on the road. Derrick glanced into the backseat and felt around inside his leather shoulder bag until he found his tape recorder.

He checked the rearview. The single headlight remained way back.

"If they're back there, why aren't they coming?" Amy said.

"They're either going to follow us right into town, or that's not them."

She noticed the mini recorder, looked out her window, and rubbed hard at her forehead with the palm of her left hand.

"If it *is* them, where will we go when we get to Trenton City?" she said. "I have no place to go."

"I'll call Jack. He was either going to a hotel or to Randalls' place. Don't worry, I'll make sure you're safe. We need to get you to a hospital or a doc-in-the-box, or something."

"I'll be fine. What's with the recorder?"

They made eye contact.

"I want you to tell me all you know about Demler-Vargus." He held it out to her, but she didn't move.

Some thirty seconds passed.

She looked down at it and snatched it, wincing as she did. "How do you turn this sucker on?"

• • •

"Brrr. It's gonna get into the teens tonight for sure." Travis stomped the snow onto the rug in the kitchen and shut the door behind Claire. He was trying to keep things light, knowing she was worried about Spivey's girls.

"I'm calling over there again." She handed Travis her coat, kicked her shoes off, and walked in her stocking feet for the phone.

"Honey, they ain't there," Travis said. "There's a million places they could be after loosing their daddy."

"Something's not right," Claire said.

"They're probably mourning with relatives somewhere in town." Travis hung their coats.

"But all the lights are on. There are cars there . . ."

"We don't know which cars belong to who. I'm sure they're with family. Now don't get all worked up."

Travis stopped in his tracks when he got to the TV room.

Big old, bandaged-faced Ralston Coon was nodding at him from the couch, bulky briefcase on the coffee table in front of him.

"Well, looky what the cat drug in," Travis said. "I do believe that face of yours is looking worse."

"Travis." Coon nodded. He was not smiling.

"Man, that was one heck of a fall."

The lawyer didn't reply.

Claire came in from the kitchen. "All I get is the answering machine."

"Leave a message and be done with it," LJ said.

Bo was still on the floor, polishing the guns with an oily rag.

Coon's phone vibrated on the table. He picked it up, read for a second, and began texting, one letter at a time with his chubby index finger.

The house still smelled like sausage. The fire was burning steady.

Coon set the phone down. "You boys look like you're loaded for bear." He chuckled, but Travis could tell he wasn't happy.

"We need to talk, gentlemen." Coon looked twice at Claire. "And ladies."

The dog barked out back.

"Mr. Coon, we're not going to meet with those crooks tomorrow, if that's what tree you're barkin' up." Daddy was sprawled out on the recliner in his pajamas, blue robe, and ratty old corduroy slippers, which were almost worn through on the bottoms.

"Now now, Galen, I need you to hear me out on this." Coon stood. Rusty was howling outside. "You gentlemen have an opportunity before you that will never come your way again, I promise you—"

Travis went through the kitchen, turned the overhead light off, and peered out the back door. One, two, three sets of headlights lit up the snow falling in the parking lot. His heart slammed into his rib cage.

"Git the guns, boys. We got company!"

• • •

Jack swung his car into the Randalls' parking lot, and Pam pulled in right behind him. They parked side by side. Jack got out and hustled over to her car, careful not to slip on the snowy pavement. She rolled the window down and looked up at Jack with tired eyes and a deflated expression that said she was at the end of her rope. Margaret sat beside her and the girls in back; their eyes were open wide, as if in a trance, and they wore blank expressions.

"Okay, there's Dennis," Jack said, as the officer wheeled up in a dark, unmarked squad car."

"Don't be long. We've had it," Pam said. "Really. I just want to go home."

"Okay. I'm thinking maybe I'll just stay up tonight, keep watch. That way everyone can sleep in their own beds," Jack said.

"Good. We can just go now—"

"No. We're going together," Jack insisted. "Just let me talk to Dennis—"

"What on earth!" Margaret said. "Those men have rifles. Girls, get down!"

They all looked toward the Randall house at once.

There stood the silhouetted figures of LJ, Bo, and Travis, steam rising from their mouths, guns and shotguns trained on Jack and company. Even old Galen was leaning in the doorway, pointing a pistol down at them.

"Who's there?" LJ called. "Whoever it is, you just found trouble!"

37

Derrick drove toward Trenton City in stunned silence. Amy had finished recording everything she knew about Demler-Vargus and had fallen asleep with her head against the foggy passenger window. The car that may or may not be following them remained way back, but was locked steady on them.

Derrick stared at the snow-dusted highway, shell-shocked by Amy's confessions. She claimed that she, Cecil, Nigel, and Pete were all paid various five-digit sums of cash on the first day of each month for keeping negative Demler-Vargus news suppressed. Her job was to nix and cover up anything that had to do with employee and citizen health issues, and complaints and cases against the corporation; OSHA and EPA violations; and, especially, any mention of the fiberglass product known as Streamflex. She suspected that at least two EPA officials were on the Demler-Vargus payroll.

Even though Demler-Vargus knew full well that the manufacturing process to create Streamflex was, in essence, a killer, they produced the high-priced, high-demand sheets of fiberglass like clockwork eight times a year. Each of those production cycles lasted ten days, but Streamflex was only manufactured from nine at night until three in the morning during those ten-day spans. It was shrink-wrapped and trucked off in the middle of the night to buyers and distribution centers across the country and beyond.

Jack was much closer to Cecil than Derrick was and had always looked up to the editor as a role model journalist. So much for that, Derrick thought. Not only had Cecil slowly brought the others onto the Demler-Vargus payroll, he was the one who'd thought of sending Amy away under the guise of pregnancy—but not before she had amassed a lethal amount of inside information.

Amy had learned from Emmett and Barb Doyle that Barb had undergone extensive medical testing, which determined, although tentatively, that her chronic illness had been caused by extreme levels of Fenarene.

Derrick looked over at Amy and back at the road, contemplating what the money had gotten her. A crevice was chiseled between her eyes, even while she slept. She looked bulimic. She had no friends. Her career was finished. She'd lost her family. And now she would be going to jail.

He checked his rearview. The one-eyed car had inched closer and was probably only a hundred yards back. His stomach soured. The recording in his bag would bring down the giant. He knew they wanted Amy Sheets—and him.

Amy had fought back tears when she told details about the long-time Demler-Vargus nightshift employee, Merv Geddy, who passed away from the effects of lymphoma. As it turned out, his attorney son had had an autopsy performed on his father. Catastrophically high levels of Fenarene were found. Oliver had been in the midst of filing a lawsuit against Demler-Vargus on behalf of his father when his little plane got sabotaged and slammed into the Sawtooth National Forest.

Derrick checked the rearview again.

Uh oh.

The car behind him had shifted lanes. It was coming—and coming fast.

• • •

Travis sat next to Claire on the couch in the TV room, listening to Officer DeVry as he paced the room, explaining his idea for a sting operation the next afternoon at Demler-Vargus.

Coon refused to look at DeVry. Instead, he sat smoldering because the Randalls had given up on their chance to milk two-point-five million bucks out of the cash cow. Jack had convinced them they would be walking into a death trap. But DeVry was certain the Trenton City PD could protect them well enough and long enough to get key evidence on tape.

Coon's phone vibrated for the gazillionth time. He read for a second and began pecking away. Travis wondered if clients were contacting him at this time of night, or maybe he had a mad wife at home. Nope, it wasn't that; Coon was not wearing a wedding ring.

"Tomorrow morning we can get LJ, Travis, and Mr. Coon wired with two-way recording devices," DeVry said. "Galen, we don't expect you do be in on this—"

"He's got to be there." Coon glared at DeVry. "They made that clear."

"I'm in." Galen's stubbly face was like stone. Travis was sure he was thinking about Momma, how they shortened her life, took her from them too soon.

It was time for payback.

"Fine, but we're not going to wire you; it would be too confusing," DeVry said. "We'll let your sons and Mr. Coon deal with the voices in their ears and the recording equipment."

"Are they going to be armed?" Claire said. "Can you promise they'll be safe?"

DeVry shook his head. "They won't be armed, but our SWAT team will be fully engaged. We'll have the place surrounded. Sharpshooters will be stationed wherever we can possibly put them. The building where we assume you'll be meeting has plenty of windows; we canvassed it today."

"And you'll have them on GPS, right?" Jack said.

"Yeah, oh yeah. We'll know where each of you is in the building, every second."

The room fell silent except for the crackling of wood burning in the fireplace and the gray cat scratching a piece of firewood leaning in the corner.

"Remember, if at all possible," DeVry said, "we want you to get them to admit aloud what they are paying you for—to quit pursuing them, to stop trying to prove they were responsible for Mrs. Randall's illness."

Daddy huffed and mumbled and sat up in his chair.

"Bring it," LJ said.

"Darn right," Daddy said.

Coon reached with both hands for his large briefcase and slid it onto his lap. Phone still in one hand, he wiped sweat from his forehead with the palm of the other.

"What's with Coon?" Claire whispered.

Travis shrugged.

"He's acting weird," she said. "I don't trust him."

• • •

Sitting on the edge of an antique wood chair in the corner of the toasty TV room, Jack was thrilled that the Randalls and Coon had agreed to go along with the sting . . . although Coon was unabashedly upset about it. He sat on the couch, clutching his briefcase as if he were clutching a bomb.

The meeting was wrapping up. Jack's phone vibrated. It was probably Pam, telling him to hurry up.

Instead he found a text from Patrick Roe, the reporter in Charleston who'd been dealing with the Doyles' arson.

> Sorry. Cannot get you copy of dvd from Doyles' fire safe yet, but we played it. They documented dates/times Streamflex produced. Names of people in charge. They show paperwork w/ Barb's hi Fenarene counts. Name of EPA guy on D-V payroll. Very incriminating.

Good! More proof. Now if Derrick would just hurry up and get back with Amy, they would have even more nails for the Demler-Vargus coffin.

He texted Patrick back: [[Thanks much! Anything else of interest?]]

"Jack, what did you decide about tonight?" Claire said.

Jack looked at Dennis. "Do you think we'll be all right at our house? I was thinking about staying up, keeping watch; hopefully it will only be for one night."

"Jack, I told you, you and your family is welcome to stay here," Travis said. "We got plenty of sleeping bags and all that."

"Yeah, we got all kinds of camping gear," Bo said.

"I'm staying," Claire said. "You may as well join the party."

Dennis started to answer, but got cut off again.

"Ain't nobody gonna mess with us here." LJ swept a hand toward the cache of weapons that encircled Bo, who sat crosslegged on the floor. "We're gonna take turns keeping watch."

Coon's eyes darted back and forth.

"Can I go first, Daddy?" Bo said. "Please—"

"Sounds like you're staying here," Dennis said. "LJ, I hope you have a permit for all these weapons."

Jack's phone vibrated. Another text from Patrick Roe.

> On dvd, Doyles insinuate Cecil Barton. Also mention a lawyer who works for D-V, Ralston Coon. I am trying to get permission to send you—

Jack stopped reading.

His face caught fire.

He forced himself to continue staring down at his phone.

His forehead was instantly filled with sweat, and his heart thundered.

Think this through . . . think it through.

Ralston Coon was a plant.

This meant Demler-Vargus knew everything. Including the fact that almost every key witness against them was conveniently gathered in that one tiny room.

Jack's insides screamed.

Sweat dripped from his armpit into his shirt.

Would Coon somehow notice Jack was onto him?

Jack would never have guessed that the gun strapped to his ankle would be needed for anyone other than Granger Meade.

He took a deep breath, exhaled silently, and slowly looked up.

With thick arms draped over his briefcase, Ralston Coon was tapping furiously at his phone, wearing the scowl of a troubled man.

38

Amy was still asleep, and the car that had been following them was within a hundred feet and closing. Derrick squeezed the steering wheel and swallowed back the sourness erupting at the base of his throat. The interstate was black, snowy, and virtually desolate. He could barely breathe. He thought of Zenia and their upcoming wedding day and doubted he was going to make it.

He reached over and gently shook Amy's knee. He tried to sound strong. "Hey, we got company."

Amy lifted her head, shook it, and squinted back at the car with one headlight.

It was racing toward them, directly behind them now.

The NAV showed a huge body of water coming up; Derrick remembered it from the drive over—a very high bridge. The BMW had waited until the lake to close in.

"It's the same car that's been back there the whole way," Derrick said. "Make sure you're buckled in tight."

She did so without a word.

"Call 911 again," Derrick said. "We're near mile marker 186, heading east."

The police wouldn't get there in time.

If Derrick and Amy were going to see the light of a new day, it was up to him. He had to think of something, do something.

He had to make the BMW crash—a horrific crash.

He could hear the roar of the dark car, just feet from his rear bumper. It was so close, its lone blinding headlight disappeared from his rearview mirror.

Amy looked up at the NAV. "Oh no. We're over water."

The car rammed them. Derrick's breath was snatched away. It felt like an amusement park ride someone else was controlling. He gripped the wheel like a vise to keep the car straight.

The other car released and dropped back, teasingly.

"Well?" Derrick said.

"I can't get them! I've barely got a signal out here," Amy said.

"Keep trying!"

The other car veered into the left lane and sped up until it was next to them.

The car's passenger window buzzed down.

A gun came out, pointing at them . . .

Derrick ripped his foot from the gas an instant before the gun exploded in a flash. A muffled *bam.*

It had missed.

The BMW slowed and was right beside them again in an instant.

Its window went up.

"Hang on!" Derrick said.

The BMW dived at them.

Crunch.

Derrick felt helpless as his car slammed to the right, right, right—too far!

Sparks exploded as the SUV ground against a short concrete wall—the only thing separating them from a three-hundred foot drop into a huge Ohio lake.

The dark car was entangled with his.

The bridge in front of them was long. Very long.

Derrick fought the wheel, forcing it left, gunning the engine.

Amy shrieked as the sparks continued to fly outside her window.

"Can you stop?" she cried.

"No!" If he did, it would be over.

"I'm gonna try something," he said. "Hold on."

There was nothing to lose.

The muscles in his jaw tightened, and Derrick floored it.

Both cars roared. Friction mounted. The red car continued to press them right, but Derrick insisted on squeezing in front.

He broke free!

For an instant Derrick and Amy were in the open!

"Good!" Amy cried. "Go!"

Derrick had the accelerator to the floor, but the SUV had no more to give.

The BMW roared up in the left lane to within twenty feet of them.

"This is it!" Derrick was sweating profusely.

"What are you gonna do?"

"Slam on the brakes. Brace yourself."

"Oh dear," Amy mumbled. "Oh, please help us . . ."

The BMW had no problem catching back up. It eased up next to them. Derrick kept checking for the gun at the window, but saw none.

"God help us," he whispered.

The millisecond the BMW bent toward them, Derrick bashed his brake to the carpet.

Amy screamed. They both jolted forward, then backward.

The other car catapulted to the right—just missing them.

Derrick and Amy careened left, left . . . screeching . . . sliding.

The other car exploded in a nasty cloud of sparks and flames as it hit the wall.

Derrick finally brought the SUV to a halt, its lone headlight shining into the wall on the left of the bridge.

Their anguished breathing was the only sound.

The smell of burnt rubber and gas and antifreeze enveloped them.

The other car . . . Derrick looked back . . . it was gone.

Gone!

Like a magic show, only a cloud of smoke remained where it had hit the wall and flipped over the side.

Amy's head dipped. She shuddered and began to cry.

Derrick examined the black highway. There wasn't another set of headlights in sight.

He took an enormous breath and flopped back in his seat.

Without looking at him, Amy reached over and grabbed his hand.

They sat in utter silence.

Two souls that would live to see another day.

Derrick covered Amy's hand with his. "Let's go home."

• • •

It was getting cold again in the car, and Pamela wished Jack would hurry up. The girls were nodding off in the backseat and Margaret couldn't sit still.

"I could sure use a drink," she whispered.

"Mom, please," Pamela whispered back. "I don't want the girls to hear that." She was about to start the car so they could get some heat, when she noticed movement to the side of the Randalls' house.

It was two men, coming down the narrow steps of a neighbor's home, a double-wide trailer. They wore dark overcoats and gloves. One had removed a glove and was doing something on his phone. The other carried a large cardboard box.

Wait . . .

The one on the phone resembled the man who had followed them. But it couldn't be.

Margaret must've seen the alarm on Pamela's face; she quickly spotted the men.

"That's the guy who chased us!" she said.

"Shhh." Pamela looked back at the girls, who were both asleep. "Stay calm."

"That's him!" Margaret screamed in a whisper. "We've got to tell the policeman!"

The lights of a small car blinked.

It was the silver car!

The trunk popped open. It partially blocked her view, but Pamela saw the one man set the box in the trunk. They squared off, talking.

Pamela fumbled for her phone.

39

Jack was trying desperately to figure out how to play this thing. Would Coon try something? It seemed farfetched. But why was he clutching his briefcase like that? His wide forehead was covered in sweat and he was pecking away at his phone as if it was his lifeline. Jack's mind reeled.

He had to let Dennis know. Or should he act now and talk later? Try to reach his gun? Force Coon to stand down and then explain his alleged involvement with Demler-Vargus?

His phone vibrated. He reached for it slowly, still feeling self-conscious, as if Coon knew Jack was on to him.

He looked at the screen. It was Pam. Maybe he could somehow signal to her to get help.

"Excuse me," Jack said, and answered the call. "Hey, hon, we're almost done—"

Pam's voice came fast and furious. "The man who followed Mom and me is right outside the Randalls' house—right now."

Jack replayed the words in his head.

Coon and the guy in the silver car were working together!

"He's with another man." Pam's voice wavered. "They're standing . . . at the trunk of the car that chased us. They just left that trailer behind the Randalls'."

Spivey Brinkman's house! What had they done to Jenness and Tatum?

All the pieces of the puzzle swirled in Jack's head at once.

He had to *act*.

"Okay." He tried to sound calm. "I understand, and I'll take care of it. You sit tight, okay?"

Coon put his phone in his pocket and eyeballed Jack.

"Why can't you talk, Jack? What's wrong?" Pam said. "Is everything okay? Are you in trouble?"

"Yes, yes we are," Jack said. "So I'll talk to you in a little bit."

He hung up before the call gave him away.

Coon squared up his briefcase and opened the lid with the contents facing him. Suddenly he stood, unveiling a large black gun. "Everybody stay exactly where you are."

Claire let out a scream. LJ cussed. Jack's head went fuzzy, as if this were a dream.

"This is loaded and cocked." Coon's voice cracked. "Officer, put your right hand high in the air and use the left to undo your holster." Coon's gun hand shook. "Bo, move away from the guns. Hurry up."

On hands and knees, Bo scampered to Galen.

"Coon, you don't want to do this," Dennis said.

Coon moved fast toward the policeman and pointed the gun up below his chin. "Just do what I say."

With a hand up, Dennis calmly undid his holster buckle and lowered it to the ground.

Outside, Rusty barked.

Jack sat forward, elbows on knees, getting his hands as close as possible to the gun strapped to his ankle.

"Coon, what do you think you're doin'?" Travis said. "You ain't gonna—"

"Shut up, Travis," Coon said. "DeVry, sit on the floor, next to Claire."

The officer slowly did as he said.

Jack hoped Pam had called the police.

But those men were outside—*now*.

The veins in Jack's wrists and temples pounded. He had to do something.

The police radio blurted a shot of static. "Officer DeVry," came a female voice. "What's your ten-twenty? Over . . ."

"Don't even think about answering that," Coon said.

Dennis nodded and held up his hands.

It was probably better if he didn't answer—maybe they would send help.

"My job is just to hold you here. That's it." Coon's nose dripped.

"So you been in on this from the start," LJ said.

"No . . . no." Coon moved the gun across the room, pointing at each of them. "I was helping Galen." He spoke as if he was trying to convince himself. "Demler-Vargus, they . . . they assured me there was no wrongdoing. They simply wanted to make sure they gathered any outstanding accusations—"

"Did you poison Daddy?" LJ pointed a bony finger, nostrils flaring.

"It wasn't my fault. Their people got involved." Coon shook his head. "I . . . they . . . my job was just—"

"They paid you to get all Daddy's evidence," Travis said. "And what else? Kill him? Kill us?"

"No!" Coon whipped the gun toward Travis. If Coon turned twenty degrees more, his back would be to Jack.

"They promised me you would be compensated," Coon said.

"So I'm right. You was double-dippin'," Travis said. "And look what it got you. You're goin' down, boy."

Coon wiped the sweat from his forehead with the wrist of his free hand.

"It backfired. I admit it. That's why they ganged up on me." He pointed to the bandages on his face. "Because I refused to play any part in hurting anyone! I'm out of it after tonight. If you just do what I say, I'm not going to hurt you—"

"But someone's goin' to, ain't they!" LJ lashed out. "You're no better than Judas. If you do get away, I hope you do what he done . . . spill his own guts out."

"Don't count on it," Coon said.

The police radio blared again. "Officer DeVry, do you read me? What is your ten-twenty, please? Do you read me? Over . . ."

"Ignore it," Coon said.

"They'll be here any minute," Dennis said.

But the officer didn't know those men were outside. What were they planning? What had they already done to Jenness and Tatum? Jack's fear spilled out in words.

"Who's outside, Coon?" he said. "Who are those guys? What were they doing at Spivey's house?"

Coon whirled around toward the door, as if Jack had seen the men standing there.

Dennis squinted at Jack, trying to figure out what he knew. The others watched in confusion.

The dog howled outside.

"Shut up!" Coon yelled. "Everyone just shut up. I've had enough!"

He latched his briefcase with one hand while keeping the gun trained on them with the other. Sweat dripped down his nose and onto the briefcase. He threw his coat over his arm, grabbed the briefcase, and backed toward the door.

Jack eyed Dennis, then LJ and Travis.

Dare they dive for the guns?

DeVry must've seen the wildness in each of their eyes. "Everybody just sit tight." He spoke evenly. "He's not going to use the gun. Jack, what do you know about others outside?"

"Shut. Up!" Coon fired a round into the ceiling.

Claire screamed as drywall crumbled to the floor. Bo jammed his fingers into his ears. Travis embraced Claire. LJ clenched his teeth, chomping at the bit to strangle Coon.

"I'll use it!" Coon said. "I've gone this far. Don't make me shoot you."

Bang.

The distinct shot of a gun rang outside the house.

An animal whimpered. Rusty?

Coon's eyes danced. He backed all the way into the kitchen and dropped the coat and briefcase on the table. "Do. Not. Move." He turned his head, separated the slats in the blinds, and looked outside.

Jack's cue! He ripped up the cuff of his pants, undid the Velcro on the holster, and yanked the gun out.

Dennis and LJ were in motion for the weapons on the floor.

Jack racked the slide and trained the gun on Coon with trembling hands.

Coon had to have heard the commotion, but he was frozen, staring out the window.

His big shoulders slumped. "What the . . ."

Then he ripped at the blinds like an animal and smashed his face against the glass.

"Nooooooo!"

40

Pamela was about to have a nervous breakdown as she tried to keep her mother calm and the girls asleep. Something was wrong in that house. After Jack hung up so abruptly, she called the police and told them about the two men outside, and that Officer DeVry was inside.

"Did you hear that noise?" Margaret glanced at Pamela and glared back at the house.

Pamela thought she might have heard a faint pop.

"It sounded like a gunshot. Pam, we've got to do something." Margaret leaned over the dashboard, peering at the strange men who stood talking, half hidden behind the trunk of the silver car, about forty yards from the Randall house.

"I don't know what more to do, Mom. Officer DeVry is armed. Jack's armed. What more can we do . . . we've got the girls—"

"Since when is Jack armed?" Margaret said.

"I'll tell you later."

"Jack signaled they were in trouble," Margaret said. "He's going to be in bigger trouble if those guys go into the house."

Pamela's mind spun.

"Start the car," Margaret ordered. "At least it'll distract them. Let them know someone else is here."

It might be a good idea.

But she didn't want to attract the men to the car . . .

Should she call Jack again?

Surely the police would be there soon.

A howling orange dog came prancing around the corner, out of the shadows, heading toward the men.

It was freezing in the car, because it hadn't been running for some time. The windows were starting to fog.

Pamela could see steam rising from where the men stood, conversing.

The dog stopped about twenty feet shy of them, but continued barking.

"I can't figure out why—"

Before it could register in Pamela's brain what she was seeing—one of the men lifting a gun toward the dog—the shot flashed. Its muffled *pop* jolted Pamela out of her dreamlike state.

The dog yelped and scrambled back into the shadows.

The men arched backward, laughing, then bent down into the trunk.

"Start the car," Margaret fumed. "If you don't, I will!"

When had her mother gotten such courage?

But the girls . . .

"We need to act!" Margaret said.

"Mommy?" It was Faye, awake.

"What's going on?" Rebecca sat up.

Pamela turned to the girls. "Sit back, honey, and get your seat belt on." She could barely breathe. "Both of you, buckle your seat belts."

"What's happening?" Rebecca tilted her head with a puzzled look. "What are those men doing? What do they have?"

Pamela felt a hard tug on her arm. Margaret's eyes were enormous, her mouth agape as she stared in horror. She was squeezing Pamela's hand so hard it hurt. Either she didn't want to frighten the girls or she was too scared to get a word out.

Pamela forced herself to look.

The men were hoisting huge canisters from the trunk of the car and shuffling with them toward the house.

Alarms blared in Pamela's head.

"Start the car." Margaret's shallow voice sounded like a ghost.

The men were hunched over from the weight of the tanks and struggled to lift and rock the canisters, back and forth, liquid sloshing out the spouts.

Everything flicked to slow motion.

The engine turning over jolted Pamela.

Her mother had started the car.

"What are they spilling?" Rebecca said.

"You've got to *drive!*" Margaret screamed. "We've got to save them."

Pamela's head dropped. She glanced at the steering wheel, the dashboard lights, the gear shift.

"Move over!" Margaret was coming onto her side.

"No." Pamela looked up. Saw an opening, right into the grass. "Girls . . . hold on. We've got to help Daddy."

She put the car into drive.

"They see us!" Margaret said. "Go! Move!"

Both men set their cans down and stared in the direction of the car.

"What's wrong with Daddy?" Fay's voice bumped from the back.

The men whipped their coats back and grabbed their weapons.

"Dear God, help us." Pamela gritted her teeth and punched the accelerator.

41

"Drop it, Coon!" In a flash, Dennis had his weapon braced in front of him and was moving quickly toward the kitchen where Coon stood glued to the window.

Jack moved in behind him with his gun drawn.

The others had armed themselves and were following suit.

Coon's gun clattered to the floor.

"Pam called me earlier from the car." Jack's heart thundered. "Two men came out of Spivey's house—they're outside."

Coon turned around, his face stark white. "We've got to get out!" He broke for the door.

"Stop!" Dennis said. "On your knees."

"They're gonna torch the place!" Coon dropped to the floor and covered his head with his arms. "They're gonna kill us all! If you try to leave they'll shoot. I know—"

"Watch him, Jack." Dennis eased open the door, gun clutched to chest, and worked his way around the doorframe to the porch.

Jack heard sirens far off.

With his weapon pointed at Coon, Jack went for the door right behind Dennis. He needed to get to Pam and the girls.

"LJ, watch Coon," he said.

Boom, boom. Boom, boom, boom . . .

The shots were so close, they reverberated in Jack's chest.

He hit the cold air just as Pam's car slid sideways to a halt ten feet short of the two men lying on the ground with steam wafting up from their chests.

Dennis's arms were locked in front of him, gun smoking, pointing at the two men he had just put down.

Jack leapt down the steps and took off for Pam's car.

He smelled gas, natural gas.

The two men had to be dead, their bodies riddled with bloody holes. Their guns were near them on the ground, along with two large gas cans. Ralston Coon had not been seeing things.

Pam's door bounced open; she practically rolled out of the car and into Jack's arms.

"It's about time." She was crying and laughing at the same time.

Jack hugged her for all he was worth. "It's over," he said.

Margaret was out on her side and had an arm around each girl, facing them away from the dead men.

Travis ran up, gun in hand. "LJ's watchin' Coon," he said, as DeVry came toward them.

"You smell that?" the officer said.

"It's comin' from Spivey's!" Travis said.

"Oh dear." Claire took off for the trailer.

"Wait, Claire!" Travis and DeVry were right behind her.

"Go." Pam pushed Jack. "I'm okay."

"Sure?"

"Go!"

Jack took off too, gun in hand, the dog barking somewhere behind.

Just then a big SUV with only one headlight and a bashed front end came roaring around the corner and swung into the Randalls' parking lot. It was Derrick, with Amy Sheets in the passenger seat.

Thank God.

Jack kept going toward Spivey's place.

Officer DeVry was yelling for Claire to wait until he got there before going in.

The sirens were closer.

Every light in the house was on at Spiveys', but not a sound came from inside; it was dead still. The overpowering smell of natural gas was thick in the cold night air; it made Jack nauseous. If the men had torched the Randall place, Spiveys' double-wide would have blown too.

Please let them be alive . . .

Dennis and Travis kicked in the door as Claire looked on with her mouth and nose muffled in the crease of her arm.

"Claire, you better stay back." The officer took a giant breath of outside air and dashed inside. Travis and Jack followed.

No one in the living room or kitchen.

"In here!" Dennis called.

Jack and Travis followed his voice to a back bedroom. Jenness's wheelchair sat empty. Jenness and Tatum were on the floor near the bed, both unconscious.

Too late?

Jack bent down and hoisted Jenness over his shoulder and rocketed out, out, out—into the cold night air.

Dennis and Travis had Tatum and were right behind him.

Everyone outside came running toward them—Bo, Claire, Galen, LJ . . . and even Derrick.

"Jack!" Derrick yelled. "I got Amy! We got everything on tape . . ."

Jack's vision jumped off track.

Uh oh. Blurry.

The gas . . .

He couldn't get Jenness much farther.

Blue and red lights lit up the trees.

Good.

With the last energy he could muster, Jack delivered Jenness into Claire's outstretched arms . . . and everything went black.

42

It was a damp, misty morning several days later. Jack was already at the office and the girls were off to school. With coffee mug in one hand and the morning edition of *The Trenton City Dispatch* folded in the other, Margaret shuffled over to Pamela in her robe and slippers, and handed her the paper.

"Look at that story." Margaret pointed at the top headline. "Read right through to the end. You are going to be very proud of your husband."

"Thanks, Mom." Pamela set her journal aside, unfolded the paper, and began to read.

> Girls attend service for father,
> beloved Trenton City resident Spivey Brinkman
>
> List of Demler-Vargus Cohorts Grows,
> Includes *Dispatch* Execs, EPA Officials
>
> By Jack Crittendon
> Jenness Brinkman watched from her wheelchair while her sister, Tatum, stood close, holding her hand. After an attempt on their lives five days ago, the sisters were grateful they were well enough to attend the snowy funeral service for their father, Spivey Brinkman, along with an overflow crowd at Trenton City Memorial Gardens yesterday afternoon.
> Being charged for the natural gas poisoning and aggravated assault of the Brinkman girls is the CEO of the Demler-Vargus Corporation, Leonard Bendickson III. He is the alleged ringleader in crimes that have left himself and 17 others connected with Demler-Vargas behind bars and awaiting arraignment in the Cook County Detention Center.
> District Attorney Edwin Hendricks says Bendickson is a suspect in the hanging death of Spivey Brinkman; the arson deaths of long-time Trenton City residents Barb and Emmett Doyle; the plane crash that killed attorney Oliver

Geddy; the attempted murder of former *Dispatch* reporter Amy Sheets; and the intentional homicide poisonings of Betty Jo Randall, Merv Geddy, and a growing list of Demler-Vargus employees and eastsiders, more of whom are coming forward daily.

Bendickson is expected to plead not guilty to these and other charges—including conspiracy, bribery, money laundering, and fraud—and will then await trial, likely without bond.

Other Demler-Vargus employees to be arraigned this week on related charges include Bendickson's son, Devon Bendickson; attorneys Harry Dorchester and Eli August; bodyguards Doug Frost and Peter Rosseti; and plant foremen John Clifton, Howard McPeek, Wanda Stark, and Seth Broschel.

The Demler-Vargus plant on Winchester Avenue has temporarily been shut down by OSHA and the Trenton City Police Department.

Regrettably, a number of *Dispatch* employees will be arraigned this week as well, on charges ranging from aiding and abetting, to accessory, obstructing justice, and accepting bribes. They include Editor Cecil Barton, Assistant Editor Nigel Waheed, City Editor Pete Forbes, and former reporter Amy Sheets.

Two unnamed officials from the EPA and local attorney Ralston Coon will be arraigned this week as well; their charges are pending.

Tomorrow afternoon at 1 p.m., atop the steps of the Trenton City Courthouse, *Dispatch* reporters Jack Crittendon and Derrick Whittaker will receive Awards of Bravery from Mayor Kathryn Stepanovitch for their efforts to uncover the corruption within Demler-Vargus.

Pamela folded the paper in her lap and stared at her mom. "He didn't tell me he was getting an award. I can't believe it."

"He deserves it," Margaret said. "It's a shame that Amy Sheets girl is going down with the ship. She did try to help, in the end."

"Jack told me the charges against her might be mitigated because she cooperated. I hope so."

"I think you should get the girls out of school and take them with you to see Jack get that award. It's going to be special."

"Absolutely," Pamela said. "And you're coming too."

Margaret crossed her arms. "Are you sure?"

"Yes, Mom, you're part of the family. We want you there."

"And you're positive you don't mind me sticking around a few more weeks? Sometimes I feel like a fifth wheel."

"Mom, we insist. You're a big help with the girls. They love having you here."

"What about Jack?"

"Having a built-in babysitter? Are you kidding? He's fine with it."

"Speaking of babies, honey . . . you think you'll find out what it is, so I can get busy sewing and shopping?"

Pamela smiled and shook her head. "No way. You know my policy, Mom. We don't find out until it's born. The surprise is what gets me through the pregnancy."

Margaret came over and sat down next to Pamela. "Well, if this baby is anything at all like you or your husband, you're going to be very proud parents—very proud indeed."

CrestonMapes.com